W9-AVD-284

To Jackie with
many Thanks and
all best wishes —

Jerry Fahnista
4-08

THE STRANGE DEATH
OF NAPOLEON BONAPARTE

ALSO BY JERRY LABRIOLA

Murders at Hollings General
Murders at Brent Institute
The Maltese Murders
Famous Crimes Revisited (coauthored with
Dr. Henry Lee)
Dr. Henry Lee's Forensic Files (coauthored with
Dr. Henry Lee)
The Budapest Connection (coauthored with
Dr. Henry Lee)

THE STRANGE DEATH OF NAPOLEON BONAPARTE

A NOVEL

BY

JERRY LABRIOLA, M.D.

STRONG BOOKS

All rights reserved. Except in the context of reviews, no part of this book may be reproduced or transmitted in any form or by any means, electrical or mechanical, including photocopying, recording, or by any information storage and retrieval system, without permission in writing from the publisher. For information contact:

Strong Books
P. O. Box 715
Avon, CT 06001-0715

Copyright © 2008 by Jerry Labriola

First Printing

ISBN 978-1-928782-70-4

Library of Congress Control Number 2007927201

Published in the United States of America by Strong Books, an imprint of Publishing Directions, LLC

The sale of this book without its cover is unauthorized. If you purchased this book without a cover, you should be aware that it was reported to the publisher as "unsold and destroyed." Neither the author nor the publisher has received payment for the sale of this "stripped book."

Printed in the United States of America

To my wife, Lois,
for her patience,
understanding and inspiration.

ACKNOWLEDGMENTS

I wish to give special thanks

- —to everyone at Strong Books, especially Brian Jud and Ellen Gregory;

- —to Susan Jordan and Sandy Uitti for their expert reviews;

- —to Bobbi Miller, Beverly Kallgren, Serene Hackel, Barney Laschever, Dorothy Adamson, Alan Davies, Graham Rossiter and Dr. Ann Bunch for their generous assistance;

- —and to my daughter, Sue, for her insightful suggestions.

PROLOGUE

This is a book of fiction. Perhaps a more precise way of phrasing it is that the story line and present-day characters are fictional but the historical references are on the whole accurate. Every effort was made to preserve historical facts.

The controversial Napoleon Bonaparte was doubtless a brilliant military leader. Yet that is not the thrust of this story. It is rather whether or not he was murdered. In recent years conflicting evidence has surfaced that his cause of death was arsenic poisoning. Some claim he used the chemical as a recreational drug, a common practice at the time. Some maintain he was fed the drug surreptitiously in order to hasten his demise. Still others believe he inhaled it from the wallpaper dye at Longwood, his residence on St. Helena for the last six years of his life. And some state he died of stomach cancer, as his father had.

With respect to the construction of the book, the following are worthy of mention:

—I have taken the liberty of presenting all dialogue in the English language to avoid the complexities of French versus English.

—The roles of the Talleyrand family, the machinations of the marshals associated with French General Michel Ney, and the existence of Lady Beckett stem entirely from my imagination.

—There may be parts of the book that readers may wish to skim over or skip entirely: the history of places, the careers of famous people, war strategies and others. Elmore Leonard once said, "I try to leave out the parts people skip." With all due respect to that masterful mystery writer, I have not done so. I leave it for readers to decide.

J. L.

Chapter 1

In affairs of state one must never retreat, never retrace one's steps, never admit an error—that brings disrepute. When one makes a mistake, one must stick to it—that makes it right!
—Napoleon Bonaparte, 1812

Tuesday, May 16
Early morning

The e-mail was puzzling. At least that was Paul's first impression. His second was shock. It read:

Dear Dr. Paul D'Arneau:

I represent the executive committee of *Gens de Vérité*, an organization in France that has been in existence since the fall of Napoleon Bonaparte in 1815. We are a private group that has never been part of the French government.

You of course know that there are many theories about the emperor's death. Was it natural or was he murdered?

I hope you don't take it as an intrusion into your private affairs, but we are aware of your international reputation as a scholar on the History of the Early Modern Era and of your unfortunate resignation from the Yale University faculty, for reasons that do not concern us. But what does concern us is your extensive detection work in matters historical. Your two Interpol contacts at the recent symposium in Lyon on *The Theft and Illicit Traffic in Works of Art and the Spoils of War* speak highly of you. They attended your lecture and still comment on your ability to have combined the responsibilities of heading up the history department at a major university with those that must be involved in helping recover historic and priceless artworks. We are also impressed with your rescue of that stolen vessel in Kuala Lumpur.

Now to the reason for this message. We wish to hire you to investigate the death of the emperor. Murder or natural death? It is, of course, the coldest of cold cases. We are prepared to offer you six figure compensation. Also, all paid expenses including travel, wherever it takes you. Lodging and all other necessities in France or elsewhere would be high quality. Personal security would be provided, should that be required.

Paul looked off to the side. What is this? Some kind of hoax? He scrolled down to see who the author was:

Leon Cassell, President
Gens de Vérité

Paul returned to the message.

If you reach conclusions about the death, with satisfactory documentation and evidence, we will add a bonus of one million U.S. dollars. So to be clear, Dr. D'Arneau: this sum would be in addition to the base compensation. If you are unable to arrive at a satisfactory solution, base compensation would remain yours to keep. What is it you Americans say: win-win?

If you are interested, we will send a four-person delegation to meet with you in the United States to work out specific details. They are distinguished members of *Vérité*: our secretary who is a military expert; an academic historian who, if you wish, could work with you full time while you're in Paris or beyond; a scientist; and myself. My background is in teaching and law enforcement.

Final points: (1) Since three of us received undergraduate and post-graduate training in your country (Boston and New Haven), and the fourth taught there, each of us speaks fluent English, (we even use your idioms!); (2) During any stays in France we would be available for consultation, day or night. We are in a position to open many doors for you;

(3) If you do accept our offer, we ask that you temporarily not mention this communication to anyone except to those you trust with your life. You might decide to refuse our offer and then inform others about it. We have discussed this possibility and determined that there would be no damage done to our cause, for we only seek the truth.

I ask the favor of an e-mail reply within 72 hours.

Paul reread the message—dwelling on each sentence—barely able to contain himself. The shock he continued to experience was not one of surprise but of jubilation, for what he had been unable to do on his own was now being offered to him on a silver platter. It all related to his lack of sufficient resources, both financial and logistic, for several investigations abroad, and to the manuscript he'd submitted to a university press that he'd tried to force from his mind. The editor in turn sent it to Yale's administration officials. Evidently it was the final entry in their year-long litany of complaints against him—a veritable wunderkind who had risen through the university's ranks to become at forty-four the Nathaniel Bennett Chairman of the Department of History. Among other things, they accused him of insubordination, and labeled him a "regressive mythologist", no longer a bonafide historian. *A renegade*. Then when the manuscript arrived it was all they needed: something concrete, less subjective, the final straw. Writing a book with in their words, "the most far-fetched theories about Napoleon's death and the scandalous side of his life is an unacceptable impropriety against the chair you occupy and the faculty you represent, even if your manuscript is a work of fiction."

The crux of Yale's complaint was not Paul's contention that Napoleon might have been murdered, a view held by many others, but that he had cited a list of possible suspects, including his prime one: Charles Maurice de Talleyrand-Perigord, a moderate leader of the French Revolution and an ally-turned-opponent of Napoleon. It was Paul's targeting of Talleyrand that had infuriated university officials, although they offered no explanation why.

Thus, he was urged to step aside, not only from the chairmanship but also from the faculty entirely; and encouraged to devote full time to his *real* passion of hunting down stolen artwork. Although Paul was a tenured professor and as such couldn't be unceremoniously dismissed without more serious cause, such as moral turpitude, he figured the university might find ways to make life miserable for him if he didn't cooperate. Besides, had he challenged the dismissal and was allowed to stay on, any residual resentment would have been misery in itself. He therefore offered no rebuttal and even turned down an opportunity to negotiate for a more favorable financial settlement.

Paul winced when the phone rang at 6:30 a.m. *It has to be Jean.*

"It's you, right?" he asked timidly.

"Right. You're up at this hour?"

"Aren't I always?"

"No. I just took a chance."

"What's the matter?"

"Oh, Dr. Spade phoned the whole staff last night. He's called a meeting for seven this morning."

"Why?"

"To discuss some stupid government regulation before he flies to Texas today. Some kind of lab conference."

"So? Go."

"I will but maybe I won't see you this morning and I want to so badly."

"Yeah, but take care of business first."

"I'll see if I can leave early. We can still ..."

"Have a quickie?"

"Paul, I *hate* that word! Makes me feel, well, used."

"What would you rather call it?"

"A shortie."

"But how do you think that makes me feel?"

They agreed that Jean would try to break away from the meeting at seven. Paul decided not to mention the e-mail development because doing so on the phone would neither do it justice nor convey his mixed feelings about it.

The severance with Yale had occurred a week before, and Paul was not totally surprised, as he had seen it coming. The real surprise was that once it had sunk in he was more disappointed than he'd expected to be. The news had spread across the New Haven campus like an unexpected spring squall, and he was at least heartened by calls from saddened but understanding colleagues.

For too long, Paul had been rooted in the world of academia: heated faculty meetings, endless gatherings of the state's literati and intelligentsia, formal dinner parties and the like. All of which he detested. But now he had a vision of complete freedom in his quest of stolen paintings, sculptures, antiques, and with police help, of attendant criminal networks. He had even forged an uneasy alliance with European con men who specialized in illegal "digging"of art treasures, and found this potentially valuable, albeit dangerous. He had weighed the risks and determined that as long as he remained vigilant, they were worth taking; that they allowed him to escape the "Yale box"; that finally he could answer only to himself.

Beyond all that, Cassell's offer would add another layer to Paul's vision: he could investigate whether Talleyrand was indeed Napoleon's killer. Perhaps he could even uncover fresh forensic evidence to support such a theory.

He read the message a third, then a fourth time. But why an e-mail for something presented as sensitive? Wasn't Cassell afraid of hackers? Why not a certified letter or some intermediary, a courier of sorts? Then again, Paul may have been exaggerating his own importance. Clearly, if he hadn't been thinking about his dismissal and his theories on Napoleon, he might not have opened the e-mail at all. Its recorded subject was "Important Paris request", ordinarily a sure bet for the spam heap. But a possible connection to Napoleon was too hard to resist, and although he was right on that score, he still wondered about being duped by a crackpot, or even worse, about being ensnared by some sinister foreign group. Call it paranoia, he told himself, but something seemed terribly wrong. Cassell spoke of a 200-year-old conundrum and an organization still groping for a solution. But willing to pay a king's ransom for it? Furthermore, why a secret if Paul accepted but not a secret if he refused? And the reference to personal security didn't bother him; it alarmed him. Besides all that, how and why did the Frenchman know about the situation at Yale?

A trim, straight-backed and powerfully built six-footer, Paul might have been mistaken for a career marine officer. One would think he must have been an athlete during his undergraduate days, but in fact he had never visited a ball field or a gym except as a spectator, preferring the giant stacks of the university's Sterling Memorial Library. His head, held high on broad shoulders, wandered little in conversation, his dark eyes intent, like a cat staring at an invisible shadow. He had black, wavy hair, an economical but warm smile and a square jaw. Some thought his craggy face reflected perpetual disaster; most considered it distinguished, well suited to his academic interests; while a few, mostly women, warmed to those rare occasions when it would turn blotchy because he was embarrassed, angry or otherwise emotionally challenged. He felt that way now.

Paul grew up in New Haven in the shadow of the Yale Bowl. Both his parents—retired to an Arizona condominium—had also been teachers. He often recalled his mother, born in Marseille, France, filling dinner times with tales of her native country's heroes. She had taught French and Spanish at the high school he'd attended. His father, a mathematician, was professor emeritus at Columbia. Paul believed that his happy and stimulating upbringing, particularly on his mother's side, had influenced the direction of his life's work and his fascination with French history.

He sat at the far corner of his spacious living room

in a tiny area straddled by ceiling-high windows and containing a drop-front desk, matching chair, an antique phone, computer, printer and a small maple filing cabinet. The desk and chair, both originals in the Biedermeier style of the early 1800's, had been given to him as a fee for investigative work on behalf of a museum in Vienna. Guests invariably hailed the room as most elegant, the jewel of his pre-Victorian home, a room cluttered with Hepplewhites and Chippendales and copies from the days of Louis XIV. There was even a Duncan Phyfe settee and a copy of a long-case clock in walnut decorated with floral marquetry, dating back to 1700. But in answer, Paul was quick to proclaim such elegance as faded and preferred to look upon the room as a depository for his art recovery labors. And he'd never heard it mentioned, but he was convinced that the pieces smelled their age—plus or minus a few decades—and that therefore he could attach a particular century to each new arrival without checking its history.

He looked around, his eyes settling on a wall of books—some forensic, some mythological—but the vast majority historical. He had authored or co-authored at least a dozen, one titled, *Napoleonic Strategies* and the most recent, *St. Helena: Napoleon's Final Defeat*. He had written as if he himself had been at battles like Waterloo, or at the Egypt Adventure, or in the Peninsular War and the Russian Campaign. Or in exile with the emperor at Elba and St. Helena. He knew the era well, but felt secure with his private collection to consult. Once his own books had been published, he couldn't recall ever referring to them as resource material. This could change, he thought, if the French assignment were legitimate, and if he took it on. In fact, some early drafts of his manuscripts might prove even more valuable for there were endless issues he had left out of the final versions.

It was 7:30 in the morning, a half-hour after the time when Jean would usually open Paul's front door with her own key and steal into his bedroom to kiss him awake. She would be on her way to work at the Connecticut State Forensic Science Laboratory, usually arriving at eight. Sometimes at Paul's insistence she reported later, at 8:15 or eight-thirty. As a longtime forensic anthropologist there, she never needed an excuse. More than once he would remind her that the bones could wait.

But he had arisen early and still in robe and pajamas, downloaded the e-mail. Then despite his reservations, dashed off a reply, for he'd ultimately decided to learn what he could by long distance. It was at times like this when he wished he had a wife, when he could have shared both the contents of the e-mails on the spot and the turmoil of the past few days. Once again, he briefly entertained the notion that Jean's persistent entreaties for marriage had merit, but as usual that option received short shrift. This time around he was absorbed in whether or not he had acted impulsively in answering the message from France.

Yet he rationalized that he would indeed consult with her before entering into anything definite with one Leon Cassell, if that was his real name. He would check on it and on other matters concerning a so-called *Vérité* group. By now, both personally and through his own law enforcement contacts including Interpol, he had more sophisticated ways of handling preliminary investigations than during his earlier days as an academic historian-cum-detective of sorts.

Besides, his response had been simple enough:

Dear Mr. Cassell:

Thank you for the e-mail, for the generous offer and for the confidence you expressed in me. The best I can do at this point is to say that you have piqued my interest. I am willing to meet with the delegation, not "to work out specific details", but to explore the possibilities and to ask questions. I would have to evaluate the answers before making a final decision.

Best regards,
Paul D'Arneau

Paul was still at his desk, trying to reconcile uncertainty with exhilaration when he heard the key in the door. He sprang up as Jean Gaylord walked over.

At five-feet-eight, she was nearly as tall as he and, at forty-two, two years younger. A widow, she had met Paul five years earlier at a symposium on "The Recovery of Stolen Art." He was one of the speakers. They exchanged business cards. Over many months, Jean would inform gathered friends that when she arrived home that evening, a message awaited her on her answering machine. Professor D'Arneau it seemed had asked her out to dinner and a concert the following weekend. But Paul, winking, would counter that it was she not he who initiated their close relationship, that she had invited him to her place for a sleep over. They eventually became lovers and spoke regularly of marriage, but Paul insisted—and Jean reluctantly acquiesced—that before "settling down" he must first get over the hurdle of extensive research, extensive writing and extensive travel in pursuit of plundered paintings, sculptures and antiques. The hurdle was over four years long with no end in sight.

"Why the silly grin?" she asked, removing a black trench coat. Her slim, shapely figure shuddered with cold and she rubbed the palms of her hands together. She wore the clothes of her hands-on job: white slacks; overhanging loose white top with identification tag; white moccasin shoes. She shook her head like someone trying to dislodge raindrops and ran her fingers through auburn hair, brushed severely back from a round and faintly freckled face. She rarely wore makeup except for naturally textured lipstick. "Everything about you is natural," Paul said once. "That's why you're so attractive. You don't need any help."

"Is it raining out?" he asked.

Jean forced a smile. "That's my Paul," she said. "A question to a question: 'You really like movies, don't you?' … 'Movies?' … 'How do you feel today?' … 'Feel?' … or 'Today?' The answer is yes, there's just a drizzle out there but it feels like snow."

She nestled into his outstretched arms and kissed his ear. "So, answer my question," she whispered.

Normally, he would tighten his grip, comment on her latest fragrance and accuse her of resorting to chemical warfare. Instead he said, "What question?"

Jean pulled away and cocked her head to the side. "Uh-oh. Now what? More from the university?" She eyed him suspiciously. "C'mon Paul, something new happen?"

"First, tell me how the meeting went?"

"Not much to say except that Spade could have filled out the forms himself. Everyone was fuming."

Paul paced in a circle, turned and said, "I'm not sure I did the right thing." He felt his face tingle and knew its skin had become blotchy.

Jean read both e-mails and registered little emotion, stating simply that she would reserve comment until they moved into Paul's favorite room.

Much like the characterization of Winston Churchill's Chartwell home by William Manchester, Paul's study was a metaphor of himself, steeped in the past. Jean had given it several names—sanctuary, hideout, refuge—but mainly the Chest Room, for its score of chests, Italian, French, English, Egyptian, all dating back several hundred years. They helped fill the spaces between say, a sixth-century Greek chair and a seventh-century Assyrian stool; or between an antique marble bench and a gothic oak table. Paul however preferred to call it a sitting room where he could retreat to think and write, although he did most of his serious thinking while pacing, and the bulk of the writing at his beloved standing desk. He even ate many of his meals there, gobbling them down while standing, justifying that his self-cooked preparations weren't worth sitting for anyway. He was willing to admit however that such behavior might signify an edgy streak.

There were windows on two sides, overfilled bookcases on three and in a corner, a pair of overstuffed armchairs that seemed out of place. One, its tweed surface worn thin in spots, bore testimony to Paul's frequent but less serious stretches of reading and thinking.

The drizzle had turned to a fierce, noisy rain and with it the morning light quickly faded, bringing a fresh, heavy fragrance indoors, the kind you recognized as part of the bloom and moisture of the season.

They sat in the easy chairs, facing each other.

"Well?" Paul asked.

"Let's wait and hear," Jean replied.

"That's all?" he said, "Let's wait and *hear*?"

She leaned forward. "Forgive me. I mean, I think you worded your response perfectly and now we wait. If an answer ever arrives, I don't see anything wrong in meeting with his group. Meanwhile, we can both analyze every sentence of his message, if you want to."

"I don't think that's necessary," Paul said, his thoughts divided. He crossed his arms over his chest, a move he always described as defensive. "But don't you think this is right up my alley at just the right time?" he asked.

"Yes, I do. I'm just less trusting than you, I guess. If it's legitimate, it's a godsend."

He knew that she was aware of her propensity for caution. Not infrequently he would scold her for being the scientist's scientist, never one to jump to conclusions before she had all the data to pore over. But before that she would speak almost blandly about crime scenes and suppositions and circumstances, as in circumstantial evidence. So this kind of reaction was nothing new to Paul.

"Besides," she continued, "I'm still stewing over your dismissal. I don't see why you didn't fight it as a matter of principle."

"I've already gone over that with you." He made no attempt to hide his annoyance. "The situation was hopeless. It had *noire* written all over it."

Jean focused on his eyes. "Meaning?"

"Meaning they were gunning for me because I dared to buck the establishment, just like I bucked conventional wisdom in my manuscript. Come to think of it—and you haven't heard this before—I wasn't bucking the establishment as much as not keeping pace with its changing attitudes."

"But you know universities, Paul. They're liberal."

"I'm not talking liberal or conservative. Screw them both. I'm talking legacy. They can be as liberal on the social issues as they want. I could care less."

"That's 'couldn't'," she said.

"What?"

"You *couldn't* care less." She looked sheepish.

Paul took only a moment to understand what she meant and then snapped, "Damn it, Jean, don't correct me when I'm in an uncorrectable mood!"

She lowered her eyes. He rose, took several steps as if to walk the length of the room, then returned to sit again.

"You changed the subject," he asserted, "and I'm doing the same thing. It all boils down to this: either Napoleon died naturally or he was murdered, maybe poisoned by arsenic. At least that's what people have been saying lately, since they found it in his hair samples. And let's not forget accidental arsenic poisoning. If it was murder, no one—but no one—has come up with a credible murderer and a credible motive. There's a treasure trove of suspects but none to be believed as the actual killer. Well, I went into that in the manuscript in great detail. Came up with my own suspects."

Neither spoke for a few seconds.

"Mind if I change the subject again?" she asked.

"Be my guest."

"You referred to legacy. Whose? Theirs?"

"Anybody's. They just don't believe in it anymore. Before you know it they'll call everything mythology unless it's shaded by new things. Untested new things. That's not history."

"But if I get what you're driving at, you're leaving your own legacy. You've had a wonderful university career: the history chair, the awards, the citations, the honorary degrees of a man twice your age."

Unimpressed, Paul said, "But they claim I changed over the last year." He stiffened his back. "I didn't change; they did. And why in hell do I have to accept the fact that I can't hold onto the past?"

"Well you don't have to accept it anymore. And you have a whole new career ahead of you, whether you receive another e-mail or not. Don't let it eat at you, Paul. You've got the freedom now; look at it that way."

He watched his foot tapping the floor and realized that Jean had noticed.

She got up, moved alongside his chair and drew him close. Gently patting his head she said, "You've really had enough for a single week."

Paul brushed aside the remark, eased away and palms upturned said, "Look, you read most of what I wrote. Was it that outrageous?"

"Well …"

"Forget it. I've got a chance to verify most of it now. Providing we hear back from Paris."

Chapter 2

Jean started to leave at 9, later than usual. Paul promised to call her at the lab if he heard from Cassell anytime soon.

Nothing other than conversation had occurred as they took turns expressing varying degrees of suspicion, of doubt and of hope. After a long and ardent embrace at the door, Paul, his thoughts elsewhere, said softly, "Tomorrow."

Jean smiled and closed the door behind her.

Paul returned to his study to pace. He had postponed his usual morning juice, toast and coffee, preferring for now to sift through probabilities and possibilities, a favorite phrase for his students, and a habit whenever he was faced with unanticipated developments. Another phrase he liked was, "In its sand dune simplicity", words he had once uttered while gazing over the dunes in the far reaches of Cape Cod.

Doesn't that apply here? Simplicity. Simply wait.

He finally had his meager breakfast and after showering was beginning to lather his face when the phone rang. He cursed the timing as he crossed over to a desk in the study and picked up the phone with a wet hand.

"Hello, Paul. This is Leon Cassell. I may call you

Paul, may I not?" The voice was firm and raspy, the kind Paul associated with serious smokers.

Paul tensed and knew that in an instant his skin would turn blotchy. But he spoke at once. "Well, good morning. Shall we make it Leon and Paul?"

"Yes, of course."

Paul had the urge to laugh as he visualized himself and characterized the moment: nude except for the towel around his waist; clumps of shaving cream beneath his ears; on the phone with a likely significant force in Paris, about to discuss something that might change an entire life. Or more than one.

Instead he said, "You're calling from Paris, I take it?"

"Yes, indeed. Paris. Is this an inconvenient time for you?"

"Not at all. I'm glad you called. You got my e-mail?" Paul was aware that most of the pleasantries had been questions. Questions that were not vital, that would soon be replaced by substantive ones. And hopefully by meaningful dialogue. His mind shifted to overdrive, on the qui vive.

"Yes, I did," Leon replied, "and I can understand any reservations you might have about our offer. Taking first things first, I suppose arranging our meeting with you has the highest priority. May we set a time and place? We can meet there in New Haven you know."

"Are you sure? You'll probably be flying into New York's J.F.K. I can meet you in the city."

"No, no. This meeting is our wish and therefore must be at your convenience."

Paul was slow to respond. "Very well then," he said, "Yale's library—Sterling Memorial. You know of it?"

"Oh, yes. I believe my e-mail mentioned post-graduate training in the States. I'm the one in the delegation who studied more than two years at Yale, and I remember many hours among the stacks there. Can you secure us a room to use?"

"That'll be easy." Paul was certain he still had some clout at the library.

So far, so good. On familiar turf.

"And speaking of the delegation, Paul, let me give you the names of the other three, all from Paris. There's Vincent Broussard, the historian. He's young, mid-twenties but very, very astute. Then our military man is Maurice Delacroix. Mid-sixties. Finally, the best-looking of the bunch: Sylvie Ranet. About forty. She's attached to the Academy of Sciences, which is part of the Institute of France. In fact for at least five years she's headed up one of its most important committees: *Comité Académique des Relations Internationales Scientifiques et Techniques.*

Paul got the gist of it as he scribbled down the information.

Leon continued. "I think they would all be helpful to you. We've discussed the situation at length. They're very much looking forward to our trip over. And in case you wonder about my age, I'm sixty-seven and in my thirty fifth year as president of *Vérité*. Also you must be told that the Institute considers our organization a rival, but I'll explain when we see you. Let's say for now that that group is satisfied with the natural death theory and they don't want anybody rocking the boat."

"But what about Sylvie? You said she works there."

"Correct, but neither the Institute nor even her

academy knows that she's one of us. In fact only a handful of our own full membership even knows. She stays away from our meetings but I keep her informed."

Paul had gradually relaxed over the course of the conversation. Until then.

"Does she attend academy meetings?" he asked.

"Yes."

"So she's a spy for *Vérité?*"

"You might say that."

A brief silence accentuated the sound of the rain.

"Tell me," Paul said, "does your full membership know about your contacting me? The offer, and all the rest?"

"A couple do but only the delegation knows the details. We're the executive committee."

"Which includes Sylvie?"

"Which includes Sylvie."

Paul raised an eyebrow. "Now wait," he said. "Sylvie doesn't go to meetings but is on your executive committee. How often do you meet?"

"It's ad hoc. Four times a year perhaps."

"At your call?"

"Of course."

"And the money you're offering me for my services?" Paul continued to choose his words carefully. "Where will it come from?"

"From our treasury. It's a very old treasury."

"I assume the dispersal of funds is also at your call?"

"Yes. But I prefer to call it 'appropriation of funds.'"

Paul was concerned about the revelations but felt

he had temporarily pushed hard enough. He excused himself, held the phone loosely against his hip and faked a prolonged cough.

"We never set a time to meet," he said, returning to the phone.

"We can be at Kennedy at noon the day after tomorrow, Thursday, and at Sterling by two-thirty." He sounded like an airlines representative.

"Good," Paul said, avoiding the obvious detail about transportation from airport to library, but sure that Leon would have no problem with such arrangements.

"Very good at this end too," the Frenchman said. "And do bring Jean along if you wish."

Paul felt his eyes widen as if he'd regressed to viewing a childhood horror movie. "You know of Jean?" he asked incredulously.

"Of course. Until Thursday then. Two-thirty. Sterling. Main lobby."

Paul heard a click before he had a chance to clarify what he had just heard. For a moment, he couldn't decide whether to stay seated and ponder over the call or to see if *Vérité* had a website, something he just realized he should have done before. One thing was clear: the call had generated more questions than answers.

He rose slowly and made for his computer, suddenly ambivalent about the whole deal. *Is this the fabulous opportunity he'd imagined, or was he to be a pawn in some sort of French game with a Napoleonic twist? And was Jean being included?*

He booted up the computer and searched for a website or for any reference to the ancient *Gens de Vérité*.

There was none.

It didn't take long for Paul to call Jean on her cell phone.

"Where are you?" he asked.

"In the parking lot. Why, what's up? You sound funny."

"Guess who just called me. The French guy from the *Vérité* group: Cassell. He knows of you!"

"He what?"

"He knows your name."

Paul sensed from the lull that she was thinking hard. He was too, even as he had punched in her number. Thinking hard about an offer out of the blue, from Paris no less. Until Cassell had mentioned Jean it had sounded almost perfect. Now he had doubts. It had seemed so clear-cut. Now it smacked of something ominous and Paul wasn't certain what that was.

"I'm not at all surprised," she finally said. "Don't forget, that's a big job, with big bucks. He's probably done background checks. Knows more about us than you realize. I don't really blame him."

"Hmm." It was all Paul could manage.

"In fact," she added, "I'm rather impressed. One, that kind of diligence is better than something slipshod. And two, a phone call is better than an e-mail. Shows he means business."

Paul cleared his throat and said, "You're such a scientist."

"Really, Paul, don't you think so? My sense is that this is a make-or-break event in his life. He's probably thought it through very carefully and he's got to be thorough. In my humble opinion he's found the perfect person. And …" Another lull.

"And what?"

"I have this strange feeling. Nothing serious, just strange. I don't know. Like he's sure about what you're capable of doing, and once he found out about the Yale thing he grabbed at the chance to have you on the case full time. He never mentioned the dismissal on the phone, right?"

"Never. Only in the e-mail."

"No doubt he didn't want to offend you. I mean verbally. What else did he say?"

"Before I get to that, you know what's really bothering me? How did a guy like that find out about the Yale mess? The media didn't play it up." Paul was thinking out loud. "First he knows what he wants done. Hears about me, figures I might be up to the challenge … then just as you said, finds out I was fired, and boom, he moves in?"

"Something like that."

"But it's the timing. How did he know about Yale?"

"Who knows? Maybe he has friends around here. Look Paul, my dearest, stop fretting. Get the answers later. What else did he say?"

Paul sighed. "The main thing is that the delegation's coming here Thursday. We're supposed to meet at Sterling. Two-thirty. It's like it was all prearranged. A nice, neat package. That's when he mentioned you. Said you could be there too."

"He doesn't waste time does he? We think of it as a great opportunity but he doesn't want to miss his own opportunity. You want me there?"

"I really do. First go-around. Another pair of eyes

and ears. That sort of thing. Can you get away?"

Jean's voice appeared to deepen. "You want me there—I'll get away."

Paul continued as if her answer were a foregone conclusion. "We need background checks on the four of them, before the meeting if possible. I could do it through Interpol but you could do it quicker. You know, your friends in the investigation unit." Before she could respond, Paul started to read her the notes he had taken on Leon Cassell and his three associates. He concluded by labeling that part of the phone call as "too pat."

"Enough to go on?" he asked.

"That should be plenty. And Paul?"

"Yes?"

"Sounds like you're revving up."

"I wouldn't say that. No, not really."

Chapter 3

Thursday, May 18

Sterling Memorial Library, an example of Gothic revival architecture, always reminded Paul of a cathedral, its fifteen floors towering above the other buildings surrounding Yale's Cross-Campus. Hundreds of stained glass panes and a main circulation desk modeled after an altar did little to impugn that impression.

The rains had continued on into the early night, but morning had broken to a clear, cerulean sky, and that afternoon as Paul pulled his late model Toyota into a solitary space four blocks away, he could feel the sun's rays through the windshield.

Parking was a problem in the Sterling area and ordinarily he would have been beside himself as he emerged from the car. But he felt energized over what lay ahead, at least of what possibly lay ahead, for the questions he'd assembled would require the kinds of reassuring answers that stripped away his misgivings: Cassell's knowledge of Jean; his depiction of *Vérité's* treasury; the business about Sylvie. And Paul was cautiously confident that the delegation would provide the right answers. He had gone over the questions a dozen times, yet had a list of them in the breast pocket of his blue blazer just in case.

Briefcase in hand, he walked slowly as it was only 2:15, definitely too early to appear. His mind had hardly stopped churning since the initial e-mail from France and once again he focused on the twin particulars suddenly thrust upon him: a career switch from academia to full-time investigation and a chance to delve into the mysterious death of one of history's most fascinating characters.

As agreed upon, Jean was waiting near a landmark bicycle stand fifty yards from the main entrance. Paul spotted her beyond students hurrying about and some faculty members he recognized. They didn't see him and he was glad.

Once at her side she took hold of the lapel of her jacket. "You see, I wore a blue blazer too. That's a good omen. Maybe I should have included a tie."

Paul kissed her on the cheek, then motioned toward the library. "Notice any people walking in together," he asked, "like a delegation?"

"No, but I just got here."

"Where did you park?"

"Over on College."

Paul snapped his fingers. "I always forget that street," he said. "Tell me though, did your pals come through with the background checks?"

"Uh-huh. Late last night. Everything seems to be on the up and up."

"Good. I think we're ready then. Let's go in."

He was aware of a bounce to his step as he led the way through a heavy oak door into a vestibule containing the same old but scrubbed smell that always triggered memories of his undergraduate days. The small space was lined with poster boards of flyers announcing upcoming library events. Paul pushed open the inner door and allowed Jean to enter first.

"I haven't been here in years," she said quietly.

"I haven't been here in days," he countered. "This could be my last for some time."

They paused at the near end of Sterling's cavernous nave which Paul surveyed in a single sweep, including the empty visitors' chairs on the right, several study carrels, and off to the left, an area housing a massive card catalogue system now made obsolete by modern computer technology. He had once inquired why the old system had never been dismantled. History, he was told.

Except for several staff people and a student or two, the nave was deserted.

Paul motioned for Jean to follow as he began the long walk toward the main circulation desk at the far wall. Both took soft steps in a failed attempt to minimize the echoes. They passed an elongated display case that featured writings and memorabilia of the nineteenth-century scientist, Thomas Henry Huxley. A single sentence on a piece of rag paper caught Paul's eye: "The great tragedy of science (is) the slaying of a beautiful hypothesis by an ugly fact." How many facts might he unearth in the near future and if any, would they be perceived as "ugly"?

A few feet from the desk Paul smiled nervously at several familiar staff librarians before glancing into two large reading rooms that projected out on each side. A few young men and women seated there looked like students. Turning, he noticed the librarians from the corner of his eye. They had huddled to exchange whispers.

As they headed back toward the entrance, and one of six private rooms Paul was certain was available for the meeting, he spotted two men entering the nave. Each carried a small handbag. Even from a distance of three hundred feet, he could tell that one of them was much older than the other—and larger. Immense in fact. *But if these were from the delegation, where were the other two?*

"Are they the ones?" Jean asked.

"Looks like it. Man, he's huge!" Paul checked his watch. It was precisely two-thirty.

They quickened their pace. At the same time, the men came forward, and the four met with broad smiles of recognition. They shook hands and the large man spoke first.

"We meet at last, Paul. You look a bit younger than the picture on the dust jacket. And I'm so pleased that you were able to make it, Jean. I'm Leon Cassell and my associate here is Vincent—Vincent Broussard."

Paul recognized the raspy voice. "Welcome to New Haven," he said. "You had a good flight I trust?"

"Yes, indeed," Leon replied.

"And the other two? They'll join us later?"

"Sylvie and Maurice? No, I'm afraid they couldn't make it. Last minute developments back home. But you can spend time with them when you come to Paris. Would that be soon?"

"If all goes well here, I'd say absolutely." Paul said. "Actually, I'm confident that within the next half hour we can firm up the … the …"

"Mission. Let's call it the 'mission,'" Leon said with a flair.

"Excellent," Paul said. He looked around the library. "Maybe, in honor of this place, how about the 'Sterling Mission'?" He thought there was no harm in approaching the meeting as if the deal were a foregone conclusion.

"Perfect. Let's hope the findings are just that," Leon said.

"You mean 'sterling'?" Jean said, hardly disguising an eagerness to become engaged.

"Exactly, Jean, exactly," Leon said. "Now then, do we have a quiet place to confer?"

Paul pointed to the side. "I didn't make arrangements but do you remember the niche rooms?"

"Ah, yes. I remember them well. Attractive décor, right? And one always seemed to be available as I recall. But that was a long time ago."

"Let's check," Paul said. He let the Frenchmen lead the way and for the first time realized the extent to which both men's appearance differed from what he'd expected.

Leon, well over six-foot tall, was stooped and paunchy, a three-hundred pounder if he ever saw one. He had thinning brown hair, a hawk nose, wide mouth, large yellow-shaded front teeth and a wispy white mustache. Marked creases appeared seared into his forehead, and a perpetual squint did all but hide the deep blue of his eyes. His right thumb and index finger were decidedly yellower than his teeth. But it was his girth you noticed. And his towering presence. Nevertheless, there was a gracefulness about him. Jackie Gleason had the same thing when he did his classic jig.

Jean tapped Paul's shoulder and cupped her hand near his ear as they continued bringing up the rear. "Look," she whispered, "I'll just be a casual observer, okay?"

Paul whispered back, "But observe well."

"By the way, Leon," he said, "how did you get from

J.F.K. to here? A limo?"

Leon stopped to answer. "No, Laurence drove us. He's one of our contacts here in the States. He'll meet us outside in less than an hour and we'll be off. Sorry to breeze in and breeze out, but unfortunately some duties call back home. Especially for Vincent here. And you know, there is an advantage in doing it this way: zero jet lag. But of course we'll be talking much more in France as we go along."

The mention of Vincent reminded Paul that he hadn't yet addressed or paid much attention to him. He waited for the opportunity.

They approached a wing of the library that contained the six small rooms and Paul signaled them to enter one he knew as the Linonia and Brothers Room. It was unoccupied. On the far side, four casement windows opened out onto the Selin Courtyard. There was a window seat below, three walls lined with books, several small tables with lamps, a large center table with green leather chairs and off in a corner, a small red leather couch.

"Vincent," Paul announced, "you get first pick at the table."

"Well thanks, Dr. D'Arneau," Vincent said.

"No, no," Paul said, "if we'll be working together make it 'Paul' for heaven's sake." He noted that Vincent, as in the case of Leon, had no trace of an accent.

"By any chance, would you be the one who studied in Boston?" Paul asked.

"Yes, I am. Harvard. Sylvie graduated from there. Raved about it, so I did my graduate work in history there. Four years. Some of your books were required reading, sir."

"Those poor students," Paul remarked with a wink. "And please cut out the 'sir'. It should be just plain 'Paul.'"

"Yes, sir," Vincent said. They all checked with one another and smiled.

Vincent was slight of build and jockey-like short. He had long black hair, gaps between his teeth and delicate features. Yet, he was an arresting young man with a softness in his skin, his bearing and his dark brown eyes. Not a weak softness there but a resilience, the hint of reconciliation if called for.

Both Frenchmen were impeccably dressed. Each wore a light blue shirt under a gray suit with sharply creased trousers. Only their ties differed: Vincent's a striped blue and gray, Leon's a solid rust.

Vincent chose one of the chairs at the long table. Leon squeezed his large frame into the one next to him. The other two sat opposite them. The Frenchmen took out writing pads from their inner breast pockets. Paul removed his wristwatch and placed it before him, much as he had done in his classroom teaching days. Jean sat expressionless, her hands folded demurely on her lap.

Leon was about to speak but Paul beat him to the punch. "I'd say we get down to business," he said, "but before that, I'd like to clear up something: Why me? I mean … you could have had your pick of many fine professionals … in your own country for example."

"That's a very important question," Leon said, "and it deserves a very special answer. First, we didn't want a Frenchman. Call it the need for objectivity. Second, I've—that is, all of the delegation—has read both your books on Napoleon and we like your approach. So many writers are either 'Napoleonist' or 'Bonapartist'. Either seems to skew their beliefs and writing. You appear neutral and that's what we wanted."

Directing his attention toward Jean, he said, "I hope it's not insulting if I explain the difference." Her face brightened as if expecting just that.

"Well," he said, "the best way to put it is that a Napoleonist is one who holds Napoleon in the highest regard as a man and leader, whereas Bonapartism connotes an authoritarian method of governing."

"I see," Jean said deferentially.

"And third," Leon went on, "we can't have a person who's an expert in criminal investigations only, or a person who's an expert in Napoleon history only. No, we need *tous les deux*—both of them. As a matter of fact, more of the former rather than more of the latter. And you, Paul, are that person."

Paul pressed the issue. "But," he said, "you *do* know that my investigative experience is in the area of stolen art treasures, not, for the sake of argument, in the area of deliberate versus accidental poisoning? Right?"

"Yes, I do. Now I wouldn't pretend to instruct you in how to proceed in this case, but it seems to me that you'd have to rely heavily on old, maybe misplaced or forgotten records and correspondence and memoirs—that sort of thing. So it's a question not of *stolen* treasures necessarily, but of *lost* treasures."

A prolonged silence filled the room. It was obvious to Paul that the president of *Vérité* had given much thought to his choice of investigator. Paul carried it one step further: the million dollar-plus remuneration in itself not only justified the gravity of the mission, but also put a stamp of approval on his selection. Paul concentrated hard to keep his face from blotching; he was only partially successful. Finally he said, "I'm honored you look at it that way." He was afraid it was a feeble response, but it was what came out and that was that.

Leon scribbled something on his pad. Vincent noticed and followed suit. Leon looked over at Paul and features compressed, said, "Now it's my turn to clear up something."

Paul was still disgusted with himself for showing his emotions and decided on a sterner demeanor. "That's why I'm here," he stated.

"Logically, I should inquire if you've ever thought much about the nature of Napoleon's death, but in reading between the lines of your books, I think it's clear that you have."

"You think right."

"And?"

"No, Leon. It's too early for that."

"But certainly you must have a hunch."

"Certainly."

"Well?"

Paul was determined to keep his ground. "We're playing games now, aren't we?" he said. "Actually, I have a new manuscript in which I suggest murder as a possibility, but in due course I'll provide you with my definitive answer."

"I take that to mean that you're definitely on board?"

Paul scratched the back of his middle finger, not for the first time. He glanced at Jean. "Definitely on board," he said.

His smile was thin but the others grinned as the Frenchmen reached over to shake his and Jean's hands.

"No doubt you were a great influence in the decision, madame," Leon said.

"The *major* influence," she replied, broadening her grin.

Leon shifted in his chair. "Now that that's settled we can proceed with details and unanswered questions on both sides, hopefully with great mutual trust. You said before, Paul, that you'd share your early thinking about Napoleon's death, but I would ask: perhaps after you get started, you'll share current developments?"

Paul's response was immediate. "Now what does that mean?"

"I mean in the course of an investigation like this, there are bound to be unexpected, shall we say, traps that turn up."

"I believe I know what you mean, but that's a strange way of expressing it."

"Oh?"

"I mean 'traps'. Why not say 'secrets'?"

"Secrets then."

Paul took out an index card and pretended to write down something significant. Instead he wanted a breather to assess why the meeting felt surreal thus far. On one hand, there was in the gentlemen opposite them this French-flavored antithesis: in looks, in size, in style. It was almost comical. And on the other hand, something hardly comical: these very men flying in from Paris for a single hour's meeting to firm up a lucrative and challenging pact that would redefine Paul's life and, who knows, might even redefine history. Yes, definitely surreal.

Leon continued. "Now for a potentially sensitive subject which we needn't go into if that's your wish."

"I know what's coming and I don't mind one bit."

"We know of your dismissal but not the reason why. Care to comment?"

"Sure. Two reasons primarily. Number one, in my new manuscript—which the Yale higher-ups analyzed—I gave a list of possible suspects, if Napoleon really was murdered. One of them was Talleyrand. That upset them; I'm not sure why. And second was mythology. They claimed I went beyond the thinking that myths are simply a teaching tool—to help understand many things before science came along to offer facts—that eventually I began believing the myths themselves. And that's plain bull! Just because I quote mythology doesn't mean I believe it de facto. Even the great classicist, Edith Hamilton, suggested that myths lead us back to a time when the world was young and people had a connection with the earth and nature, with trees and flowers and hills and seas, unlike anything we ourselves can feel." Paul was speaking faster. "In other words, through myths we can retrace the path from civilized man who lives so far from nature, to man who lived so close to it. What's so wrong with that?"

Leon leaned on an elbow, his eyes glued to Paul's. Vincent was writing furiously. And Jean looked like a student who wished the class were over.

"I see nothing wrong with it," Leon said. "I would think that historians more than anyone else need to appreciate the value of mythology."

"Precisely," Paul said. "Toynbee, the famous historian, wrote something that's stayed with me for years. The essence of it was that history grew out of mythology and that anyone who starts reading the *Iliad*—you know,

Homer's *Iliad*, the Trojan War— anyone who starts reading it as history will find that it's full of fiction. But just the opposite too: anyone who starts reading it as fiction will find that it's full of history. They're intertwined." Paul felt some dampness at his collar line. "And that's the extent of my love affair with mythology."

"But why would Yale object to that?" Leon asked. "For that matter, why find fault with your Talleyrand theory? Even now, many others feel the same way. After all, the emperor and he were allies at first but then became bitter enemies."

"On Talleyrand, I have no idea. On mythology, they charged that I was using my position as a bully pulpit to disseminate ancient myths as if they had never been replaced by scientific facts … ." Paul stopped abruptly. "Oh, I guess I've already said that. Sorry for preaching, and for quoting everybody, but sometimes just a single thing can set me off."

"Understood," Leon said, "and in this case, that happens to be someone quibbling with you about your own field. I do the same thing when it comes to law enforcement. Well, let me say that your dismissal was unfair and not well founded. It's the university's loss, but an enormous gain for the wider community."

"Thanks, Leon. And by the way, how did you know they let me go?"

"Someone at the Institute told me."

He couldn't put his finger on why, but Paul felt the response was a side step. The feeling was reinforced when Leon quickly slid into another subject: "Of course you know by now, Paul, that *Vérité's* premise has always been that Napoleon was murdered. We want to know if that definitely was the case, and if so, by whom. The Institute is irritated with us for having the gall to take such a position. Pardon the pun."

Paul squared himself for emphasis. "It's my premise too, but we'll see. If the delegation can open doors for me, I'm confident we'll find the answer, maybe even some secrets or 'traps' as you call them."

"You'll be surprised at the clout we have in our country, especially Paris. In my e-mail I made a point that we're not government sponsored. But we have connections at the highest levels, and even with many private and, I would say, powerful groups. The politicians, the industrialists, the rich and famous—we know them all. Some are members. I believe you call them movers and shakers here in your country. And through them almost anything can be arranged. So 'open doors'? Yes, wherever and whenever."

"Good. Which reminds me: how much time do I have for the project?"

"As much as it takes. Your expense account will be unlimited and your compensation remains the same. I'll elaborate on that before we leave in…" Leon consulted a gold watch he'd drawn from a jacket pocket. "…in about thirty-five minutes."

Paul's eyes narrowed. "The Institute won't try to block anything?" he asked.

"No way!" Leon shot back. He took out a gold-colored handkerchief and dabbed around his mustache. "Even so, may I suggest you work undercover as much as possible? I don't mean changing identities or wearing a disguise and all that. But don't broadcast who you are and what you're doing for all to hear. I think you'll be able to move around more easily at the beginning. Then if some things need to be done that might be more public—of necessity—so be it. We can handle the Institute, any time at all."

Paul nodded his approval but not before noticing that Jean hadn't changed her expression.

Vincent looked at Leon then at Paul. The shorter Frenchman raised his hand.

"One second," Leon said, "just to finish my thoughts. It's funny how one word can trigger them. 'Time'… we're talking 'time.' How to put this? Paul, can you contact me at the end of each day so we can compare notes? At least until the mission gets rolling?"

"Okay, I'd welcome that." Paul feigned enthusiasm, wondering what notes he'd receive from Leon each day. But there was the matter of a Frenchman's perspective on French territory. And of his opening doors.

"Splendid. And yes, Vincent, you were about to speak. I thought you never would."

Vincent straightened his tie and said, "Well, I have a couple of questions for you, ah, Paul. You'll be starting in Paris soon?"

"Probably tomorrow if I can catch a flight out."

"Fine." Vincent's voice deepened. "I've already made reservations for you at Le Meridien Montparnasse on rue du Commandant Mouchotte. You can arrive anytime you wish. Will madame be accompanying you?"

"Not yet," Paul replied, "and thank you."

As Vincent pushed an envelope across the table he said, "This will take care of the reservations for both of you, as you please. And one other thing: after you arrive at the hotel and get settled, please let me know. I can be ready to drive you anywhere at a moment's notice. The envelope also contains ways to reach all four of us."

"Again, thank you. Driving me? I think I know my way around Paris so I'll use taxis. But who knows? Maybe later I'll take you up on the offer, especially if I need another set of ears."

Once Paul realized that breaks in the conversation were becoming longer and more frequent, he decided to bring up the three questions he'd held in reserve.

"Why do you need to have Sylvie as a spy at the Academy?" he asked, putting on his best expression of disbelief.

"Elementary," Leon said. "To see what the whole Institute is up to regarding discrediting *Vérité*. And we're doing it through Sylvie's branch. It might sound complicated but it's really not. You see, the Institute has five branches, all academies: Fine Arts; Ethical and Political Science; Inscriptions and Belles Lettres; the Academy of Sciences, which is Sylvie's branch; and the French Academy which is merely a bunch of intellectuals who would say anything to get a rise out of other intellectuals."

"Get a rise out of other intellectuals?"

"See? As I've said, we even use your idioms."

Paul, taking notes, underlined some words and said: "Got it, I guess. Next then: How did you know about Jean? You mentioned her during your phone call."

"Your relationship was simply brought up during our due diligence on you."

"Well that's logical, isn't it?" Paul responded.

Jean nodded as if representing the others.

"And about *Vérité's* treasury," Paul said. "Your group is solvent, right?"

"Very solvent," Leon answered. "From our inception there's been …"

Paul broke in. "No need for that," he said. "Your 'very solvent' is all I wanted to hear." He reached into his pocket for the slip containing the three questions, tore it in two and returned it to his pocket.

Leon shot the others a knowing smile.

"While I'm at it, Leon, let me finish up. Only a few more. You both know our professional backgrounds. Can you comment on yours?"

"Of course, " Leon said, "A logical question. I'm surprised you didn't ask sooner. In my younger, and thinner, days, I worked as a captain for both our National Police Force and the Prefecture of Police in Paris. But for the past dozen years, I suppose I'd best be called a roaming educator. For a while I taught criminology at one of our Grandes-*Écoles*; then I lectured regularly at the Paris Police Museum; and finally now, I teach a course on Corrections, Crime and Criminology at the Sorbonne."

Jean broke her silence. "Very impressive."

Meanwhile Paul stared at Vincent, saying, "And you teach history at …?"

"Also at the Sorbonne," Vincent interrupted. "Only now it's called the University of Paris. You might find it ironic that the original College de Sorbonne was suppressed during the French Revolution and reopened by Napoleon in 1808. Today the university has many colleges and the 'Sorbonne' has become a colloquial term for the entire collection. I've just started there."

Paul gave Vincent an appreciative nod and turning again to Leon said, "Getting back to *Vérité*, how many members do you have?"

"Over a thousand," Leon said triumphantly. "We even have some American members. They've either worked here on long term assignment or have moved here for good."

"And seeking the truth is admirable, but other than our mission project, what other kinds of things do you do?"

Leon looked prepared for the question. "First of all we limit our energies to the greater Paris area. Basically we take up causes as they develop. At the heart of it is our effort to get at the truth, to go beyond the façade of political and special interest rhetoric. For example, we'll soon be taking up the cause of preserving our city's five hundred parks and gardens. Certain industrialists claim that's too many, that they hurt industrial development and the creation of jobs. Fact of the matter is that these same industrialists have histories of corruption—graft and the like. We're very proud of our work in conservation. Just as you strive to conserve works of art, we want to conserve our natural resources. There are those who say we're nothing more than a glorified advocacy group, but we're much more than that. Advocacy groups and governments come and go but *Vérité* remains a constant."

"Makes sense," Paul said, glancing sharply at the other three. "I have just one more question. "If we're successful in our … our sterling mission, what will you do with the information?"

"Announce the truth," Leon said.

"Movie, TV show, a book? Some public blowup with the Institute?"

Leon appeared incredulous. "That's to be decided."

"Hmm," Paul said. "Well I'm sorry if I sound

intrusive, but okay, that's fine, clear. Now, any remaining issues from your end?"

"Yes, the financial one. The sum of $200,000 has already been deposited in the Union de Banques Suisses: the Union Bank of Switzerland. Another million has been deposited in escrow. This will be for you upon the conclusion of a successful investigation. As for your personal expenses, you will have a running account at the hotel; and do keep track of all outside expenses. If you're wondering about something resembling a contract between you and *Vérité*, I can dispense with that very quickly. From your end, the money deposited in your name amounts to a contract of sorts—a guarantee, if you will. And from our end of the bargain your word is sufficient."

"Understood," Paul said, his eyes glued to Leon's. "Thanks for your trust, and I mean that."

"One final thing you should know," Leon said. "I own a light plane that can be available to you at any time. A German *Breezer*. Covers over five hundred miles before refueling. Plus I have access to a helicopter if the situation requires one." He placed both hands facedown on the table, looking as smug as Vincent had.

Leon checked his pocket watch again. "Well," he said, "we have little time to spare in getting back to Kennedy."

All four rose. Paul replaced his watch and picked up his briefcase. The other men, their handbags. They exited the library as a unit and paused near the entrance steps. Paul expected to walk the men to an awaiting car, but Leon insisted they bid farewell on the spot.

"Remember," Leon said, lighting up a cigarette, "please contact us when you get to Paris. And Paul ..."

"Yes?"

"Because of this meeting, and I think I speak for Vincent, I'm more confident than ever. For truth's sake, I think we have the right mission. And I *know* you're the right man for the job."

He wheeled around and led the way toward College Street before Paul had a chance to respond.

Facing Jean, Paul shook his head. "Breeze in, breeze out all right," he said. "Well, what do you think?"

"I like the guy. Both of them. Accommodating. I don't think you'll have any trouble working with them." And then she asked as if she knew the answer: "Paris first?"

"First and foremost, if only to meet the other two. Agreed?"

"Agreed. When?"

"As I said in there, as soon as I can get a flight."

"You sound wired."

"The mission's exactly what I wanted … I think."

But while Paul too thought the men would be accommodating, his primary concern at the moment was whether or not he was up to the task. He felt edgier than before the meeting. His mind wandered off for a spell, soon focusing on the disparate matters of Leon's size and the mission at hand. *Big man, big challenge.* And now he was certain that his knowledge of the Napoleonic era would serve him well. He'd have to reread sections of his own two books on the subject, and even some of the material he hadn't included in the final manuscript drafts.

Paul shared and amplified his thoughts with Jean. He expressed his delight in being able to chase after history, but he also hinted he was intimidated by the many missing pieces in the Napoleon Bonaparte story, those he hadn't been able to find during meticulous research for his latest books. Trying to locate the pieces and position them into a coherent whole would be a colossal achievement, especially in the face of Leon Cassell's story which, Paul sensed, had its own missing pieces.

"Well, let's sleep on it," Jean said.

"What's that? 'Let's' means 'Let us'", he said with a devilish smile. "You mean together?"

"I hadn't meant it that way, but now that you mention it … ."

Chapter 4

Friday, May 19
Paris, France

Late the next morning, Paris time, Paul's plane touched down at the Charles de Gaulle Airport. Earlier, he had phoned Leon of his success in booking the flight from New York, and was advised that *Vérité's* military historian, Maurice Delacroix, would be asked to greet him at the Meridien Montparnasse Hotel.

Paul was about to board a shuttle into the city—it had been his custom on several other trips to Paris—but in stretching Leon's request to travel "undercover", he flagged a taxi. Halfway into the twenty-mile ride, he noticed the driver's shoulder twitch as the taxi speeded up, its horn sounding more often than most.

"Driver," Paul said, leaning forward, "what's going on?"

"The car behind, monsieur. It follows us from de Gaulle."

Paul turned around and saw a black Citroen tailgating them. At first he thought the reflection of the sun's bright rays were obscuring any view of the interior, but then realized that its windows were tinted. "All the way?" he asked.

"Oui, monsieur. I slow, he slow. I go fast, he go fast."

Even so, Paul made little of it for he believed no one other than *Vérité* knew of his flight plans. Unless someone were after the cabbie. Paul was more preoccupied with whether or not jet lag would present a problem. If so, it would be the first time because historically his body was easily able to adapt to a six-hour time difference.

Yet he continued to check on the car that remained in pursuit until the end of Charles de Gaulle Avenue when it veered off onto Malakoff Highway in the direction of the Eiffel Tower. The taxi then slowed to the traffic's pace along the Avenue de la Grande Armée, through the Arc de Triomphe, onto the Champs Élysées, and past the Hotel des Invalides, a complex which was on Paul's immediate agenda. He had been there before, visiting Napoleon's tomb and the military museum, but was anxious to return, this time with a more vital purpose.

As they approached Paul's hotel, he thought it odd that the cabbie had commented no further on the Citroen episode, but he let it pass. He had enough on his mind.

The Meridien barely met Paul's expectations: lobby décor in pastels, reservation desk spanning one wall, archway to a cocktail lounge spanning another, bronze statues of war heroes at every corner. What he hadn't expected were contemporary furnishings and light fixtures, an overuse of mirrors and glass, and background music from America's Broadway. Then again, the architecture of the entire Montparnasse district was modern, a fact not lost on the Parisians who, Paul had heard, complained that it clashed with all else neoclassic merely blocks away.

His room was a continuation of the lobby in style. It was clean, ample and serviceable, but its twelfth-floor view contained none of the well-known icons of Paris.

Even before freshening up and unpacking he sat on the edge of the bed, contemplating the traditional components of detective work. He had never been called upon, nor was he qualified, to investigate the usual violent crimes — murder, rape, aggravated assault and the like — but his quest of stolen treasures had required utilizing many of the same investigative components: interviews and interrogations, undercover operations, overt and covert intelligence, photography, tailing and archival research. He understood, however, that shedding light on the death of a famous emperor was not the same as investigating pilfered art. Most valuable, initially at least, would be archival research and, as the situation dictated, individual interviews. There was only one problem: beyond meeting with Maurice Delacroix and Sylvie Ranet, he wasn't sure where to start.

He also mused about his last visit to Paris, commissioned to find an art dealer who had absconded with a painting of one Catherine Worlee Grand. It hadn't registered at the time but Paul had skimmed over an article that alluded to her love affair with the noted statesman, Charles-Maurice de Talleyrand. Paul's jaw tensed as he now grasped the irony of that relationship, coupled with his claim that if Napoleon had indeed been murdered, Talleyrand had to be considered a prime suspect. Paul glanced at his luggage bag. He had brought along his research notes for both the recently rejected manuscript and his two previously published books about Napoleon.

He flinched at a knock on the door.

"Yes, who is it?" he asked.

"Maurice. Maurice Delacroix."

Paul opened the door. "Well," Paul said in surprise, "hello."

Maurice, a tall, square-shouldered man, tried to stretch his thin frame an inch taller but then gave up as he shifted clumsily to steady a cane and extend his hand. It had a fine tremor. "I hope it's not bad timing for you," he said, "but I've been anxious to meet you and have a chat."

Paul shook the hand, ushered Maurice in and said, "No, not at all. Have a seat. May I take your hat?"

"I'll take a seat, but I'll keep my hat, thank you." He tugged down on a black beret, doing little to cover the places where sideburns should have been. He was sixty-four, going on eighty-four.

His shirt seemed undersized, his tie dull and too long, and he was one of those who wore both suspenders and a belt. Paul could never fathom what that signified. Nor, in this case, could he tell if Maurice knew how to smile or simply wanted to hide a mouthful of embarrassing teeth.

The rest of his face too was a blank, smooth save for the wizened pockets around his eyes, and gray in color, like the façades at Fontainebleau Palace. Then there was the reek of alcohol, but no slurring of speech, giving the impression of a long-held tolerance to wines or spirits. Paul couldn't imagine the motor and cognitive consequences if his own breath were as heavily laced so early in the day.

Maurice lurched onto an art deco chair behind a small round table overflowing with magazines whose covers touted Parisian cuisine and nightlife. Paul moved from the bed to a similar chair from behind the desk.

"The clerk downstairs signaled me when you arrived," Maurice said. "Leon had alerted me about your touch-down time at de Gaulle, and I sat in the lobby no more than ten minutes. So, yes, good. Excellent timing. I hope it's a favorable omen for us." His speech was deliberate, with gaps between words.

Paul wanted to comment but Maurice continued, his voice turning nostalgic and grave. "Sorry I couldn't make the trip to the States. Not much notice you know. It would have been my first visit back since the days I helped out at West Point. Sylvie is sorry too — we talk regularly. But Leon briefed me when he and Vincent returned. I understand your meeting went quite well. Vincent assured me he'd call, but he never did. Predictable I'd say, like a dog near a hydrant."

Paul tried to read the man's facial expression, but, as he spoke it remained a seldom-blinking stare, his mouth in concert with nothing else.

"Why don't we get right to the point?" Maurice said. "That is, asking, answering and amplifying. Both of us. Know what I mean?" He paused and shook his head as if to dislodge a headache. "My apologies," he said. "I'm afraid I come on rather strong at times. Some people call me brassy. Not a bad term really. Reminds me of trombones and trumpets. But 'asking, answering and amplifying' is an old military slogan I often used for troops under my command — and you certainly aren't under my command, so please forgive me."

Paul teased out a demure smile and crossed his arms loosely across his chest.

"Let me begin a different way," Maurice said. "I'd like to offer whatever services I can to help you in this probe. I know Leon calls it a mission, but I see it as a probe." He placed his cane on the table. "And as such you should know where I'm coming from. I'm just as eager as the other three to solve this ... this mystery once and for all, but barring conclusive evidence to the contrary—and I mean conclusive and really to the contrary—I continue to hold that Napoleon was murdered. That's it, murdered. There is reason to believe he was being poisoned by arsenic long before he got to St. Helena."

Paul quickly asked, "What reason?"

"Examine the battles. Forget the arsenic they said they got from his hair—if it was his hair in the first place. The conduct of his campaigns doesn't lie. It can't be messed with; it's there to see. Study full throttle. You'll be only the third person to arrive at an obvious conclusion: you, me, and a French journalist I suggest you look up. I'll give you his name in a minute."

Maurice rose and cane in hand walked to the door, then back and sat again. "Hip gets stiff," he said. "Where was I? The obvious conclusion? Yes, that's it. I wouldn't want to prejudice your own analysis, but as long as you asked for the reason, you know that the prevailing theory these days is that Napoleon was poisoned by arsenic and you no doubt realize that it can be administered in small doses over a long period of time."

"I'm not clear on the relevance to the military battles," Paul said.

"His behavior during the last of them, his judgment erratic or better put," Maurice pointed to his head, "*son état mental*—his mental state." He fanned the air in a gesture of disgust. "Once the poisoning started to take hold he made error after error. Some of the things he did, or didn't do, would have been unheard of in his earlier campaigns."

"But if that were the case isn't it possible that anything erratic might have been due to mental strain alone?"

"Possible, even though the emperor was hard as nails." Maurice's voice thickened as if he couldn't take time to swallow. "Look," he said. "Take the Russian campaign. Eighteen-twelve. Errors you'd never expect. And why? You'll see. You'll put it all together. But please, don't waste time on what Napoleon *did*; look for what he *didn't do*." He was breathing heavily now. "The brilliant 'diamond-shaped' formation ... eighteen-six, against Prussia; his 'spider web' tactic; his 'square battalion'; his 'envelopment attack'. What happened to them? Abandoned for what purpose? Defeat? I commend you for your books, very well researched, very well written. But you didn't analyze with an eye toward some outside force influencing Napoleon. Like poison. He has his admirers—me, for one—and his detractors I'll admit, but along with Alexander, he must be considered the greatest military leader of all time, and as I said, some of his last battlefield decisions were way out of character. So go back. Go back and check."

Maurice searched the air for another thought. "Now about that journalist," he said. "Name's Guy Martin. He's also made a study of the emperor. Knows details you probably can't find anywhere else. He writes for the *International Herald Tribune* here in Paris. A loyal member of *Vérité*, incidentally. You can reach him at the paper if you need to talk to him."

"I'm sure I'll need to."

Paul was surprised at the sudden lapse in the one-way conversation and leaped to take advantage of it. "You game for a question or two, Maurice, ah, or do you go by Colonel?"

"Maurice. By all means, Maurice. And please yes, questions."

"Good. The first's the same one I put to Leon. You know about my background. Can you give me some idea of yours?"

"That's simple. As Cicero said, '*Gallia est omnis divisa in partes tres.*' All Gaul is divided into three parts. The same with my career: all of it military. The first part? Twenty-six years in the Foreign Legion. Became Colonel. Indochina, Africa, others. The second part: Teacher at the Special Military School of St. Cyr for ten years. Our motto was '*Ils s'instruisent pour vaincre.*' They study to vanquish. You might be interested to know that Napoleon founded the school in eighteen-two. It's where Charles de Gaulle went. Then the third part: With the Gendarmerie Nationale right up to four years ago. That's our national military police force. Mainly participated in ceremonies involving foreign heads of states or governments. Another way of looking at my background, my life if you will, is to divide it into necessary pursuits and voluntary pursuits, although 'necessary' and 'voluntary' can be interchanged, but for now I won't go into that except to say that my main voluntary pursuit was to study the Napoleonic Wars. That I have gladly done since I was a young boy."

He spoke carefully, as if it had been rehearsed, or at least recited many times before. Maurice kept at it. "And

I've written regularly, not big volumes. No patience for that anymore, just some articles, commentaries, for my favorite organizations: The Dutch Line Infantry Battalion, The French Line Infantry Battalion, Supporters of the Waterloo Battlefield, The European Napoleonic Society. You might find these groups useful. If you like I can put you in touch with their officers."

Paul opted to change the subject. "You spent some time in the United States I'm told. Where and how long?"

"I suppose you might say I was on loan to your West Point Academy: a visiting lecturer in residence for four years. Went so fast, one of the highlights of my life."

"You must have been a hit there," Paul said vacantly, his mind both on answers received and on any other questions that needed asking.

"You have it backwards. The cadets were a hit with me. But I too have a question, Paul. How long will you be in Paris?"

"Maybe just a few days to begin with, but there could be several visits, depending on what I uncover and how fast I uncover it."

"And you'll contact Sylvie?"

"Absolutely." Paul checked his watch. Twelve-noon. "Within the hour."

Maurice reached for his cane before rising. "I know you just arrived and have much to do so I won't keep you. Thank you for receiving me and listening to my rambling. Once I get going on my favorite topic ..." He gripped Paul's shoulder and reiterated his availability.

Paul was itching to get in one last question. At the door he said, "About Vincent. I thought I detected some sarcasm when his name came up. Hope you don't mind my asking, but does that mean anything? It may be important if I'm to interact with the whole delegation."

Maurice's tremor worsened. "Feel free to ask me anything you wish anytime you wish, good buddy. And yes, maybe it does mean something." He thrust his head forward. "Let's put it this way: I'm a retired military officer who still understands history and he's a young historian who knows little about military matters. Get my point?"

Once the door closed Paul let his shoulders sag as he caught his breath. He wanted to dwell on what had just transpired, but knew that some phone calls had to be made. Until a better time he simply tagged his visitor as Maurice the Military Man, a delegation member swept up by booze, age and memories.

Paul phoned Leon and Vincent to inform them he'd arrived. The three agreed to have lunch the following day. Each Frenchman's closing remark struck Paul as curious. Leon said, "When you meet with Sylvie, please don't bring up the *Vérité* and Institute rivalry as it applies to her."

But it was Vincent's that caught Paul off-guard: "Remember I can accompany you anywhere while you're here. Keep in mind I have a loaded pistol in the glove compartment of my Renault."

After explanations to a dozen intermediaries at the Academy of Sciences, Paul finally reached Sylvie. He was taken with her throaty voice. She invited him over. Since the Institute was not open to the public that day, she indicated that she would meet him at a side entrance at one-fifteen.

Paul unpacked, took a quick shower and hurried down

to the lobby's coffee shop for a sandwich, postponing any consideration of his encounter with Maurice. It was a habitual skill he'd learned through the years: if pressed for time or feeling distracted, he could clear his mind of dangling questions to make room for new ones. Then before too long he would prioritize, resolve and record his observations.

An hour later the sky turned cloudy, the air cooler, and Paul was happy to be wearing the blue windbreaker he'd debated packing. He also took along a briefcase. The taxi sped down Boulevard St. Germain, over the pont de la Concorde and took a right onto Quai des Tuileries. It slowed as they passed the Louvre and, bearing right over the pont des Arts, Paul could see the dome of the Institut de France up ahead. He knew that there was a more direct route from the hotel but guessed the driver wanted to "show off" the complex of Louvre buildings to an American tourist. Someone more cynical might have attributed it to a longer, more lucrative, taxi ride. Paul should have been annoyed but he understood, even though he didn't like to be shown a city by a native, since from experience, the more he was asked to notice the more he missed. Somewhat akin to taking pictures of one view and missing two others while fiddling with the camera. Besides, he had seen the Louvre many times before, both inside and out. At least the driver could have asked.

The woman waiting on a side door landing was hardly what Paul had anticipated. Or maybe she wasn't Sylvie. As he climbed the dozen or so steps toward her, his perspective made her look taller than her five feet but no less stunning, with green eyes, flawless skin and a punishing smile that took shape slowly. Yet it was a mole that captured Paul's attention upon reaching her level. It was a tiny round beauty spot at the vermillion border of her upper lip. She pushed back strands of straight raven hair from the corner of her eye, then extended the same small hand toward Paul. With the other she untwisted a silver cross that hung from her neck. She wore loose pink slacks and a matching tight-fitting blouse under a light blue, unbuttoned blazer.

He took her hand loosely in his fingers. "You're Sylvie?" he asked. "I expected a lab coat." He stared at the hand, not knowing whether to kiss it or shake it.

"Yes, I am," she replied, "and it's okay. You can kiss it."

But he shook it.

"Come, let's go in," she said.

She led the way past a maze of meeting rooms and through a glass corridor that opened into a large reception area with marble walls, a fireplace and a skylight. An obvious chemical odor reminded Paul of his infrequent visits with former colleagues in Yale's chemical laboratory. He sniffed audibly.

"I guess halogens and alkali smell the same in Paris as they do in New Haven," he smirked.

"What smell?" she asked.

Beige and white easy chairs were clustered about. Sylvie motioned for Paul to sit in one of them. He consented and she pulled its mate closer before sitting and crossing one leg over the other. But she hastened to re-cross them, redirecting and nearly touching Paul's ankle with her high-heeled shoe. Her left pant leg slid up, revealing a small tattoo of a black widow spider on her ankle.

"Well now," she said, her voice taking on an official air, "let's you and I get one thing settled, shall we? That lab coat business? Those days are over."

"Meaning?"

"You might say I've done it *all* here. Worked every department in eighteen years. Now, I'm part of administration, in charge of grant proposals. No money? No research. And thank God I'm where I happen to be. The problem with hands-on research is that you lose so many times and I like to win. There are so few breakthroughs. I think I'm where I belong right now. Let the others be disappointed all the time."

"So you write out the proposals all day long?"

"All day long, but much of it is boilerplate. There's just enough left to make it interesting actually. Plus I get to travel sometimes to present our case in person."

"You and your husband can make it business with pleasure?"

"No, I'm not married."

"I see. Ever come to the States?"

"Many times. We've had some generous American grants."

"How does that work?"

"They sometimes have special projects that we're particularly suited for."

"Any through your alma mater?"

"Harvard? A few."

Sylvie leaned forward. "That's enough about me. I want to congratulate you on your double careers. Outstanding for such a young man I mean. The art cognoscenti speak very highly of you in terms of what

they call your ..." She looked down at her notes. "...
your retrieval skills." She looked up at him. "I love that
phrase."

"Really? Makes me sound like some kind of dog."

Chuckling she replied, "It's how they express it in
their business, silly." She seemed to cast off her official
air. "You've been to Paris several times, I hear."

"Several times. For research."

"But certainly you've experienced some pleasures
here."

"Certainly. I like your sidewalk cafés. Great history
... great charm."

"I bet you're fun when you loosen up."

Paul couldn't think of an immediate answer.

Sylvie broke the awkward pause: "Time to get
serious, though. Are there any questions left over from
your meeting with the other team members that I might
help you with?"

He pulled his own note pad from the briefcase and
faked scanning its empty pages. "Yes. Any chance of
getting a cell phone to use while I'm here?"

"That's not a problem." Sylvie produced a tiny phone
from beneath her blazer and handed it to him. "I have
another one in my desk," she said.

Paul felt the phone vibrate and he shoved it toward
her as if it were a bomb.

"Pardon," Sylvie said, putting the phone to her ear.
"*Oui?*" She listened and nodded. "I'll be right there." She
gave the phone back to him and said, "Upstairs calling.
Mild dilemma. I can be back in a few minutes, or better
still, can we continue this later, say for dinner perhaps?"

He jumped at the opportunity. He wasn't sure

why, aside from learning all he could before starting his investigation in earnest. Or was there more to it than that?

Sylvie wrote down the name of her favorite restaurant for him—Alan Ducasse au Plaza Athenée—and they agreed to meet at six-thirty. He commented that he had dined there several times on other visits to Paris and was impressed both by its cuisine and its location, in the heart of haute couture Paris.

They got up and Sylvie clasped her arm around his and went to kiss him. Paul expected a peck on the cheek but it landed on his lips.

On the ride back to the hotel, Paul called Guy Martin at the *International Herald Tribune* and asked if he might visit with him. It was not yet two p.m. The journalist said that his friend, Maurice Delacroix, had mentioned him several times and Guy suggested that Paul drop by right then. But Paul explained that something crucial had just come up and four o'clock would be preferable. The journalist approved.

The "something crucial" was Paul's realization that events had been happening too fast and he needed time to be alone, time similar to many others through the years, when he would abruptly step back, slow the pace, sort out things. Jean and his closest colleagues could recognize the beginning of such an episode by his sudden silence and a faraway look in his eyes. She, in conjunction with her laboratory work, was more familiar than most laypeople about medical matters and whenever Paul got that way, she often referred to his having a brain spell of sorts. To which Paul would stiffen indignantly and counter with his own diagnosis of *interpretive moment.*

Paul savored such a moment in the hotel room, when he could freely attach significance to this and that, raise doubts and even be paranoid. It hadn't taken him long to remove his moist shirt, kick off his loafers and lean back on the bed.

Many thoughts and thought fragments flowed through his mind: the pesky reservation about giving up an academic lifestyle; the conversation with Maurice; why Sylvie hadn't asked him upstairs at the Institute; her inviting demeanor; a phone call that arguably could have been staged to set up their dinner meeting. But the impact of all these paled in contrast to Vincent's comment that he kept a loaded gun in his car which by implication, was available for use when they traveled together.

Nonetheless, Paul dwelled on each one and arrived at fuzzier than usual conclusions, but this was a new and in many ways unusual time in his life. And all the events following Leon's e-mail were like so many ticks of the clock. He let it go at that, reminding himself that he was in Paris after all to verify a theory about a six-generation-old death. Or to refute it.

Chapter 5

The taxi weaved through traffic toward the *Herald Tribune*. Paul's cell phone vibrated at his hip. It was Guy Martin.

"Sylvie told me you like our sidewalk cafés," he said, "and I got to thinking. Would you prefer talking over a drink or two, or do you still want to come here?"

What is this? Everyone I meet talks to everyone I'm about to meet?

"If you … well, yes, I'd like that. A drink sounds good right about now."

"*Bon.* I have three favorites, each near one another. Les Deux Magots is the most hip. Jean-Paul Sartre practically lived there. Next door is Café de Flore. Albert Camus helped make it famous. Both are usually tuned into TSF. That's our radio station that embraces American jazz like no other—from your Charlie Parker to Thelonious Monk to Ray Charles. Our music critic here at the *Trib* calls TSF the only unsubsidized station in the world playing smart jazz twenty-four hours a day, seven days a week. So if you like that for background, pick one. Otherwise, right across the street is an entirely different atmosphere: Brasserie Lipp. It's where Ernest Hemingway wrote most of *A Farewell to Arms*. Each one is nice so wherever you say. I'm in Neuilly-sur-Seine so I can be there in fifteen or twenty minutes."

Paul didn't mention he was two blocks from the newspaper. "I know them very well from previous trips. Let's go with Hemingway," he replied. "See you then, and I'm not wearing a red carnation."

"What's that?"

"I'll probably get there before you do. I'm wearing a blue windbreaker."

He notified the driver of the change in plans. As the taxi swerved sharply left to double back to the Montparnasse district, Paul caught a glimpse of the car behind them. It had taken the same abrupt turn and kept a close distance before changing course, an uncomfortable ten minutes later. He had peered back at it repeatedly and had no doubts it was a black Citroen. He puffed out a deep breath.

The same car, twice.

The Brasserie Lipp hadn't changed much since Paul was there last, nor much perhaps since it opened in the late 1800's during the Franco-Prussian War. It had grown to be known among the 12,000 cafés in Paris as the best literary meeting place, having won the Legion of Honor in 1958, commemorating that distinction. Many thought that if there had also been an award for the best beer, sausage and sauerkraut, the Lipp would have won it, hands down.

To this day, some still argue tongue in cheek whether or not the giant publishers Gallimard, Grasset and Hachette Livres settled nearby because of the literary intellectuals who frequented the area. It was in fact one of the reasons why Paul had spent most of his "leisure" time there while in the throes of compiling material for his most recent book, and even writing parts of it, just as Hemingway had turned the same terraced haunt into a place for work. Such a public relations coup was never lost on its proprietors who accepted, even encouraged, the café's nickname: Hemingway Place.

Paul had read the plaque displayed under the awning the last time two years ago, when *St. Helena: Napoleon's Final Defeat* was in its infancy. And now, waiting for Guy, he shielded one eye against the last traces of the fading sun and read it again, taking more pains than before to digest every word. It was written in both French and English.

ON THIS SPOT, ERNEST HEMINGWAY WROTE:

The beer was very cold and wonderful to drink. The pommes à l'huile were firm and marinated and the olive oil delicious. I ground black pepper over the potatoes and moistened the bread in the olive oil. After the first heavy draft of beer, I drank and ate very slowly. When the pommes à l'huile were gone, I ordered another serving of cervelas. This was a sausage like a heavy, wide frankfurter split in two and covered with a special mustard sauce. I mopped up all the oil and all of the sauce with bread and drank the beer slowly until it began to lose its coldness and finished it and ordered a demi ...

It was turning breezy and Paul was tempted to sit and warm up inside but decided he would more readily capture the ambiance he remembered if he simply turned up the collar of his windbreaker and took a seat at the empty table beneath the plaque. Besides, he knew that the conversation he had in mind with Guy, coupled with a beer or two, would raise his thermostat.

The faint mustard and onion aromas too were the same. Only the music wafting from within the café proper was different this time, but still nostalgic — World War II nostalgic: Edith Piaf and *La Vie en Rose*. All that was required to complete a perfect retrogression was the appearance of Vera Lynn and *Lili Marlene* or *The White Cliffs of Dover*.

Within minutes, a short chunky man appeared at the corner, stopped to survey the tables, and despite a cigarette dangling from his mouth, flashed an aha smile at Paul. He hurried over as Paul stood. Their handshake was firm and long, as if either they hadn't met in years or they were about to arm wrestle.

"You'd better be Paul," the man said, smiling more broadly. "I know I'm Guy." His speech was also hurried, its cadence a dramatic contrast to Maurice's.

"Yes *sir*, Guy. Thanks for coming." Paul stared at the cigarette and Guy crushed it into an ashtray.

"Good to meet a man from the States," he said. "I spent twelve years there working for the paper. New York."

He was nearly a head shorter than Paul, with a puffy face that recessed his eyes and a ruddy nose that stood out against a pale complexion. His flint hair seemed ironed, almost glossy, and at the sides ended too abruptly to be considered his own. A gray mustache appeared to be pinned on, pencil-thin in contrast to thick, low-set eyebrows that swept straight across, even encroaching on the bridge of his nose.

He wore black, pleated trousers and a yellow, hand-tied bow tie over a dark brown shirt rolled up at the sleeves. Specks of light reflected off the spaces between pens inserted into a plastic pocket protector.

They sat and looked at each other. Paul felt comfortable with the man he guessed was either side of fifty in age.

Finally he said, "You're probably wondering why I contacted you. I've been asked to research the death of …"

"Yes, I'm aware of that. Leon and Maurice both told me. I know about the delegation too. We're all good friends. Well, most of the time anyway. Leon and I especially. We keep in touch on a regular basis. And I believe Vincent's a definite asset."

Paul thought for a moment. "Maurice thinks very highly of you, you know. Why aren't you part of the delegation?"

"I *am* really but because I'm a newspaper man—an investigative reporter—Leon believes that the more I know, the more I might leak out by accident. He's dead wrong of course. It's a funny relationship, the delegation and me. I'm not officially part of the group but I go to the quarterly meetings of the full membership, give opinions. Leon keeps me abreast of everything important to us. So if he thinks I might accidentally … hell, that could apply to any of us … anyway, you figure. I suppose you might say I'm a de facto member. But back to good old Maurice. He may think highly of me as you put it, but the feeling isn't mutual. Maybe that's a bit harsh, but you should know where we stand if you're to deal with us. He drinks too much and his brain has a few chinks. The Foreign Legion for example. I'm sure he brought it up. Fact is, he was never in it. It's one of his favorite fancies."

"Then why is he part of the delegation?"

"Because he's got Leon snowed, and he does know his military history. Just be careful."

"But did he teach at West Point?"

"Oh yes. I'll give him credit for that. Must have done a decent job too or they wouldn't have kept him on."

"What did he teach?"

"Military tactics. They say he's an expert in spotting enemy errors — in the planning and on the battlefield. But again, be careful. You might want to double check some of the things he says." Guy's expression turned anxious. He changed the subject.

"Let me say right off, Paul." He leaned closer and lowered his voice, but its cadence remained rapid. "Sooner or later the subject of arsenic will come up. As they say in the States, 'sure as shootin'. My take on it is that it was fed to Napoleon in small doses from about 1812 on."

"By one of his own men?"

Guy shrugged. "Hard to tell. But how else to explain his military blunders?"

"Yes, but why give it in small doses?"

Guy shrugged again, took out a cigarette pack, paused and returned it to his side pocket. "I can only speculate. Maybe because it was a convenient way to do it. Maybe because they thought it was less detectable that way. Maybe, and this is far-fetched I know, maybe there was method to madness here: that whoever was doing it deliberately wanted Napoleon to fail in battle. I mean, over and over again. Before dying."

Guy waited for a response and when none was forthcoming seemed disappointed. And said so. "I'm disappointed. You don't agree?"

"It's not that. Those are all plausible reasons." Paul pressed his lips together. "But your choice of the word 'they' intrigues me. You believe it was a conspiracy?"

"Most likely and I'll tell you why in a minute." Guy hailed a waiter.

"And when he didn't die, they finished the job at St. Helena?"

"Precisely."

"By the way," Paul said, "your opinion about the gradual poisoning jibes with Maurice's."

"It's about the only thing we agree on."

They each ordered a beer.

"You have any suspects in mind?" Paul asked. "Wait! Before answering that, I should have explained." One thing he didn't want was to have his questioning smack of an interrogation. "I'm not personally interested in taking information from you and incorporating it into a book or article or anything like that. This is a mission I have in Paris, as you've mentioned you know, and I'm only looking for reasonable opinions and particularly leads that might help. I'm sure you're familiar with that. I'm being paid a handsome fee; I was assured that important doors could be opened for me; and I've been given all the time I need. Lord knows I have the time now and ..."

"I'm aware of that Yale thing too, but please continue. I understand."

The reference registered big time, but Paul didn't let on. "One lead points me in one direction," he said, "which provides another lead, then another, and so on. You know the drill. But getting back to the question: Any suspects?"

"The usual ones but no real proof. I'm talking about

St. Helena, not the start of it all during the battles. This is why I believe there was a conspiracy. You know the cast of characters as well as I do. You've written about them. Count de Montholon heads everyone's list, although I noticed you didn't go out on a limb."

Paul simply queried, "How about Talleyrand?"

"I doubt that," Guy said. "I even believe Montholon conspired with the governor of the island, Hudson Lowe — I call him *Sir Nasty* Lowe — for fear Napoleon would somehow escape and return to France to rule again."

Paul gave him a critical squint. "Have you ever put down these ideas in a column?" he asked.

Four tables over, a waiter dropped a glass. Guy appeared not to notice, instead raised his voice a notch. "Never!" he said. "I don't dare. Too much opposition around here for those points of view — and they wouldn't fly with my bosses. I've covered Napoleon in quite a number of columns, but slanted my opinions about his death toward the natural death theory — stomach cancer — or toward accidental arsenic poisoning, either from inhaling it from the wallpaper or from the incompetence of his physicians who were using it in enemas. Some even say arsenic was administered to make him sick so that the English would allow him back into France."

Guy looked satisfied with his response and, the beer having arrived, took a long gulp and wiped the foam from his lips with the back of his hand. He didn't appear to have any intention of waiting for Paul's reaction.

"So Paul, I sincerely want to assist you and through you, to assist *Gens de Vérité*. I've been a member nearly twenty-five years now, even while working out of the New York office. And if you consider it a favor, I have one to ask of you in exchange."

Paul stopped short of taking his first sip of beer. With no idea of what Guy had in mind, he said, "Anything at all."

"Our conversation should be strictly confidential because as you've already learned, my private views are different from my public views. It sounds hypocritical I know, but I rationalize that I'm not hurting anyone. I mean no harm."

"You have my word," Paul said. "But don't your bosses know you're a member of *Vérité*?" He regretted posing the question because it took up time and, judging from the way Guy was draining his beer, another one would be ordered, and he wanted the newsman to be fully coherent when the subject of the military battles was discussed. Up to this point nothing was new to Paul. It was the battles he wanted to delve into, for although he'd addressed them in one of his books, he believed his research had been sloppy and superficial. Even at that, some of what he had uncovered had been trimmed to the bone for inclusion in the book.

"You bet," Guy said, "and they know I'm proud of it. However, it's all right with them as long as I don't use my position at the Trib to advance *Vérité's* beliefs. They're very gracious that way."

Guy signaled for two more beers but Paul shook his head. "Still working on the first," he said.

It was time for the battles. Paul went ahead. "Leon tells me you've made a study of Napoleon's military campaigns. Can we go into that?"

"I thought you'd never ask. My favorite topic. But first, before I forget, you must know as well as I do,"

Guy was speaking deliberately now, "that there are many investigations taking place, criminal and otherwise, in which boxes and boxes of potential evidence are never opened. Found, discovered, unearthed, lying around, however you want to put it, but never opened. The investigators have one thing in mind. They find it and case closed. They stop looking for other things. So you must locate those boxes and look inside. I've done quite a bit of that myself but, as I've said, had to keep things pretty much under cover—the private versus public thing again. I've uncovered the possibility for example that Napoleon had an affair with some English lady who pursued him wherever he went practically, for years and years. This is the sort of thing that gets lost in the shuffle and is beyond what you can find at say the Bibliothèque."

"Years and years?" Paul asked, almost as breathless as Guy. "Even while he was held captive at Helena?"

"There and at Elba. All the authors write about his wives and lovers but here we have a kind of mystery lady. And I'll let you in on another little secret. Diaries, memoirs, letters, wills? They're available and accessible if you know where to look. But again, I'm not talking about what you can find at libraries or auctions or other public places. Private collections are the best way. Private collections from private collectors. Not only that though. Let's narrow it further: private collections from private *anonymous* collectors. They buy and sell. I have a unique relationship with most of them, so I can borrow or 'rent' information for a few days if it's in written form, sometimes only hours, depending, but I can't keep the original source materials unless they say so. And that's rare. Sometimes what you get from them isn't in written form at all; they simply tell you things. Actually that's the case most of the time. They gather information for you and they also refer to all the information on a certain topic as a "collection." Their fee for me is reasonable. It wasn't at first but now it is ...we've done business for a long time. I refer to them as '*historians*' — you know, like 'contrarians'— because what they furnish is often contrary to what history has provided us. Exhaustive research can change earlier beliefs. For example new findings about Napoleon's era popped up not only fifty years ago but also as recently as 2002 and 2005. Or how about this? The first slaves in your country were originally thought to have come from the West Indies. Now, new research this year, with excellent documentation, shows that they came from Angola. And if I may say so, Paul, what you need is just that: *excellent documentation*. I'm sorry, I get into these rambling moods."

"Not at all," Paul said. "Is it inappropriate to ask how you've earned that unique relationship with these ... these *historians*?"

"Completely appropriate. I'd be surprised if you *didn't* ask. I've been able to keep their enterprises under ..." He searched for the right word, "... under wraps I suppose is the best way to put it, to keep their identities and what they do out of the spotlight, away from media coverage. Believe me, it's all on the up and up, and they're grateful. Plus they know that whatever I learn from them and from whatever they let me examine will be kept confidential."

By then, Guy was halfway through his second mug of beer. "Just as I would ask of you. If and when you're ready to go that route, I'd be willing to point you in the right direction—a *confidential* direction."

"You have my promise," Paul said, taking his longest swig. "I'm not quite ready yet. Got to get my bearings you know, but when I do …"

"Don't forget, let me know." The request reminded Paul of Leon. "I'm at work early every morning, six days a week," Guy added.

"Any names to give me now?" Paul asked.

"I'd rather call you back. I'll alert them first and get an official okay. Incidentally, Leon and the whole delegation knows of the *histarians* and I'd be shocked if they'd disapprove of your consulting with them."

In view of Guy's revelations to that point, the subject of military battles seemed somewhat anticlimactic, especially since Maurice had already gone over the essentials, but *Maurice Delacroix was no Guy Martin*, and Paul decided to continue as planned but with a minor adjustment. For in fact his sole purpose in meeting with Guy was to confirm and embellish on Maurice's information. However, since the mention of anonymous collectors and the mystery lady had come up, Paul had lost interest in learning more from the journalist, military battles or not. Before, he'd intended to request details; now it would be a scaled down version. Furthermore, holding back his own thoughts was frustrating him. After all, he had written two massive books on Napoleonic history.

"I understand you have some personal insights on Napoleon's military campaigns," Paul said. "If you're anything like me, you probably have folder after folder on them. I should have asked if you'd take some along to refer to." He was hoping such an approach would lead Guy simply to touch upon the issue.

Guy let out a loud, alcohol-heightened laugh. "No need to. I apologize, I'm beginning to feel the beer … we should have asked for some biscuits." He engaged the waiter's eye, gestured for the check, and then turned back to Paul. "I don't need a folder. I know his principles of war by heart and keep them treasured there. But his mistakes are another matter. I wish I could store them somewhere else." He caught a fly with his hand and dashed it against the table. "Got the little bastard," he exclaimed. "You feel like listening?"

"If you don't mind," Paul said.

"Well, first off, Napoleon had a natural grasp of the essential tactics for war and the art of waging it. He would rattle off these aphorisms as if they were golden rules and early in his career they pretty much were. Like, 'A field of battle which the enemy has previously studied and reconnoitered should be avoided,' or 'March dispersed, fight concentrated', or 'When it is possible to employ thunderbolts, their use should be preferred to that of cannon.' And my favorite: 'War is an immense art which comprises all others. It is also, like politics, a matter of tact'. Guy recited the words like an evangelistic preacher. "There's almost a pious glory to them," he said, "but eventually Napoleon blasphemed that glory.

"Take the first one about reconnoitering. He broke it by attacking Wellington on the Waterloo position even though the Duke had reconnoitered it the year before. And Napoleon *knew* it."

Paul felt as though he should say something. Anything. "You and Maurice talk about this stuff?"

"All the time. Now then, along about 1812, during the Russian Campaign specifically, things began to change. His mechanics of warfare became flawed and that continued on until his pitiful fall at Waterloo three years later. That period was not Napoleon's finest—what an understatement! For in a way, the real Napoleon ceased to exist. I won't elaborate, Paul, but during those two debacles and during the Spanish and French campaigns, he violated the classic maneuvers of warfare. Most military experts say there were only seven of them. To wit …"

Paul imagined he was listening to the final draft of one of Guy's newspaper columns.

" … penetration of the center, envelopment of a single flank, envelopment of both flanks, attack in oblique order, the feigned withdrawal, attack from a defensive position, and the indirect approach. But without a doubt, the worst thing he ever said, and a dead giveaway that his mind was being altered, was, 'I have fought sixty battles and I have learnt nothing that I did not know in the beginning.' Can you imagine? Learnt nothing!"

Guy ignored a bead of sweat at the corner of his mustache. He was visibly tired. He gave a single pat to the edge of the table with all ten fingers and said, "I could go on and on but you get the idea. Maybe we could meet again if you'd like, but for now I'll end with a question: Have I made my case about the gradual poisoning of one of the greatest military commanders in history—right up there with Alexander and Caesar?"

Paul was the first to stand. "Yes you have," he said, "strikingly. And I appreciate it. I appreciate your time and I appreciate the knowledge you've shared. There's no doubt that I'll call on you again."

They exchanged cell phone numbers. Paul picked up the check from the table and started to leave but

Guy grasped his arm. "Paul," he said, "two last things. I suppose in the greater scheme of things, the first doesn't matter but that business of mythology and the powers that be at Yale. Any truth to what Leon told me?"

It was Paul's first uncomfortable moment with Guy. "It obviously depends on what he told you," Paul replied.

"That they were unhappy with your reliance on mythology."

"That's way off base. I don't rely on it; sometimes I find it instructive."

"Well if it makes you feel any better so do I."

But Paul didn't buy it. "And the other thing?" he asked.

"That mystery lady? If you decide to pursue it and learn her name, you might check out a connection with the East India Tea Company. There was some reference to it in some obscure publication, but I never followed up on it."

Chapter 6

On the taxi return to the Meridien, Paul made some notes—his summations— beginning with: "Can't believe was in Paris only 5 hrs & already met with Maurice, Sylvie and columnist Guy Martin (recomm. by Maurice)." He looked vacantly out the window until a conclusion gelled: that he shouldn't care about any tensions among certain delegation members. That he just wanted to utilize them individually as resource people. Still, he wondered what the real reasons behind the tensions were. He scribbled down highlights of each meeting and first impressions of each person. And last impressions. He had always held to a maxim recorded in mythological history—he could never remember the exact quote—that first and last impressions were not necessarily the same; that last ones required time before becoming lasting ones, which in turn could be dissimilar to the others.

He put asterisks next to several points:

Under Maurice: "Must study what Napoleon didn't do in battles. Truthful? Dislikes Vincent? Jealous?"

Under Sylvie: "Purposeful, but for what? Phone call to her arranged? Dinner tonight."

But most asterisks were assigned to Guy: "Mistrusts Maurice and probably Leon. Sweeping orations. In my

art-recovery travels, why did I never hear of *histarians*?
If Napoleon murdered, did killer really want slow death
so more battles lost? Why bring up mystery lady? East
India Tea Co.? Why ask re mythology? A resource worth
more tapping."

He also asterisked "suspicious black Citroen," then
went back to underline mystery lady.

During interviews, Paul usually shied away from
taking notes, which he considered distracting to both
parties, and welcomed the time afterwards when he could
record his summations. He looked upon that time as a
triumph of a previously cluttered mind.

He arrived at his hotel room at 5:30 and called Jean
at the lab in Connecticut. It was 11:30 a.m. there.

He apologized for not calling sooner to confirm his
safe arrival. "But everything happened so fast, beginning
as soon as I closed the door to the room."

"That's the way you like things, though, isn't it?"

"How?"

"Fast. Or else you're bored."

"Me? Or should I say 'moi'?"

Paul outlined the afternoon and mentioned his dinner
engagement with Sylvie.

"What does she look like?" Jean asked.

"Gorgeous."

"Oh, great."

"Not to worry. I'm all business."

"But what about *her*?"

"I'll handle it if she isn't."

Paul didn't know how to handle the ensuing silence,
however.

"Well, I do trust you, my love," she finally said.

"And I, you. You must know that."

Paul reiterated some of what he'd learned about the people he'd met. When the question of research came up, he said, "The way I figure it is that if new records surfaced in 1955 and again in 2002 and 2005, then certainly more must be around. But with what Guy said about those *historians*, I might not need to break my a ... to search high and low for them."

Jean laughed.

"What's so funny?"

"You don't have to mince your words with me. Don't you know that by now?"

"I'm just practicing for tonight."

Paul checked his watch. He wanted more time to review matters with her but closed with, "Look, wish me luck. I'll call you at the end of each day."

"How many is that?"

"I don't know yet."

There was less than an hour to take a second afternoon shower, shave, don a turtleneck, jacket and trousers in different shades of brown and keep his dinner engagement with Sylvie.

James Cameron wrote, "Paris is an air and a scent and a state of mind." The same can be said of the gourmet Alain Ducasse Restaurant in the Hotel Plaza Athenée. The hotel, just off the Champs-Élysées and within view of the Eiffel Tower, is a throwback to the classic French style of the early twentieth century with its high ceilings, authentic moldings, and fireplaces. Located on one of the world's most glamorous shopping streets, it's surrounded by one luxury boutique after another: Chanel, Dior, Lacroix,

Valentino. Inside, the restaurant itself is what Paul would call "classy" or, depending on the listener, "refined", with central tables, brass lamps, and red leather banquets beneath Art Deco murals. The backside of its menus refers to the scent of the dining room as that of "white tea mingled with geranium and freesia that is designed to be calming, relaxing and sophisticated."

From a distance, Paul recognized Sylvie standing near the front archway. He gave a slight wave and, walking over, admired her attire: white pleated silk-chiffon dress, gold sandals and an embroidered black silk coat that she wore unbuttoned.

They exchanged greetings. "I understand you've had an interesting afternoon," she said.

His lip curled slightly. "Guy Martin no doubt called you."

"Yes, he did. We're old friends and like it or not, you're somewhat of a celebrity."

"And you look radiant I might say."

They entered the crowded main room and the maitre d' ushered them to a corner table near a large window. String music was barely audible above the lowered conversations of middle-aged patrons, the whispers of the young set. Moving among the tables, Sylvie cited their good fortune in obtaining a reservation on such short notice.

Shortly thereafter, they agreed to forego any discussion about the mission until later, perhaps over an after dinner drink. They then dined on soupe à l'oignon, crudités, boeuf bourguignon and a fine wine while Sylvie spoke of French fashions and Parisian café society, often reaching over to touch his arm in the process. For his part,

Paul dwelled on the adventure and sometimes the peril of chasing down stolen art treasures — "170,000 of them world-wide. Of course, they weren't all my cases." He stifled what would have been a wry grin. At one point, he caught her mischievous eyes scanning his face but he didn't let on.

"And Sylvie," he said, "I've been thinking."

"Oh you have, have you?" she teased.

"Yes. Of those 170,000, there are 166 Rembrandts, 167 Renoirs, 175 Warhols and 200 Dali's." He punctuated the air with his fork. "But think of it … they can't be sold! Nobody in his right mind would touch such famous works of art, so they're probably gone forever."

"Unless you were the one hunting them down, Paul."

He disregarded the compliment and said, "Then there's the problem of forgeries. If I find a stolen art piece and later learn it's a fake … dealers tell me forged art makes up forty percent of the market. Forty percent! Then I feel obliged to return half my fee."

"So your fees are up-front?"

"Sure. It's only fair, before I put in all kinds of effort. Many's the time some Far Eastern — crooks I call them — have reneged on me and I never made a fuss because of my position at Yale."

"Let me tell you, Paul, the whole delegation knows about that policy of yours. I mean the reimbursing half thing. Even my friends at the Institute — the ones into serious art like paintings and sculpture. They say it's what separates you from the rest of the art sleuths. That's what you are, right?"

" 'Art *investigator'* sounds more elegant."

"In a non-elegant field?"

"Why so?"

"Forty percent."

He felt no blotches and chalked it up to the alcohol. As dinner wore on—the wine glasses were replenished more than once—he had increasing difficulty keeping his gaze off the swell of her breasts which he assumed she knew rose and fell with her breathing. Which, in turn, had become heavier.

He saw that she noticed him and foolishly, because he couldn't think of any other way to say it, he stammered, "Your breathing has changed."

"Yes, a bit. Happens now and then. Then was then; this is now. Does it bother you?" Her leer was unmistakable.

Paul felt reasonably in charge of himself, yet allowed his mind to drift. *I could have this woman for the night but thank God for Jean. I only wish she were here to help me. Not fair ... not at all.*

Seconds later, Sylvie announced that she, too, had been thinking. "Would you care to come to my place for dessert? I made some nice crème brûlée." She uttered the words like a schoolgirl.

Paul, his eyes as wide as hers, responded, "Your place?"

"Yes, we could easily walk there. It's an apartment only a couple of blocks away." She pointed out the window. "I'm temporarily between houses, but that's a long story. I might even stay put. I'd love you to see it. C'mon, why not? We could have our own little party."

Paul hesitated. This doesn't compute. It should be the other way around! Ah, these French women. Or, for some obscure reason, was he being tested by the delegation?

"Thanks, but I'm beat," he said, almost biting his tongue, "and you've got to understand if you don't already: I'm engaged. Name's Jean. You didn't know that?"

"Well, Leon briefed the delegation on just about everything about you. Your ... Jean ... sounds familiar come to think of it. Guess it didn't mean too much to me at the time." Her features fell. "So how 'bout that?" she said. "A rejection and a revelation, both on the same night. Lucky me!"

"We can have an after-dinner drink in the bar though, can't we?"

Sylvie looked wounded, but she slowly composed herself and, her breathing normalized, grumbled, "I suppose that's better than a complete rejection."

They quibbled over who would pick up the tab until she said, "Don't worry, I have an expense account. This is part of international cooperation, minus the dessert I'm afraid." She laughed heartily, a sign that convinced Paul once and for all that she had other things on her mind besides the mission.

If the restaurant's design was retro, the hotel's hip Bar du Plaza was avant-garde and the hottest address in Paris. The centerpiece was the bar itself, long and illuminated with cool blue lights. Paul had been there numerous times before and remembered its similarity to an iceberg or glacier. He was tempted to suggest they sit on the tall blue stools but decided that if their conversation were to turn serious, as he hoped, there would be greater privacy at a table. They took the nearest one available, sitting opposite one another. Each ordered a Rosé Royale, the house specialty.

Sylvie reached over, placed her hand on his, and said, "Look, let's you and I get one thing settled, shall we?"

"You said the same exact thing earlier today."

Ignoring the remark she said, "I haven't the faintest idea about how to help you except to answer your questions." She withdrew her hand and waited for a response.

"Okay," Paul said, "If you were me, where would you start?"

She wasted no time in answering, leaning forward, her brow pleated. "With Napoleon's lovers. I mean secret lovers, real secret."

Guy had touched on the same subject only hours before, but Paul welcomed a woman's point of view, especially Sylvie's. "Funny you picked that as a starting point," he said. "Why?"

She lowered her eyes as well as her voice. "Because much is revealed in the heat of passion. Maybe Napoleon got careless, revealed too much. And you might get some clues, like from some recorded confessions. Was there any jealousy rearing its ugly head?"

"And how's the best way to explore the issue?" he countered.

"There must be memoirs or journals or letters lying around that have never been examined or even found yet."

She knows the same *historians*? But if so, why?

"Great!" he exclaimed. It was his most emotional comment of the night, perhaps too emotional, but he let it stand. "Two hundred years of history writing out there," he continued, "and I'm supposed to uncover something new on the subject?"

Before he had a chance to retract the statement—for it suddenly dawned on him that their friendship was brand new—she reached over once again and patted his hand.

"But that's why you took the job, remember? At least that's why I think you did. We're all counting on you, and now having met you, I personally believe you can do it."

"Well thank you." Paul looked around for the waiter and their drinks before asking, "Any idea where I should spend my time? At least for starters?"

"You've probably spent time there before but you might try Bibliothèque Nationale or the War Museum at Invalides. As you know, they have volumes and volumes on Napoleon you won't find anywhere else. I wish I could put you in touch with people who know more than I do." She brushed her hair away from her eye. "You've already spoken with Guy Martin and he's clearly the number one fan of the emperor in all of France. And because of that, he's right there near the top as far as experts on Napoleonic history are concerned. Kind of an unpublished, non-university-based expert's expert. I'm sure you know of such people—if not historians, certainly mythologists."

"Oh no, don't tell me you too!"

"What?" she asked.

"Mythologists. Where'd you get that? Forget it. The delegation knows I'm into it and I'd wager they all understand. Not like that dumb Yale group." He sighed through his nose, hoping it would stem the bitterness. "Plus while we're on the subject of who knows what, I understand the entire delegation knows that the Institute is oblivious to your connection with *Vérité*. But I'm not, and I translate it into your being a spy."

"Look," she said, "Let's you and I get one thing…"

"I know, I know," he blurted, "'one thing settled'."

"I apologize," Sylvie said, "I've developed this compulsion, this obsession. Do you have any obsessions?"

"Certainly. Napoleon." *Why is she avoiding the spy label?*

She drew back, observed him skeptically, then said, "That's why you're the obvious person for the job."

He began scratching his finger.

"I once knew a man who did that same thing," she said.

"What?"

"Scratched his finger."

"Oh," he said, shoving his hands in his pockets. "I didn't even know I was doing it."

"So there must be other things you do and don't even know it, right?"

"I do?"

"There!" she cried. "Right there. See?"

"Sometimes I eat crackers too—saltines"

"You what?"

"When I get nervous."

She fed him an incredulous look. "A man like you gets nervous?" she said.

"You'd be surprised. But you're embarrassing me. Let's move on. I wanted to ask you about Talleyrand. Do you think he had anything to do with Napoleon's death?"

"Talleyrand? No, I don't. But that's only because I'm not convinced Napoleon was murdered. That puts me in the minority as far as the delegation is concerned. I'm sorry."

"Don't be sorry. You're entitled. And that's why I'm here. Not so much to identify his killer, but to determine if he was definitely killed in the first place."

"And I'll help in any way I can. Maybe if your conclusion is murder, I'll be convinced."

For several seconds, they eyeballed each other. Paul felt awkward and at the same time wasn't sure how to interpret Sylvie's facial expression, as there was still some kind of emotion there.

"Will you be going outside of Paris on this trip?" she asked.

"I'm not sure yet. Any suggestions?"

"Elba? St. Helena? Although that's practically unreachable out there in no man's land. South Atlantic. No airfield. Takes days by ship if there *are* any anymore."

Their drinks arrived, they toasted the mission and each took a sip, Sylvie savoring hers more fervently. She ran her tongue delicately over her lower lip.

"But," she continued, "just because of his exiles—six years on Helena, I think—doesn't mean you'd gain anything by going to either place. After all, that was almost two hundred years ago."

"We'll see," he said. "Who knows? I might even decide on London. A lot of where I go depends on how I do in the next day or two, if I get information that would lead me to certain places."

Sylvie took two more sips in succession. Her face hardened. "Look," she said, " I find all this so very intriguing, and please don't think I'm being too forward. You might though, because we've only just met. But I feel I've known you longer. What the heck, why not?" She fondled the gold chain around her neck. "If it's beyond France, I'd be willing to accompany you. With the delegation's approval of course. Strictly business."

Flabbergasted, Paul put his glass down, fearful he might take a swallow and choke. *What am I getting into here?*

"Well," he replied, "well, ah, that sounds like a nice offer. Very cordial. Yes, cordial. And I appreciate it. Let's see how things develop."

Sylvie downed the rest of her drink in a single gulp. "Paul?" she said, drawing out the name. "Did you ever believe that destiny takes you by the hand?"

"And what exactly is destiny anyway?" he said. He realized he answered the question with a question and quickly said, "If it's what I think it is, I suppose so." He was as unsure of where they were going with the question as he was taken aback by her offer to travel with him.

"Or escape," she said. "Did you ever want to escape from yourself?"

"Not too often," he said. "How about you?"

"Yes, but I don't mean in a sick way. If you can't escape from yourself, then I guess the next best thing is to change *le milieu*, the surroundings, and that's why I asked if you'd take me along in your travels. I value things like these: destiny, fate, escape to new lands. I like to think of them as imaginary lands. You might question why I bother with these thoughts. And I would answer that you might as well question why I breathe."

It all sounded to Paul like rationalization, concocted and delivered on the spur of the moment to soften her earlier request. He thought they should end the conversation and call it a night.

This time it was he who reached across the table, taking her hands in his. "Sylvie," he said, "I don't know if you're a sentimental scientist or a scientific sentimentalist, but either way you're most engaging. I've enjoyed the evening and you'll be hearing from me again. That's for sure."

As he was getting up she said, "May I have the last word on the subject?"

He smiled approvingly.

She beckoned him closer. He complied and she whispered, "Sooner or later, we all become sentimentalists."

Outside the restaurant, Paul reconfirmed that Paris at night was unlike any of the world's other great cities. As a stolen art hunter he had been to most of them: London, Rome, Budapest, Istanbul, Buenos Aires, Lisbon, Seville, Vienna. He again looked forward to the gleaming beauty of the palaces and monuments of Paris and its chestnut tree-lined avenues, all awash in a panoply of floodlights. The City of Light. And ordinarily a city of unrelenting traffic noise. On this night however, as he gave Sylvie a parting hug and she turned to leave, it seemed to him to be also a city of silent calm.

She had refused his offer of walking her home—"It's only a block away"—and during her first dozen steps toward her apartment, he stood mulling over the wisdom of that refusal. Then everything happened in a blur: black Citroen breaking the silence of the evening … tires screeching to a halt opposite Sylvie, three men piling out, two at her arms, one pulling a hood over her head … muffled screams of, "No! No!" … feet dragging along the pavement, body shoved into the back seat, men wedging in on either side… Citroen bursting off.

Paul was struck motionless. Sylvie had been whisked away in a matter of seconds! There had been no time to intercede, even to yell out. But he hadn't failed to notice that it was unmistakably the same car that had followed him twice before.

He stared at the car's shrinking taillights for a few seconds, then rushed back into the restaurant. He informed the nearest employee of the kidnapping, and asked her to call the police. Meanwhile he took out a card with the delegation's contact numbers and reached Leon, cell phone to cell phone. Leon's response to the news was more emotional than Paul had expected. He stated he was at a dinner party nearby but would break away and arrive at the Alain Ducasse in a matter of minutes. It was eight-thirty-five. Paul had come to picture *Vérité's* leader as "the giant" and felt that his own day's overdose of emotion had distorted his thinking when he envisioned a visibly upset giant taking a few steps across several city blocks to reach the restaurant.

A few minutes later, Leon entered the lobby at the same time as four police officers. They took turns shaking his hand warmly. Leon introduced Paul as a consultant to *Vérité,* then called the lead officer aside. He returned to Paul and whispered, "There. They'll keep it out of the papers."

With Leon standing by, the police asked Paul three questions and left.

"That's all?" Paul said, flustered. "I thought I'd be detained for a while."

"They know where to reach me," Leon said.

Paul better understood Leon's earlier claim of

"connections at the highest levels." And in the rush of excitement, Paul hardly noticed the giant's attire: a three-piece, double-breasted tan suit with vest and silver watch chain. The outfit was less then slenderizing.

In contrast to Leon's response on the phone, his mood was one of controlled preoccupation. He approached the reservations desk and asked for an empty table. Permission granted, they headed toward it side by side. Each sat heavily on adjacent chairs.

By now Paul, perhaps taking the lead from Leon, felt slightly more composed. He was eager to discuss the kidnapping and its ramifications.

"Is there any family to notify?" he asked.

"I don't believe so," Leon said. He used the butt of his cigarette to light another. "She's an only child. Her mother and father died in an auto accident and she never married."

"Any enemies?"

"Not that I know of. She's a great gal. Well liked, popular. Competent at her job."

Between responses Leon shook his head in disbelief.

Then he arched back. "Just a minute!" he exclaimed. "I wonder …"

"You wonder what?" Paul asked, feeling more like an attorney for Sylvie than a hired investigator for *Vérité*.

"Some years ago, maybe ten or twelve, she mentioned she was being stalked by a man and woman in a car. It continued on and off for a few months. She told me about it. We even called the police and arranged some intermittent protection for her. That was called off about three months later because there were no further sightings of the car. So we forgot about it. I wonder ..."

"I'll bet *she's* never forgotten though. She ever mention it since?"

"No, not to me anyway."

"And you'd be the one she'd most likely tell, right?"

"Most likely."

Paul ran a finger back and forth over his lips. "Offhand," he said, "I doubt there's a connection. Then again, maybe there could be. But that was a long time ago."

"Unless," Leon said, "unless it continued, but she kept it to herself."

"I can't imagine stalking and stalking and then finally kidnapping her ten years later."

"No, I guess you're right," Leon said, "so for now we just wait it out. I'm not sure for what though. Are they after ransom money? Or was it for sex?"

Paul shook his head no. "I doubt it because it was the same car that followed me earlier today." He then described the tailgating black Citroen and the taxi ride from the airport and, four hours later, to the Brasserie Lipp café, episodes that suddenly took on greater significance.

"Interesting," Leon said. "When I get home I'd better inform some of my detective friends at the prefecture."

"Does this mean we should postpone the mission?" Paul held his breath.

"No way!" Leon fired back. His voice seemed raspier than usual.

Paul got up and put his hands on his hips as if to emphasize the next statement. "Good. I hope it doesn't sound callous at a time like this, but I'm raring to continue tomorrow." He sat again. "Which reminds me: Elba and St. Helena?"

"Both banishment and the emperor's low points. One place wasn't too bad for him, but the other was holy hell at times. What about them?"

"Any value in my traveling there?"

"Absolutely. You never know what may have been overlooked even after all these years, and the *histarians* will prove invaluable. Guy and I discussed that option at length."

"I suppose I should ask if Helena is even accessible. It's in the middle of nowhere."

"As I pointed out in New Haven, practically anything can be arranged for you, Paul. St. Helena has no airstrip but you can reach it from Ascension Island. That's about eight hundred miles from Helena. Then from there, about a day and a half by ship. The Royal Air Force has regular flights to the Falkland Islands that stop at Ascension. We could set you up on one. It would leave from Brize Norton airbase, about an hour's drive from London." Leon paused as if to assess whether or not he had left anything out. "And you're right," he continued, "midway between Africa and South America is the middle of nowhere."

"So we're talking roughly two to three days total?"

"About that, plus the time you spend there. If you decide yes, let me know and I'll get things moving."

"Decision made. I tend to agree with you, Leon. A fresh look at both locations is a must. Let me think about the timing and I'll call you tomorrow." He had already decided, in fact, that following up on Guy's offer to put him in touch with the *histarians* was more crucial than anything else on his agenda.

Paul rose stiffly. His body told him that it could never sustain the pace of the last nine hours in Paris.

"Well, I'd better turn in," he said. "Thanks for responding so soon." It sounded abrupt but he'd had enough for one day and needed some quiet time, let alone a good night's sleep. Perhaps the jet lag was taking a toll after all; regardless, even without it, he could always tell when mental fatigue finally caught up, when his mind might not have been fair in judgment of others. In this case, the people he'd met since noon had characteristics that troubled him, some more keenly than others.

Leon's parting words were, "Please inform me of any significant developments."

All the way back to his hotel room, Paul found himself rushing—in paying the cab driver, walking through the lobby, exiting the elevator. He couldn't wait for a breather, to be alone with his thoughts. He closed the door behind him and was about to turn, lean against it and sigh when his attention was diverted to a sheet of paper directly under his feet. It looked like a hotel bill slipped under the door on checkout morning. He bent over and picked it up. It contained a single line typed in bold capital letters:

LEAVE PARIS TOUT DE SUITE

So much for a breather!

Questions raced through his mind. "Leave Paris immediately": why was it written in both English and French? Other than the delegation, Guy and Jean, who knows I'm in France and especially at the Meridien Hotel?

Were Sylvie and I being watched at the restaurant? Is there any connection to the kidnapping? He answered only the last: possibly.

He was tempted to pass off the note as some kind of joke or as a case of mistaken identity. But considering the stalking black Citroen and the fresh-in-his-mind kidnapping, how far could he go with excuses? If he hadn't been alone in the room, he would have folded the paper, put it in his pocket and dismissed it for later consideration. But he allowed himself to be shaken, to conclude once and for all that the mission he had coveted and agreed to would be perilous at best.

He had three phone calls to make. He punched in the number for the reception desk, resisting the urge to scratch a finger. After learning that no one had asked if he was a guest there, he phoned Jean in the States. It was three p.m. there. He steadied his voice and related all he could think of regarding the kidnapping and its aftermath. All except the note under the door, as he didn't want her begging him to heed its instruction and return home. But precisely that occurred when he described the kidnapping.

"That's terrible!" she shrieked. "Maybe you should reconsider staying there. I mean it, Paul. It's not worth it if it's that dangerous. You may be next and …"

"Now let's not jump to conclusions. You know, it may have nothing to do with me or the mission for that matter. Sure, it was terrible, but let's not get too uptight. Okay?"

There was no response.

"Okay?" Paul said again.

"Okay, but we've gone into a whole new realm here. What's next, bodyguards?"

Paul felt the blotches and let the remark pass. "So let's keep it together and go on as if it hadn't happened." He swallowed dryly. "I've decided to stay here longer than I'd originally planned. For starters, there's a meeting with the *histarians*. Then the trips to Elba and St. Helena; these will take time."

She offered no opposition, instead saying, "I'd make it *histarians* first, just in case they furnish you with some leads or secret information about the islands."

"Good point," Paul said, relieved. "And Jean? See if you can do a check on Guy Martin. Remember? He's with the *International Herald Tribune* based here."

They exchanged "miss you" sentiments and Paul said he'd keep her posted.

The last call was to *Vérité's* president. "Leon?"

"So soon?"

"I'm afraid so. You mentioned significant developments and this is definitely one you should know about." Paul described the plain sheet of paper and recited the brief message.

Without hesitation Leon said, "I think it's time for you to have an armed Vincent nearby, particularly when you're out of your hotel room."

"But ..."

"No 'buts', my friend. "We think very highly of you. And your safety is foremost."

Paul remained silent, thinking of Jean's "what's next?" statement.

"Yet you're also *Vérité's* grand investment. Now Vincent may not appear to be a bodyguard type but believe me, he's quick and wiry strong. I've seen him take down a pickpocket twice his size. Had martial arts training. Uses his wits. And he's an expert with pistols. I'm alerting him and I'm sure he'll agree to meet you in the lobby — at say, 8 in the morning?"

"Eight would be fine."

After the conversation Paul was slightly more relieved than he had let on. He checked the door from the outside to make sure it was locked, then readied himself for bed still dwelling on the gravity of recent events. He had never experienced such a "travel" day and certainly never anticipated a kidnapping from right under his nose and a demanding note from right under his door. *What happened, happened. But why?* He refused to buy into the obvious theory that Sylvie was being used as a bargaining chip to remove him from the mission.

As he lay tossing and turning, the last few hours fading into a half-forgotten nightmare, he searched for a bracing thought. But he couldn't find any.

Chapter 7

Saturday, May 20

At 8 a.m., Paul scanned the lobby but saw no one resembling Vincent. Still sleepy but more emotionally collected, he paid little attention to the coffee shop as he walked by.

"In here," a voice said.

Paul doubled back sharply and seeing Vincent, coffee cup in hand, gave him a knowing smile.

"I saved you a seat, Paul," Vincent said. "Have you had breakfast? Their stuff is pretty good. Lots of safe ingredients in the whole wheat muffins."

They shook hands. Paul pulled out a chair from a table near the middle of a small but crowded room. "No I haven't. And don't tell me you've tasted the muffins and you weren't poisoned."

Vincent laughed. "Sorry, didn't mean it that way. I should have used the word 'healthy'."

The shop seemed like an architectural afterthought, a projection into a heavily flowered courtyard, its ceiling a series of clear glass panels that rose to a center point. Patches of dew dispersed into new patterns. There were no booths, just square glass-topped tables for two and a counter at one end with stools fully occupied by silent morning customers. All the furnishings were done in variegated pastels. Their colors were no doubt accentuated by shafts of early morning light beaming through the ceiling and two side walls of casement windows. The air smelled of coffee and bacon.

Vincent bit into the last of his muffin as Paul ordered orange juice, coffee, salted crackers and the same kind of muffin. As he tucked the corner of a napkin into the top of his white sport shirt, he spotted a slight bulge near the left lapel of Vincent's sport jacket. "Nice jacket," Paul said, nodding toward the bulge.

"You noticed. Too obvious?"

"No, not at all. I happened to be looking for it. What kind?"

"It's a Beretta Cougar .45. The other's a Heritage Stealth 9mm."

"The other?"

"In my ankle rig," Vincent whispered. "You should know it's there. My outer right side. Just in case I'm down and you need a pistol."

Paul didn't know whether to be reassured or to recoil. He glanced at the counter. More than one man glanced back. *Or was it his imagination?*

"I don't think you'll ever need it though, do you?" Vincent asked.

Without bothering to respond Paul said, "I've got to ask you: Are you sure you're up to this? I mean following me around. My bodyguard as Leon put it. Who knows where developments might take me?"

"The answer is yes. Whatever and wherever. I'm looking forward to it."

"But what about your responsibilities at the

Sorbonne?"

"Leon's taken care of that."

"And the home front—are you married?"

"No. Engaged. Yvette's working on her doctorate at Trinity College in Dublin."

"What field?"

"What else? History. Hope you can meet her someday."

"I'd like that."

Paul's breakfast arrived and he put the package of saltines in his pocket. Vincent asked for a coffee refill.

"You know," Paul continued, stirring his coffee, "I took on this assignment thinking it would be completely clandestine, but I get the feeling the whole world knows about it."

"Hard to say, but I wouldn't go that far. It may be that you're, ah, that the entire delegation's a bit on edge, until we get rolling, so everything's magnified."

Paul harked back to Leon's initial use of the word "astute" in describing Vincent, and was beginning to agree with him. He shifted to another subject.

"Speaking of the delegation, do you and Maurice get along?"

"Why? Did he say something bad about me again?"

"Well ..."

"Truth is he doesn't care for any man under forty."

"Women okay?"

"*Any* woman is okay with him. But on balance he's a decent fellow. Wife died about five years ago and he turned to drinking. Only guy I know who uses red wine as a mouthwash. Holds it well though and he's just as sharp

as ever on military matters. Once in a while he'll go into
the business of his escapades in the Foreign Legion, but
he was never a member at all. We put up with it, so now
the stories have taken on a life of their own. Sort of sad
really."

Despite the favorable outcome of Jean's earlier
check on *Vérité's* members, excluding Guy but including
Vincent, Paul had wanted to form his own conclusions at
this breakfast meeting. It hadn't taken long. This was the
right man to accompany him on his investigative journey.
Paul was impressed with his maturity, his intellect and
his crisp replies. Moreover, Vincent's facial expressions
indicated he cared deeply about what he was saying.

But Paul had one more question. "Vincent, I didn't
intend this to be a quiz, but one last thing. Can you tell
me your definition of 'loyalty'?"

Vincent wasted no time. "Certainly," he said.
"Remember the pistol at my ankle? I indicated that if I
were down, you might need it? I didn't say 'dead', I said
'down', wounded, maybe slightly, and even if that were
the case, you could still have the pistol."

Paul stared at the young Frenchman in disbelief for
a full ten seconds. Then he held out his hand. Vincent
reached over and shook it and they both stood as if it were
a solemn ceremony.

"Today we start as a team," Paul said.

After discussing a workable but flexible schedule—
Leon's and Guy's input were crucial— they agreed to meet
at the coffee shop each morning at eight. At day's end
Vincent would accompany Paul to the door of his hotel
room. The proposed trips to Elba and St. Helena were

a different story and would be dealt with later. Without urging, Vincent stated he would stay in the background as much as possible, but Paul insisted that he remain within earshot of any important discussions they might encounter because he valued his opinions. They also agreed that they should meet with the *historians* before visiting either island.

"You have my cell phone number," Vincent said. "Keep it handy. I'll have it turned on twenty-four/ seven."

Vincent listened in as Paul phoned Guy Martin at the *Tribune*.

"You heard about Sylvie, I take it?" Paul said.

Guy asked him to call back to his cell phone. Paul obliged.

"Sorry," Guy said, "too many nosy switchboard operators around here. Yes, I know about Sylvie."

"Leon called you?"

"No. I heard about it from my main man at the prefecture. I guess you might call it a direct pipeline with the police. Please keep this quiet but I check there nearly every morning. Been doing it for years now. Then I can get printed pretty much whatever criminal stuff I want. In return, I try to make the police look good, at least never like fools. A bit conniving but no money ever changes hands so I consider it above board. Happens in government all the time. Even Leon knows about it and he's never objected."

Paul was inclined to take a dim view of the disclosure but didn't want to risk alienating one of his principal resource people. And what's this secrecy business? *First the historians, now the pipeline.* Would there be more?

"So what's your take on the kidnapping?"

"A complete puzzle. I've tried to figure it out. Maybe related to her job? I do know she's responsible for securing grants but also in deciding what grants to select. You'd be amazed at the number of competitive groups out there who want the Academy of Sciences to do their research. Was one of them given a promise and then Sylvie reneged? Or could it be a hostage-type thing? Will the Academy get a ransom note? Then there're the people at her parties. All types, all levels. Has lots of friends. Maybe one got ticked off."

"Parties?"

"She throws … used to throw … great parties. Any excuse for one, at the drop of a hat. Never seen anything like it. My wife needs weeks to prepare. Sylvie called them celebrations: getting a new client just that afternoon; some friend's good news; a birthday. Anything. Has a fantastic place over near the Eiffel Tower. Lavish. Been invited there a few times myself. She's really quite beguiling … as in charming, not deceitful. You have any ideas on the abduction?"

"None. But I haven't known her long enough to consider many options. From what I've seen though, it's hard to conceive of her having enemies." Paul shrugged and imagined the same thing occurring at the other end. "But I want you to know, Guy, that I'm ready to talk with the *histarians*."

"Good. I've already broken the ice with them. You'll be conferring with the top man. He's heard of you; can you believe that? You're a highly published author, so why not? But what a coincidence. He said you were the one who investigated the theft of … and he didn't go into detail on this, nor did I ask him to … but here, I wrote it down: the theft of Dagobert's Throne."

"Dagobert's Throne?" Paul exclaimed, his voice a notch higher. Several nearby customers looked over. "Wait a second. Who *is* this guy and where's he located?"

"Frère Dominic. He's the prior at the Senanque Monastery down in Provence. American born and educated. Moved to France in the late fifties, early sixties."

"A monastery?"

"Yes, how's that for a cover? Actually it's hardly a deliberate cover. He's been there for fifty-odd years and this informant business came much later. But it's ideal, I'd say. He's not breaking the law and any modest monies he and his associates earn are considered donations to their Benedictine Order. In fact, all checks are made out to the monastery and go through me."

"And the information they give out is accurate?"

"That's the wrong word, but it's close. As I mentioned to you before, they either lend you documents or they share tips and hearsay they've accumulated, sometimes going back centuries. They sift through it and dole out the most credible. It's up to their clients to do the checking, if there's checking to do, and since I've been dealing with them, their batting average has been fantastic. Not a thousand but almost."

"Meaning that most of the hearsay turns out to be factual?"

"Correct. *More* than most."

"But what's the proof?"

"Information jibing with other information, over and over. Documents turning up that reflect the original thinking. Diaries and memoirs finally located. That sort of thing."

Paul liked what he'd heard and, checking his watch, asked if the prior might see him as soon as possible.

"I'll call him right now. But first, what's the deal on that throne affair?"

"Oh that? Some years ago, I was hired to trace it down. It's a replica of a bronze armchair owned by the Abbey of Saint-Denis just north of here. It had great value since it was a perfect facsimile of a relic from the Middle Ages and, as I understood it, the original belonged to the Merovingian king, Dagobert I. Well, when all was said and done, I found that it wasn't missing at all, just misplaced. So I returned half my fee to the Abbey. That created quite a favorable reaction in ecclesiastical circles and I would guess Dominic got wind of it."

"Interesting," Guy said. "You dealing with any missing whatever right now?"

"Yes, two Fra Angelico paintings missing since the," Paul felt a blotch coming on, "I can't believe this—it never dawned on me—missing since the 1790's, and that, my friend, is squarely at the beginning of the Napoleonic era!"

"Some coincidence, but then again, Renaissance art and all. It's about the time he invaded Italy, I think."

"You think right. That's why they scattered six small panels of his frescoes. Pretty soon two were unaccounted for. *The Golden Saints*. I'm commissioned to find them. Haven't put much time into it I must admit and now of course it's on hold entirely."

"The golden what?"

"Saints. That's what they're called: *The Golden*

Saints"

"Let me try the prior and I'll call you right back. What if he's willing to meet with you today?" The change of subject was seamless.

"Where exactly is the monastery?" Paul asked.

"In Gordes, about 450 miles from here. I know Leon offered you his plane. I've been on it several times myself. Uses a very experienced pilot. You'd fly into Avignon; then it's about a half-hour drive to Senanque. So you can be there in about four hours."

Paul deemed this to be the legitimate beginning of the mission and was anxious to get started. His answer required little reflection. "Why not? If it's a yes at his end, it's a yes at mine. But first, see if you can reach him. I'll wait to hear from you. Oh, and one other detail: if it's a go, tell him that Vincent Broussard will accompany me." Paul went on to explain that Vincent would serve as an "extra pair of eyes and ears" during the mission and Guy labeled it a smart move.

Vincent took out a pad and made some notes while Paul finished his breakfast. Within minutes, his phone vibrated at his hip.

"Good news, Paul," Guy said. "Frère Dominic can see you this afternoon at four. That should give you plenty of time. I told him you'd be there unless he heard otherwise. The monastery is maybe two miles north of the village in Gordes. You shouldn't have any trouble finding it. He said the south wing is clearly marked. His office is on the second floor. You'll be greeted there by the sub prior or second in command. Oh, and one additional thing about the prior—don't be thrown off by it. He'll feed you legitimate information but, more often than not, he'll slip in something cryptic or ambiguous. Likes to play mind games. I've used him myself to get inside information for some of my stories. I write it all down as he's talking and later on I find this, like, off-the-wall double entendre that I have to clarify on my own. Then he'll call a few days or weeks later and ask how I made out. So the vast majority of the stuff is legit, a tiny bit might or might not be—like dropping clues and planting red herrings in mystery writing. Weird."

Red herrings? Mind games?

"You should also be aware that I've informed Leon about this," Guy added.

Paul thanked him and indicated he would keep him advised of the visit's outcome and any developments related to it. He then phoned Leon about the hastily drawn up plan and learned that the plane and pilot could be ready within two hours—sooner if necessary. Leon said that he had flown into Avignon and driven to Gordes many times; that the region was one of the most beautiful in all of France; and that in more practical terms, the trip should prove beneficial to the mission.

Paul checked the time: eight-forty. "Eleven would be perfect," he said. "By the way, where do you keep the plane?"

"At a little airstrip east of the city. It has no name but I call it de Gaulle Junior. You're taking Vincent with you, I hope? He knows the location."

"Yes, of course. I'm with him now in fact. We should work well together."

"Fine, fine. I know you will. You *must*. Will you be staying overnight?"

"No. I can't imagine our discussion lasting more than

an hour or so. I'd like to take off by six. Six-thirty if we decide to catch a bite."

"Okay. Our pilot… name's Ansel. Been with me for years. He'll keep himself busy until you're good and ready to leave. No need to rush. You should be back to your hotel by eleven at the latest. Good luck, Paul."

"Thanks. And I've been meaning to ask: are all the other delegation members kept informed of things like this?"

"Anything and always," Leon replied. "Of course, Sylvie's, ah, indisposed right now, but she'll know in due course, God willing. So just to make it clear—as soon as any member receives news worth sharing, it's shared immediately. That's one of our agreements."

"And only the delegation knew of Sylvie's spying function, right?"

"Right. Unless she told someone else, which I doubt."

Paul revealed the essence of Guy's and Leon's remarks to Vincent before they rose to leave. On the way past the counter, Vincent nodded to someone Paul had noticed staring at their table twenty minutes earlier.

Chapter 8

The flight to Avignon took the anticipated three hours, during which Paul hardly spoke, preoccupied with Sylvie and her fate. For whatever reasons, he was drawn to her, no question. She had entered his life as one of the "truth seeking" delegation, though Paul had difficulty reconciling such a membership with her role as a spy against *Vérité's* rival, the Institute of France — and through it, the whole Academy of Sciences. Plus the fact that the Institute was her employer! But the Sylvie at dinner was a different woman, even if one put aside the sexual overtures. And now she had been whisked away, right before his eyes. *If she is returned safely, should she be a travel companion?*

Ansel stayed behind at the airport while the others rented a car and, Paul at the wheel, drove the twenty-two miles to Gordes, a medieval village perched on the southern edge of Plateau de Vaucluse. Its dry-stone bories tightly set against the base of cliffs had served the Resistance well during World War II. Paul and Vincent followed the signs and proceeded north another two miles on a road that wound through rocks and valleys and forests, and eventually a narrow valley embracing the Cistercian Abbey Notre-Dame-de-Senanque. Before long, a purple hue would spread through its fields of neatly arranged lavender and over miles of woodlands beyond; for now, thousands of gray-green plants lay dormant, ready to reach their full bloom and famous perfumed scent in mid-July. It was 3:45, May 20.

Paul expected to pass through a security gate and see monks milling around. He saw neither. Silently they strolled through an empty parking area and approached the dome-topped entrance marked South Wing. An unlocked door opened into a rotunda-like space with beige walls. Paul was curious about the walls' surface: smooth masonry or rough wallpaper? He ran his fingers over one section. Masonry.

Aside from a plain metal umbrella stand, there were no furnishings. The lighting was adequate but the floor was uncarpeted, its sheened oak blending with wooden benches built into the periphery. The smell of must seemed appropriate, although it was not overwhelming, in contrast to the ticking of a clock that echoed about them. Overall, the atmosphere was stark and austere, almost ominous, the kind Paul associated with old-time horror films. He looked down empty wide corridors and discovered more of the same.

Vincent inspected a winding staircase on their right while Paul stood in the center of the space, trying to decide whether the abbey's interior possessed atmosphere or mood. He settled on mood. And again, what of the monks? *Were they off praying?*

In an anteroom upstairs, the sub prior, a middle-aged man in a white cassock, was all business. He remained seated behind an old table used as a desk, introduced himself as Frère Rudolph, and addressed them as Dr. D'Arneau and Dr. Broussard.

"Frère Dominic is expecting you," he said. "You may go right in. But wait! You don't have anything dangerous in the briefcase, do you?"

Paul affected a smile and answered, "No, unless you consider some reference notes and a few crackers as dangerous. I'll show you if you want."

"No, that won't be necessary."

Paul thanked him and opened the door to a large inner office. A lanky man with bushy white hair and sunken cheeks stood behind a larger version of the table outside.

"It's a pleasure to meet you both," he said. "Welcome to Senanque." His voice was high pitched though soft, one you might predict emerging from such an asthenic figure. He reached over to shake Paul's hand. "You're a very generous man," he said. He then shook Vincent's hand, pointed to three chairs near the table and asked them to sit. He walked around to join them.

"Generous? That's kind of you," Paul said, "but what makes you say that?"

"Dagobert's Throne."

"Oh, that thing. It's only fair."

"Plus your reimbursing dealers when what you recover is a forgery."

He knows about that too?

"That's admirable," the prior said, "and also sensible, especially with archaeological finds. Sensible because indirectly you may be helping defeat terrorism."

"Terrorism?"

"If I were a betting man, ah, let me put it a different way. I'm not allowed to bet, nor would I, but if so I'd say it's a good bet. I understand those things are shipped from

the Middle East by the hundreds of tons. Surely some of
the money is hoarded by criminal elements and eventually
some of that reaches terrorist groups."

Paul didn't intend to cover the topic and said simply,
"Thank you for receiving us, Frère Dominic. So happy
to meet you too."

"Please call me Dom. Everyone else does."

"We hate to take up your time," Paul said, really
wondering what he did with it.

"Not at all, gentlemen, not at all."

The prior wore a white collar and lavender blouse
tucked into black pants pulled high on his hips. A large
silver cross hung from his neck. His facial skin appeared
tight and remarkably wrinkle-free as if it had never
experienced the sun. But it was his nimble smile that
intrigued Paul the most, at one time full and rich, at others
taking seconds to form and only a moment to disappear.
The term "disjointed" came to Paul's mind.

He was also intrigued by the number of books
surrounding them, in floor to ceiling bookcases on two
sides and stacked on counters that rimmed the room. He
could read the spines of the largest of them and noted that
the majority bore historical titles.

He circled the room with his finger. "I assume you've
read every word?" he said facetiously.

Dom gave one of his disjointed smiles. "Naturally,"
he replied. "I never liked the designation 'history buff'
because people might believe I read in the nude, but I
suppose that's what I am." All three laughed, Vincent the
loudest.

"Yes, indeed," the prior continued, "and as it involves
you, I can put the Napoleonic era into a context that
might interest you. I've read about the importance of the

Stone Age through developments in ancient Egypt and in the civilizations of Mesopotamia and Sumeria and Babylonia; in the battles of the Hittites and the Persians and the Assyrians; through the glory of Greece and the grandeur of Rome, as they say; and on into the Middle Ages. And I've read and reread the sad details of terrible wars—revolutionary, civil, worldwide; the rise and fall of the Hitler and Stalin dictatorships in Europe; anti-colonial sentiment in Africa and Asia; flaming battles for independence in Kenya, Algeria, Mozambique, Angola and Rhodesia; the Mao Tse-tung cultural revolution in China; Israel's six-day war in Egypt; internal turmoil in Russia, Nicaragua and the Philippines; skirmishes in the Falklands and Granada and Northern Ireland; the rise of terrorism and the 9/11 attacks; ongoing events in the Middle East."

Paul had followed the discourse suddenly thrust upon them and felt out of breath. *Had this been rehearsed?*

The prior went on. "So what am I driving at? Simply this. In all my study—and I must admit—for better or worse, I don't just read, I study. In all of it, I have never come across such an obvious, abrupt change in the behavior of an army general as I have in the person of Napoleon Bonaparte. It's flagrant. It's what I would interpret as schizophrenia, at least as far as his military acumen is concerned. But even his political decisions suddenly became grossly flawed. It was like night and day—both militarily and politically."

The prior had been twirling a pencil as he spoke. He tossed it onto the table and said, "I'm sorry, I didn't plan this. Sometimes I get carried away, but then again perhaps it sets the stage for something I *did* plan. You see,

Guy Martin briefed me on the nature of your investigation
and I believe I can help. It's amazing that no one but you
has come forth—to this place I mean—to inquire not
about Napoleonic history but about Napoleonic truths.
They're satisfied with the legend but I assure you, other
possibilities are legion." He leaned closer to Paul. "And I
would say that it's up to you to pursue the possibilities and
either discredit them or factualize them. Is that a word?"
He leaned back. "Another point up front: Please don't feel
obliged to follow through on any of my suggestions for
that's all they will be—suggestions."

"I understand." Paul said. "But before we get to that,
I'd like to say something, then ask a question or two."

"Certainly," Dom said. He folded his hands on his
lap.

"Guy also briefed us. That is, on you. And we're
extremely impressed ... and grateful that you're willing
to help. I want to assure you that we understand the
conditions: complete confidentiality; payment of a fee—or
rather a donation—made out to this monastery. Just let
Guy know the amount and I'll submit a check."

Dom nodded. "I assure you, it won't be much. We
commend you for taking this on. It excites all the *historians*.
And history has been waiting for it for years."

"Thank you," Paul responded. "Now, a question: Can
you tell us where you get your information?"

"All clients ask me that and my answer is the same:
no, I cannot. However our sources go much deeper than
the persistent rumors we analyze. I've been here over fifty
years. Sometimes visitors say things to me here that they
wouldn't say in public—you know, on the outside."

"Okay, next then. You're called an '*historian*'? Guy

says it's a play on the words 'historian' and 'contrarian'.

Dom flashed the smile. "Yes, I know," he said, "and don't let Guy mislead you. He tells everyone that he made up the word, but '*historian*' was coined by yours truly. I believe it's a *good* word. Germane. Apt. We do, after all, hand out secret information that runs contrary to recorded history."

"You just referred to 'we'. The other *historians*? Are they here?"

"No, not at all. I'm the only one here at Senanque—the one assigned to you. Our rule is one *historian* per client. We found that to be best for all concerned. Dealing with a committee can be awkward. For both sides. The others come from … let's say all walks of life."

"And speaking of others, do many monks reside here?"

"Yes, many. But I'm not at liberty to give out the number."

"Hmm … if I may ask then, where are they?"

"At a special prayer meeting in our auditorium. I'd have you join us but once the doors are closed and prayers begin, no one else is allowed in. That applies to me, to the sub prior, to the sacrist, the circuiter, the chamberlain, the almoner, any of us. And if it applies to leadership and to all our monks, it must apply to visitors. I hope that makes sense to you."

"It does make sense, and maybe it was none of my business anyway."

Dom stared at Vincent. "And, young man," he said. "Do you have any questions?"

"No sir, I'm just here to observe … unless … yes, I do want to know a couple of things." He straightened in his chair. "Do people often come here to seek your advice?"

"Not too often but often enough. The other *histarians* take their turns and we like to engage clients one at a time because the group confers on each case—which helps eliminate misinformation. So I'd say a client arrives here about once a month. More frequently during the Easter and Christmas seasons when emotions run higher and they want certain problems solved."

Both Vincent and Paul took out their note pads and penciled in a note. "And do you have such a thing as a success rate?" Vincent asked.

"It's hard to measure because we don't always hear back, but I suspect that because of the scope of your mission, as Guy put it, I'll hear back from you. And you'll hear back from me. Several times, I'm sure." The prior looked dissatisfied. "Let's put it this way: I'm as committed as you and your whole committee to settle the disputes about Napoleon once and for all, and ..."

Paul interrupted. "You used the plural."

"You mean 'disputes'? Yes. It isn't simply a case of whether or not he was murdered. There's much more to it than that." Dom took out a red manila folder from the table drawer. "It seems to me that you can launch your own attack on the, ah, disputes by concentrating on three fronts: the emperor's lovers, his last two battles and his postmortem disappearance."

"Postmortem disappearance?" Paul exclaimed.

"Exactly. After his death, the ceremony on St. Helena was well recorded and documented. What was *not* recorded is that there was ample time and opportunity to steal the body. And rumors are still rampant. That's why you definitely must go there and investigate. To my knowledge no one else ever has—with that possibility in mind."

The prior handed Paul a card. "Here's the name and address of our *histarian* on the island, in Jamestown. Name's Thatcher Drinkwell. We're old friends. He already knows of your mission and that you're likely to see him. Look him up. He's the constable there and can be trusted."

Dom waited while Paul and Vincent made more notes, Paul reluctantly. Finally Dom said, "With regard to the lovers, you know of course that Napoleon had more than most for that era. But one woman in particular stands out." He ran his finger down one of the papers in the folder. "Her name was Lady Beckett—that's with two t's. From London. She was a top executive with the British East India Tea Company and from all indications, a female Lothario. Guy may have mentioned her to you as the 'Mystery Lady'. The most I can reveal now—because we're still studying her lineage—is that as she grew older she became more feeble, and the more feeble she became, the more she opened up about her relationship with Napoleon. She apparently wrote extensively about that part of her life and called it her 'ruby years'."

The prior began to quote word-for-word from the folder. "She wrote that 'the ruby symbolizes great value, wisdom, costly glories and prized treasures.' She referred to the citing of these in the bible: in Job and in Proverbs." He looked up, his face glazed with incredulity. "Think of how the words apply to Napoleon. Prized treasure? If the relationship was as expected, he certainly was that to her. Wisdom? In good health, he had that in full measure. Costly glories? This is the one that astounds me in its relevance to him. He had glorious triumphs but at what cost? Thousands of men were lost. Great value? On balance, he was all of that." Dom closed the folder and set it aside. "We'll talk further about this as more information comes in."

"Ah, the 'Mystery Lady'", Paul said. "I was wondering if anything would confirm what Guy told me." He wanted to elaborate but he also wanted to hear more.

"That brings me to the military battles," Dom continued. "It's essential that you visit his 'First Island of Disgrace' — that's my designation. So in addition to St. Helena, please go to Elba. It will be worth your while. If you were to ask me whether visiting the islands should be one of your top priorities, I would answer that it should be your whole list. We have reason to believe that he made a monumental decision and hatched some sort of plan on Elba. Understand, those are two separate things: decision and plan. The decision had to do with the contents of his will. The plan, as I've said, was hatched on Elba but not documented by him until late during his years on St. Helena. It was related to his two terrible defeats in Russia and France. But related in a way one would not expect. Our *histarian* there can elaborate. He's the curator of the National Napoleonic Museum. It's really two buildings, arms if you will: one in Portoferraio, Palazzina dei Mulini which was the official residence of Napoleon and his sister, Paolina; and the other three miles away in San Martino, his summer home, Villa San Martino. Name's Clive Weaver. Been around awhile. He's older than I am, which means he should be dead. He was with the British Museum early on. Spent winters on Elba, then moved there thirty, forty years ago. I strongly recommend that you have a look at his collection of cartoons."

"Cartoons?"

"Yes. They show that from 1800 to 1815 the battles between Napoleon and the royalists were waged even in the arts. In 1814 for example, merchants showed only portraits of Louis 18th and caricatures of Napoleon. A little while later the reverse was true. Then back to Napoleon as a cartoon character. No guarantee but they might reveal something useful for you within such changing attitudes. But to continue with our *histarians*: They're each learned and experienced. Been with our group as long as I can remember. They speak fluent English, of course, coming from British families and that's why I chose them over some others."

"About those cartoons though, wouldn't Weaver have seen something suspicious in them by now?"

"Maybe yes, maybe no. And even if he has, who's to say he would necessarily share the information? I for one always thought there might be something important to learn from them. A secret enemy of Napoleon for example. Or a would-be assassin. You'd bring a fresh perspective."

Paul thought for a moment and asked, "Wouldn't it be wise for me to see if I can find out what I need simply by phone?" He chose the words carefully to get his exact meaning across. And he uttered them knowing full well that he *had* to make the trips, but he wanted to express one last devil's advocate position.

The prior picked up his pencil and began twirling it again. "No," he stated. "They won't give out anything by phone. I'm afraid it's face-to-face or nothing. They're strict about it. We *historians* all are. Don't forget, they may have materials to give you. I don't know. I do know they don't trust the mail and they shouldn't if they have sensitive materials for you." He placed the pencil back down carefully as if he didn't want to break it.

"So you see," he continued, "the trips may be arduous but you won't be sorry you made them. Even if you find nothing significant on your own, it's speaking with Weaver and Drinkwell that matters. They won't come here so you must go *there*."

Paul entered Weaver's name under Drinkwell's and was about to comment but the prior preempted him.

"One final point," he blurted. "You've no doubt read of Michel Ney?"

"French Marshal Ney? Certainly. Napoleon's 'bravest of the brave'."

"Correct. Well, when Ney switched his allegiance away from Louis XVIII back to Napoleon, the king's sympathizers, including four of the emperors' former marshals, began to meet regularly. They voted for Ney's execution. It's all in the personal letters of those marshals. To a man, each refers to minutes kept at the meetings. And here's the good news: Thatcher Drinkwell has the original letters!"

Paul gawked in disbelief. "Besides referring to the minutes," he said, "what else is in the letters?"

"He didn't give me the details, other than something about their doing away with Napoleon."

"And who were the marshals?" Paul readied his pen.

The prior reopened his folder. "Dominique Perignon, Auguste Marmont, Jean-Baptiste Jourdan and Claude

Victor. Jourdan was president of the court that sentenced his fellow marshal Ney to death."

Paul listed the marshals under the names of the contacts, then said, "I'm sure we both know of arsenic supposedly found in high concentrations in Napoleon's hair samples after he died. Any evidence he was murdered, or could he have inhaled the arsenic while he was living on St. Helena … from the dyes in the wallpaper and curtains at Longwood House?"

"There's no clear proof of murder thus far but maybe the marshals could have tried to kill him. Maybe they conspired. I think it's well known he sometimes used arsenic as a recreational drug. Many people did in those days. Whether or not they slipped him more when he wasn't looking, I have no idea, but I think Drinkwell and the letters can help you with that."

"How about Talleyrand?"

"As a murderer? It never crossed my mind but I'm not the expert here. Weaver and Drinkwell are though. At least that's their reputation."

"One last point," Paul said. "Why would you have an *histarian* on both Elba and St. Helena? They're dots on the map."

"Because they've been around—have many, many contacts."

Amid a protracted silence, they glanced at one another. All three stood. There was a round of handshaking and thank-you's.

"So I take it you'll travel to both islands soon?" the prior asked.

"Very soon."

"Good, I'll alert both men."

Dom pulled a six-page pamphlet from the folder saying, "Very often a unique portrayal of a land can give insights into the character of its famous past residents — even their secrets. This is titled, 'Elba the Refuge, A Different View.'" He handed it to Paul saying, "Here. I hope you'll find this informative. It gives a little different slant. I don't have one on Helena but you've written so extensively about it that you could probably put one together as we speak."

Could this be the ambiguous thing Guy warned about? Or was it the cartoons? Or both?

At the door, Paul turned to their host and said, "Tell me, do you like Napoleon?"

"Let's say if I'd been around in his time, I'd have admired him."

The trip back to Paris provided Paul with ample time to evaluate what had just transpired and to determine his next course of action, knowing full well that there would be many other courses to follow. It was their order that gave him pause. He wanted the investigation to go smoothly, its parts in proper sequence, yet integrated. He concluded that the order probably made little difference and he was inclined to let it go at that. One thing was clear: visits to Elba and St. Helena were a must. *Before that, however, shouldn't he spend some uninterrupted time on the military battles?* After all, any clues that were not apparent in reading over the draft notes of his Napoleonic Strategies might turn up and serve him well as he prowled around the two islands. Not only that: the notes for his *St. Helena: Napoleon's Final Defeat* would be important to review before exploring the island on which the emperor died. Advantage military battles. He was glad he had taken the notes and final manuscripts to Paris and was determined to hole up in his hotel room and scrutinize them for whatever new insights they contained.

His attention shifted to Frère Dominic. Paul characterized the prior's remarks as a blend of suggestions and pronouncements — plus a dash of something he couldn't put his finger on. Hyperbole? Stealth? Harking back to the heads-up that Guy had provided, Paul couldn't differentiate between "clues" and "red herrings", leaving only one alternative: check them all out. And Dom's last comment seemed odd. If he only *admired* the emperor, had he skewed information so as to make Napoleon look worse then he might have been? Or would he in the future? He asked a half-dozing Vincent for his opinion and found that the Frenchman had wondered about the same thing. Paul also told him that the next day, Sunday, would be devoted entirely to isolated study in his hotel room and that his services would not be needed. He assured Vincent that he would otherwise contact him and when prodded, Vincent said he didn't know what to make of the prior.

His nightly call to Jean focused on the monastery adventure. Fatigued, he dispensed with specific details, grouping them all into a single broad category he termed "leads." He did however stress the prior's insistence that some time be spent investigating Elba and St. Helena in person.

"But what about Guy?" Paul asked her. "Did you get a chance to run a check?"

"I did. He's clean and highly regarded in his field."

"Excellent. That's a relief."

"You had doubts?"

"Not really. It's just that 'highly regarded' has a nice

ring to it."

Paul inquired about Jean's work and her general well being and apologized for not having done so during earlier calls.

"My job's never boring so I'll always like it. And except for missing you, I feel fine. Still a little worried, but fine. Take care, Paul; you sound exhausted. Spread things out. Get some rest."

Paul's parting comment was that he would try but that when important things materialized "out of the blue", it meant they were unanticipated and that sometimes they needed tackling on the spot. He knew the comment was two parts vague and one part informative.

The sound of Jean's voice and her motherly advice had served as temporary solace. Very temporary. After the call, Paul began to feel unnerved, perhaps even angry with himself. He acknowledged that he should have considered the Senanque meeting a major plus, yet there was this nagging uneasiness and he couldn't decide on its cause: the nature of the prior's advice or that same lingering doubt about his taking on the Napoleon assignment in the first place. In spite of some promising leads and some interesting yet enigmatic French players, he hadn't yet fully dismissed that doubt.

And there was the entire Sylvie issue and her three roles: spy, unsuccessful seducer, potential traveling companion. Then she went and vanished! Paul snapped his fingers.

"Like that!"

Chapter 9

Sunday, May 21
8:50 a.m.

P aul had fallen into bed at 11:15 Saturday night and awoke at 8, as drowsy and unsettled as when sleep had finally come. By the time he returned from a breakfast of a single poached egg, toast and coffee, and secured the chain at the door, his head felt like an over-inflated soccer ball. Everything seemed so complicated by then, yet he was determined to form a simple plan of action for the day. He believed he had made the right decision in reserving time for study, alone in his room with his two published books on Napoleon, the new manuscript that had rankled Yale officials, and his several folders of research notes for all three. His goal was to address two questions. One, did Napoleon's military conduct deteriorate significantly from 1812 on? His recollection was that it did, but he wanted to reaffirm it and to answer the question why. And, two, how did the emperor die?

He doubted he would find much of value in the new manuscript or its notes as most of it was fresh in his mind and had addressed different aspects of the emperor's career, especially those involving his robust love life. Its tentative title made indirect reference to that very issue:

The Male Mystique of Napoleon. And he had taken pains to distinguish between where knowledge ended and imagination began.

Since checking into his room nearly forty-eight hours before, Paul hadn't noticed its mismatch of furniture pieces. Until now. All but one were contemporary in style. The exception was a desk snugly tucked into an alcove. It was of another era, perhaps Napoleonic: a large heavy desk with a marble-topped surface and curved, crossed legs like the legs of the Roman curule. He knew that its appearance conformed to the Empire style but its presence confounded him; it was as if it had been placed there for his benefit.

The phone rang. Paul's friends and closest associates knew that when he was receptive to a call, he answered "hello?" but when he was annoyed, he answered "yes?"

"Yes," he said and heard a soft click, the kind you get when the caller expects to hear a different voice. It could also have signified a legitimate error and Paul, dismissing it as just that, slid his chair closer to the desk.

Uncertain where to begin, he finally decided that a quick appraisal of the materials he possessed, especially his notes, was as good a place as any. He thumbed through them and discovered a combination of basic facts he knew by rote, and information he had either neglected or treated lightly in compiling his last two books. Most of the neglected material was painstakingly written in longhand on 5 x 8 colored cards with a title for each one, notably: *Early Life and Military Career; Rise to Power; Mistakes and Defeats* (two cards); *Loves and Marriages; Military Domination; Political Achievements; Decrees; Nepotism; Banishments; The Fall.* He recalled that his intentions had been lofty at the time—meticulous, scientific—but once he had filled the cards with facts, he hadn't referred to them again. It was now vital that he review the information carefully. He had never considered himself an expert on Napoleon's life. He had dwelled more on the emperor's battle strategies than on what some of the cards contained. His previous book, *St. Helena: Napoleon's Final Defeat*, dealt with the last six years of his life when he was out of power. Like the prior, Paul admired Napoleon and wished he had studied and written more about him.

He started with a white card, mulling over each paragraph, each phrase, each word, like a decoder trying to extract some hidden meaning:

<u>Early Life and Military Career</u>

Born Aug. 15, 1769 on island of Corsica in Mediterranean. Parents Carlo and Letizia Ramonlino Buonaparte, members of noble Italian family. Father prominent lawyer. Mother beautiful and opinionated. Age 9: French military school at Brienne-le-Château, near Troyes. Age 15: chosen for elite *École Militaire* in Paris. Graduated following year. Age 16: commissioned second lieutenant (artillery) in French army. Captain 7 years later (1792). During early part of 10-year French Revolution (1789-1799) joined radical political society (Jacobins). Thus opposed royalists (supporters of French monarchy) early on. Age 24: Brigadier general after heroic victory against British at Toulon (1793). Age 26: Major general after successfully defending National Convention against royalist supporters (1795). Used point-blank cannon fire ("whiff of grapeshot"). New government (The Directory) installed.

The next card was gray:

Rise to Power

Assumed command of meager French army unit against Austrians on Italian-French border (1796). Defeated them and later, an additional handful of armies larger then his. Following year France and Austria signed Treaty of Campoformio which sealed an enlarged territory for France. His star continued to rise. Had become well-known authority on military strategy and timing. Did not mind announcing his secret: Start battle while holding back large reserve. Decide on weakest point in enemy's lines and penetrate at proper time. (I assume he didn't mind who knew about this approach for he could use it or not use it, thus keeping enemy guessing and off stride). His political ambitions grew but decided to wait. Invaded Egypt to destroy British trade with Middle East (1798). Won Battle of the Pyramids. Month later French fleet defeated in Battle of the Nile by Lord Horatio Nelson. Turkey formed alliance with Britain and Russia and declared war on France. Defeated Turks in Egypt at Abu Qir. Austria joined Britain and Russia to form coalition against France and defeated French army in Italy (Napoleon not there—still in Egypt). Sailed for France and greeted as super hero because of Abu Qir victory. People turned allegiance away from Directory and toward Napoleon. He seized control of government (1799) in Coup d'État of Eighteenth Brumaire. 10-year French Revolution ended. Directory replaced with Napoleon's Consulate and he became ruler of France. As popular figure ...

The phone rang and Paul answered, "Yes?"

"Sorry to bother you." Paul recognized Vincent's voice, the words louder and faster than usual. "I just got this call and we figured you'd better know about it. I phoned Leon first. Briefed him on Senanque, but he wants you to contact him when you can."

"But what about the call you got?"

"About ten minutes ago. It was a gruff voice. Not a good connection—probably a cell phone. He stuttered a lot. I wrote down what I could remember. He said we should have known that the lavender's prettier in July. Said I should stay away from the Meridien. That I should tell the American to mind his own business and go home. He said that twice. Then he hung up."

Paul took out a small package of salt crackers brought up from the coffee shop and placed it on the desk. "Have you ever heard the voice before?" he asked. He couldn't help rushing his own words.

"No. You all right?"

"Yes, of course. Studying my head off, that's all."

"You know, I'd feel better if I came over, Paul. I'll

plant myself in the lobby, check out the people coming and going."

"That would be boring."

"I'll bring a book."

Instead of continuing along that line, Paul thought out loud. "So they know we went to Senanque. But how? Do we have to assume they know our whereabouts at all times, whoever 'they' are?"

"I think we're forced to think of it that way. Keep our guards up. Look, I can be downstairs in a few minutes. You agree?"

"As you wish."

"Just keep going. Make believe I'm not even down there."

Paul hung up the receiver gently, preoccupied with the new development—and its import. He got up to check the door, munching a cracker on the way.

When he returned to the desk, he dropped into its chair, resolved not to be sidetracked by yet another warning. He finished the last sentence of the gray card:

> As popular figure, Napoleon ruled with impunity. Officially first consul of the three-member Consulate, but other two bowed to his decisions. Became, in effect, dictator.

Paul counted the remaining cards. There were eight to go but his concentration was shot by Vincent's call. A perfect antidote popped into his head: a change of pace, a surcease from the rat-a-tat-tat of the card entries. He needed to recapture the mindset of his last two books, particularly *Napoleonic Strategies*, hoping it would improve not only his focus but also his mood. He had suddenly turned sullen. Consumed, threatened—and sullen. A funk atypical for him. So he selected three vibrant passages he'd incorporated in the book and paced about slowly as he read them aloud, repeating them several times to expurgate the boredom, cleanse the mind. What's more, he enjoyed reading them, particularly if they pertained to Napoleon.

He had written the first passage to answer the question: Was Napoleon a god or a fool? Preceding it was a comment attributed to a French captain who claimed that one day in the distant future, when enthusiasm and animosities have died away, "a man free from passions, consulting the thousands of volumes written, and that yet are to be written, will be able to find truth in the well."

The passage itself came from a work by Pieter Geyl: *Napoleon: For and Against*:

> To expect from history ... [such] final conclusions, which may be obtained in other disciplines, is ... to misunderstand its nature ... It is impossible that [any] two historians, especially two historians living in different periods, should see any historical personality in the same light. The greater the political importance of an historical character the more impossible this is. Is there anyone whose decisions have been more affected by the ever-widening network of international relations than Napoleon? Is there anyone whose decisions have had greater consequences for the whole of Europe?

The second passage was more descriptive of Napoleon the man and referred to the differences between his pre-1812 and post-1812 careers. It was written by David Gates in his book, *The Napoleonic Wars, 1803-1815*:

> ...the Napoleon of 1803 seems to have been a very different person from the Napoleon of ... 1812, with contrasting aspirations. Among other things, his capacity for work, his cerebral powers, including his phenomenal memory, and his not inconsiderable courage make him stand out as an extraordinarily gifted man. However, he was mortal just like the rest of us and was aware of the implications of the physical deterioration to which we are all subject, commenting in 1805 that: "One has only a certain time for war. I will be good for six years more; after that even I must cry halt." He did not; and we must wonder why ... his final defeat [Waterloo] was both costly to achieve and a long time in coming. It required no fewer than seven coalitions and 12 years of incessant warfare.

The third, from the same book, alluded to Napoleon the military genius:

> Napoleon ... excelled at seizing the initiative and imposing his will on his opponents. While, as one of his aides confirms, he 'never devised any other than a vague plan, preferring to take counsel of opportunity, a system more

conformable to the promptitude of his genius', like a chess master, having chosen a particular gambit to open a game, he was almost unerringly good at predicting his adversary's response, allowing for any contingency, misfortune or opportunity which might arise, and calculating the risks and benefits of every possible course of action ... He fought all of 60 battles in his career, emerging victorious from nearly all of them.

Paul sat again, not as purged and energized as on other occasions. The phone call from the stutterer still bothered him. But one thing was certain: if he were to receive a call from that person, he would recognize the voice as the same one that issued the warning to Vincent. *Small consolation.*

He picked up the last eight cards and merely glanced at each one, unable to galvanize any motivation to continue with the entire collection. He decided to read only two more, figuring that the total of four, plus an examination of battles won or lost since 1800, should give him a definitive answer to his first question: Did Napoleon's military abilities deteriorate from 1812 on and, if so, why? Or at least pave the way for the answer. But he would first call Leon.

"How was the visit with Frère Dominic?" Leon asked.

"Excellent. He's a fountain of knowledge."

"Vincent told me that, but I wanted to hear it from you. You have some leads then?"

"Several. The guy, ah, the prior really knows his

stuff, I'd say."

"Care to share any of them?"

"Not at all. They're engraved up here." Paul pointed to his head. "In my brain. He called Napoleon's military acumen schizophrenic. Then he mentioned the murder possibility and advised that I should concentrate on his battles, his lovers and—get this—his postmortem disappearance."

"Schizophrenic and postmortem disappearance? What did he mean?"

"He meant an abrupt change in behavior; said it was flagrant. And the disappearance? I'd have to apply the old standby to this one: motive, opportunity and means. He claims the opportunity was there and probably the means. Never covered motive but said my checking things on St. Helena was essential."

"Well, we all agree with that. What else?"

"He listed some personalities to look into: a lover named Beckett, various French marshals of that era. Then the campaigns—said Napoleon had some mysterious plan that I might clarify if I went to Elba. He gave me a contact person there—another *histarian*. And for Helena, too."

"That would be Clive and Thatcher. They're both excellent. Did Talleyrand's name come up?"

"Yes, I brought it up. He said he doubted he was a murderer, and that's all."

"I see." Leon teased out the last word. "Well, you have a good deal for starters. I'm sure you'll be talking to him again. Generally, when he gets absorbed in something, he puts out his tentacles toward his other sources, and new information comes flowing back. Did you get that impression?"

"What, that he's absorbed or that he has tentacles? Ah, sorry, Leon. Guess I'm punchy."

"That's okay, you have much on your mind. Actually, it was quite funny."

"I could use a little humor right about now. Anyway, the thing he said was something vague about lineage and about Elba. That he'll get back to me."

"Marvelous. So what about the islands? Elba first?"

"Elba first."

"When?"

"As soon as possible. Leave in the morning? Can you arrange it?"

"Yes. I'll have Ansel fly you there — Airport Marina di Campo. He'll have to refuel in Marseille. That's about three hours plus from here. Then Elba's another two hours or less, so you'd better allow five hours total."

"Where would we stay?"

"Hotel Fabricia. In Portoferraio, ten minutes from the airport. Very impressive. Four stars. Everyone recommends it. I'll make arrangements."

Paul wrote down the name. "And Helena?"

"I'll have the plans when you get back. In the meantime I'll contact the R.A.F. As I said before, they'll fly you to Ascension Island and from there you sail on the Royal Mail Ship ... for a day and a half. Ansel can get you to London in no time at all and from there to Ascension on an R.A.F plane is about three hours."

"You've taken both trips yourself?"

"Neither one. I simply prepared in advance of your decision."

"I did a little preparing too," Paul said, scratching his

finger. "Let's see, today's Sunday. If we leave for Elba in the morning and stay there through Tuesday—that gives us nearly two full days, which should be plenty. Then we return here mid-day Wednesday, and maybe Thursday set out for Helena."

"And keep your stay there open-ended?"

"That's a good way to put it. As far as I can see, the whole mission is open- ended." Paul spoke without disgust or frustration.

"A healthy outlook at this stage," Leon said. "Means you're keeping an open mind. Remember back at the Sterling Library? I stressed we want objectivity and neutrality and that you, Paul, are the person for the job."

Paul liked both Leon's use of the word "healthy" and his vote of confidence. These, together with talk about the trips, lifted his spirits.

"Leon, I'm sorry but I still see a loose end or two. Shall I mention them now or later?"

"Now. And don't be sorry."

"Well, number one: While we're doing our thing on the islands, what will our pilot do?"

"Ansel? He'll come home and return for you when you're ready. Just give me a call."

"Okay, then, number two: Can Vincent take his pistol on a private plane?"

"From our little airstrip? I'll handle it."

"How about on the R.A.F. plane to Ascension Island?"

"I'll handle it."

"And on the ship from Ascension to Helena? ... I know, you'll handle it."

"*Exactement.*"

Paul laughed audibly but received dead silence in return. Apparently Leon took his connections seriously.

After settling on a 7:30 liftoff from de Gaulle Junior, they ended the conversation on the usual Paul promise to keep the giant informed.

Paul felt relieved that he needed only two more topics to make an informed judgment about Napoleon's post-1812 military abilities. He also dwelled on several other now vivid memories: that he had required two cards for the next topic: *Mistakes and Defeats*; that he had arbitrarily chosen the very date of 1812 to begin the summaries; and that Napoleon's military performances seemed to have begun to sour at about the same time. And on this point, he recollected one other thing: that Napoleon had violated his own military principles. Paul had culled the principles from numerous reliable sources and now picked only ten for review. The first blue card read:

Mistakes and Defeats

Violation of Principles and Examples of Lost Battles:

Nothing is so important in war as an undivided command. For this reason, when war is carried on against a single power there should be only one army, acting upon one base, and conducted by one chief. Example: Russia (1812).

The keys of a fortress are always well worth the retirement of the garrison when it is resolved to yield only on those conditions. On this principle it is always wiser to grant an honorable capitulation to a garrison that has made a vigorous resistance than to risk an assault. <u>Examples</u>: Ciudad Rodrigo and Badajoz (1812).

To act upon lines far removed from each other, and without communications, is to commit a fault which always gives birth to a second. The detached column has only its orders for the first day. Its operations on the following day depend on what may have happened to the main body. Thus the column on any sudden emergency either loses time in waiting for orders or acts without them and at hazard. <u>Example</u>: Salamanca (1812).

When two armies are in order of battle, and the one has to retire over a bridge while the other has the circumference of the circle open, all the advantages are in favor of the latter. <u>Example</u>: Leipzig (1813).

A fortified place can only protect the garrison and arrest the enemy for a certain time. When this time has elapsed, and the defenses are destroyed, the garrison should lay down its arms. All civilized nations are agreed on this point, and there has never been an argument except with reference to the greater or lesser degree of defense a governor is bound to make before he capitulates. <u>Examples</u>: Burgos and San Sebastien (1813).

The second blue card read:

> There is no security for any sovereign, for any people, or for any general, if officers are permitted to capitulate in the open field and to lay down their arms, in virtue of conditions favorable to the contracting party, but contrary to the interests of the army at large. <u>Example</u>: Outskirts of Paris (1814).

> To authorize a general or other officers to lay down their arms in virtue of a particular capitulation, under any other circumstances than when they are composing the garrison of a fortress, affords a dangerous latitude. It is destructive of all military character in a nation to open such a door to the cowardly, the weak, or even to the misdirected brave. <u>Example</u>: Hamburg (1814).

> A general-in-chief should ask himself several times a day, What if the enemy were to appear now to my front, or on my right, or my left? <u>Example</u>: Quatre Bras (1815).

> It is an approved maxim in war never to do what the enemy wishes you to do, for this reason alone, because he wishes it. A field of battle, therefore, which he has previously studied and reconnoitered should be avoided. <u>Example</u>: Waterloo (1815).

Infantry, cavalry and artillery are nothing without each other. They should always be so dispersed in cantonments as to assist each other in case of surprise. <u>Example</u>: Waterloo (1815).

Paul placed both blue cards side-by-side, stared at them for a few seconds, then shook his head. *How could I have ignored the obvious? How could this glaring string of defeats have made no impact when preparing Napoleonic Strategies? Such outcomes were rare before 1812. Granted, some of his subordinates acted independently, but Napoleon was the leader.*

A red card was next, the last he would read. He included it in his review because its subject matter might have affected Napoleon's concentration on succeeding battles. It was, in fact, one of Paul's contentions in the new manuscript that had been roundly rejected by Yale officials:

<u>Loves and Marriages</u>

Had many mistresses but only two wives: Josephine Beauharnais and Marie Louise of Austria. Mistresses: Marie Walewska. Désirée Clary, Pauline Foures, Mademoiselle Georges, Giuseppina Grassini and one he referred to as the mystery lady. Of the two wives: Josephine was the more famous. Born into nobility in West Indies. Was herself mistress to various leading French politicians before Napoleon and even during their marriage. He wanted son as heir to succeed him but she bore him no children. For this reason and because of sound strategic (military) reasons, he married young (19) Austrian princess, Marie Louise. Divorce from Josephine was reluctant on part of both parties. Marie Louise was great niece of Marie Antoinette. The marriage did nothing to end friction between France and Austria, but his young wife gave him the son he wanted, François Charles, born in 1811, who became King of Rome. Of the mistresses: Polish countess Marie Walewska and Napoleon had two illegitimate sons; actress Marguerite-Josephine Weimer (Mademoiselle Georges) made her acting debut in 1802 at age fifteen; Giuseppina Grassini was an opera singer who performed at La Scala; Pauline Foures divorced her husband after beginning affair with Napoleon in Egypt in 1799; and Désirée Clary, a Marseille silk merchant's daughter, eventually became Queen of Sweden.

Paul reread the list of mistresses. *A mystery lady? The same one Guy had referred to? I wrote this stuff myself. How did she escape my full attention?*

He returned to the notes on Marshal Michel Ney and each of his four comrades in arms whom the prior had fingered as possibly poisoners of Napoleon, and who had voted for Ney's death by firing squad. The four men had served a long stretch in La Grande Armée and each had risen to the rank of marshal. Paul found a description of Ney as a "soldier's soldier" and a list of his widespread battles: Neerwinden, Mainz, Hohenlinden, Jena, Friedland, Bussaco, Boradino, Smolensk, Lutzen, Leipzig, Quatre Bras, Waterloo. He especially pondered the defeat at Waterloo in 1815—part of the Hundred Days War—but found nothing out of the ordinary. Nor could he find any hint of the prior's claim, so the idea of a murder conspiracy would have to await whatever Paul might unearth on the islands. *If he found anything there.*

On the issue of arsenic poisoning, certain things were clear to Paul, and he framed them as questions. Had Napoleon's mind been systematically altered by the substance or had he merely softened in his desire to attain power? The whole tenor of the wars that enveloped Europe between 1803 and 1812 versus those from 1812 on was much different. Paul saw a distinct dichotomy. At times even peaceful coexistence seemed a possibility but Napoleon shunned that option. Or even if he really wanted to be softer, in his altered state of mind, had he pressed on, much like a drunk who takes greater, even unthinkable risks? Again, Paul would pursue the issue on the islands.

Two final notations puzzled him. They were in his notes about St. Helena. The first was a group of seven names bracketed together but he didn't know why: Balcombe, Greentree, Brooke, Doveton, Leech, Bennet, Rutledge. He had penciled in a large question mark outside the bracket.

The second, also question-marked, was a reference to a codicil to Napoleon's will. Paul knew copies of the will were freely available but he had never examined one. The codicil might present a problem, however.

He sorted out the cards and papers and reinserted

them into their folders. Several minutes later the phone rang.

"It's me again," Leon said. "Are you wearing a hat?"

"Wearing a hat? What are you talking about?"

"Well if you are, I'll ask you to hold onto it. Sylvie's back."

Chapter 10

Paul had changed into a dry shirt between setting aside his last folder and answering the phone. It took Leon's statement a few moments to sink in and even then, he wondered whether or not he had heard wrong. He also wondered why his fresh shirt collar had dampened so fast. He checked his watch. It was one-forty. *Five hours of grinding study. No lunch. Startling message. Distortion.*

"Sylvie's back. That's what you said, right?"

"Uh-huh. Just got off the phone with her. She escaped, ran out into the street, hailed a motorist and went directly to the prefecture. She's there now."

"Was she harmed?"

"Not in the least. They locked her in a storage room. Untied. Never questioned her about anything. Brought her food on time. She didn't recognize any of them but said they were young. Said she could explain more later this afternoon at the party."

"The party?"

"She wants to throw one. They'll take her statement, then drive her to her apartment. I got on the phone with them, told them to downplay the entire incident and assign her a bodyguard for the time being. She completely balked at that. She's tough. Always has been."

"But she's ready for a party? How could she think

of one now, at a time like this?"

"She wants to celebrate her escape. That's Sylvie."

"Are you going?"

"Yes, sir. And she wants you, Vincent, Maurice and Guy there. I think you should go, Paul. We'll get the scoop on what happened and it'll give us a chance to reunite as a group and compare notes."

"What time?"

"Five. By the way, I told her you're leaving for the islands tomorrow. She wants to go with you."

"She told you that?" Paul didn't wait for an answer. "What do *you* think?"

"I like the idea. You, Vincent and Sylvie. Sounds like a great team to me."

Paul had at least two hours to fill. He considered a nap but decided he was too hyped-up. Hyped-up, unsettled, baffled. There seemed to be so many stimuli assailing him in such a short time span, some he believed helpful, others distracting, and the newest one inscrutable, namely Sylvie. She had proven to be as puzzling as some of the characters in Napoleon's life and this latest incident and its aftermath—the kidnapping and the party plans—simply expanded the puzzle.

Then there was the matter of his summation notes. He could have used the time to bring them up to date. But he had had his fill of notes for the day so he reconsidered and opted for a nap after all.

His alarm sounded at 4 and he staggered into the shower. He could still feel the pull on his arms and picture the misty image in the nightmare: his own body dangling from a rope in the middle of nowhere. Twisting and screaming, he was afraid to let go.

Sylvie's "apartment" was not an apartment at all. Situated on an avenue between the Champs-Élysées and the Eiffel Tower, it was one in a string of four folk-Victorian structures with only an alleyway separating them. One would have classified them as single-story town houses had they been connected. Inside, the living and dining areas were contained within an open space wrapped around a narrow kitchen. Overall the design was varied. Furniture pieces were formal, hardware distinctly decorative. The main space had walls of white paneling and rough-cut blocks of gray natural pumice. Paul noticed paintings with ornate frames, fantasy mirrors, murals behind fluted columns and chandeliers suspended from high-beamed ceilings. Waist-high cherry cabinets rimming three walls offered fresh flowers, fine china and linen, sparkling silverware, champagne and a bottle of cognac on a silver platter.

Paul and Vincent had driven over together. Paul spotted a police car parked across the avenue. Its occupant waved at them.

Vincent saluted back. "That's good old Chester," he said.

"Chester?"

"Yeah, he's our favorite at the prefecture. Swears he was named after all the trees around here."

They approached the front door, found it slightly ajar and walked in. Leon, Maurice and Guy were seated in a circle of easy chairs, laughing at an apparent joke. Paul caught Guy's last line. "No," he said, "I work for a French, not a Spanish newspaper."

A teenage girl in a blue dress and matching blouse with a logo over her left chest was carrying plates of food from the kitchen to a large table in the dining area. She wore a tiny white apron.

All three men stood when Paul and Vincent ambled over.

"Here they are," Leon said. "Have a seat. Sylvie said she'd be out in a minute."

"We've seen it before," Maurice said. "That's when it's hard to believe she's a scientist—when she's more like a Parisian grande dame."

"A grand entrance by a grande dame," Guy chimed in. "Frankly, I think she's been waiting for you, Paul."

At that, Sylvie appeared, rushed over and hugged each of them, Paul last. She stepped back. "Thank you all for coming," she said. "I needed you." She looked as though she were fighting back tears.

"Hail the conquering hero," Maurice shouted. "I mean heroine."

"Some heroine," Sylvie retorted. "I ran into the street as fast as I could."

She wore a tan suede jacket over a white turtleneck sweater; burgundy jeans with abstract geometric patterns; brown boots; and a beige necklace of shell, wood and Lucite along with matching earrings. A far cry from the casual clothes the others wore. Except for Leon. He was decked out in another double-breasted suit, this one black. Paul guessed he didn't own any casual clothes.

"There's the bar, gentlemen," Sylvie said. "Please help yourselves." She motioned toward a well-stocked portable bar half as long as one sidewall. "And there are some canapés on that table near the canapé. I love saying that!" She pointed in the direction of what Paul recognized as a French sofa.

Paul poured two burgundies and handed one to Sylvie saying, "Just like on Friday, I assume?"

"Just like on Friday," she answered. "Thanks."

While the other four men took turns fixing their drinks, Paul ushered Sylvie aside and whispered in her ear, "Where did she come from?" He pointed a finger toward the girl in the apron.

Sylvie in turn whispered: "That's Bernadette, my favorite. Works for a caterer I use. They bring over terrific spreads in no time flat."

"Well I hate to sound discourteous," Paul responded, "but if we happen to get into some confidential talk, will she still be around?"

"Not at all. She's usually in and out. Prepares the table and leaves without even saying goodbye. But she's the best. I do the cleaning myself after everyone's left."

Paul could feel her breath as she enunciated the last few words. "I can help if necessary," he said.

Sylvie leaned back and engaged his eyes. "I can *make* it necessary," she declared.

"What about Vincent? I came with him."

"Oh, I forgot. He may not want to stay."

"We can ask him."

"That's okay. We can make it another time." Sylvie's head drooped. "So it's not necessary after all."

"What's not necessary?" Leon bellowed as he strode toward them.

Paul didn't miss a beat: "That we be discreet in our conversations. We'll leave the serious stuff until the professional help has gone."

The others joined them. Guy was waving a champagne bottle. "I propose a toast!" he exclaimed. There was a chorus of head nodding as all six gathered together. Vincent broke away and rushed back with a tray of glasses. Guy popped the cork. Maurice hiccuped.

Glasses filled and raised, Guy said solemnly, "To Sylvie and her safe return. God is good."

Bernadette, faintly smiling at Sylvie, slipped inconspicuously along the far wall and out the front door.

Each person took several sips of the champagne before Leon, looking directly at Sylvie, said, "We've been avoiding the issue—your captivity. I for one believe it must have been horrendous for you. I don't know how you can be so calm after an ordeal like that."

Sylvie focused briefly on each man, swallowed hard and explained. "I talk to myself. I keep insisting that this thing didn't happen to me at all."

When no further words were forthcoming, Paul said, "That's one way of handling it."

Sylvie's expression brightened. "The other way," she said, her voice rising, "is to *throw a party*! So welcome to my little place."

They sipped some more before Sylvie resumed: "And, gentlemen, as I look back, it was no big deal—but I have to admit it was scary. The worst part was wondering what they were up to. But nothing happened, so there's not much to talk about really."

"How did you manage to escape?" Maurice asked.

"The storage area had stacks and stacks of wooden crates, some filled with who- knows-what, some empty. At least they were light. I decided to look behind some of the light ones against the wall and, voilà, there was a door! Unlocked. So I ran out. Simple as that."

Some questions and answers came in spurts:

Guy: "Did they say why they did it?"

Sylvie: "They never said a word, about that or anything else. It was real spooky."

Guy: "But didn't you inquire about it?"

Sylvie: "Yes, of course, but they just gave these sickly smiles and said nothing."

Guy: "Do *you* have any idea why they did it?"

Sylvie: "I racked my brain and came up with zero. I'd like to think they were simply out to scare me and would eventually have released me unharmed. But that doesn't compute either. Scare me over what?"

Paul: "Did they stay there with you?"

Sylvie: "No, they left by the front door, locked it and never came back the whole time except to bring food."

Vincent: "Did they carry firearms?"

Sylvie: "No."

Maurice: "Did you recognize any of them?"

Sylvie: "No, they didn't even look French."

Maurice: "What, then?"

Sylvie: "Maybe Middle Eastern?"

Paul thought Sylvie must feel as if she were on a witness stand.

They talked further about the location of the warehouse, police notification and whether or not she got any sleep.

"There was a cot there. I managed. And they were completely polite and humane at all times."

They discussed the outcome of the monastery visit for Sylvie's benefit; she was hearing of it for the first time.

Leon, who led the discussion, indicated that they would take up details of the Elba and St. Helena visits once they had eaten.

They moved to the dining table and in relative silence feasted on shrimp chowder, diced lamb with cumin and apricots, potatoes au gratin, mixed vegetables sprinkled with crushed croutons, caramel apple cake, and a choice of red or white Bordeaux wine.

Leon, who was the last to finish, patted his lips with a napkin and said playfully, "Which brings us to the island trips." He outlined the proposed itinerary and offered his reasons for urging Paul to go forward with travel to both islands, despite the difficulty in reaching Helena.

"Now, Sylvie," Leon said, leaning across the table, "are you serious about wanting to go?"

Sylvie smiled demurely and replied, "If Paul thinks I can help, I'll be happy to go along." She walked into the kitchen as if knowing there would be discussion about her.

Inquiring eyes shifted to Paul. "That would work out fine," he said. "Sylvie, Vincent and me."

"Amen," Maurice said. "And, Paul, good buddy, we all know of the threatening note you received." He grasped his cane and jabbed the handle in Vincent's direction. "Stay close by them, Vincent," he commanded.

Back in his hotel room Paul made some summation notes before phoning Jean to report Sylvie's safe return. He described the party and indicated he'd heard before about her propensity for throwing them on the spur of the moment. "But I never thought this kind of moment would qualify," he added.

"Good for her though," Jean said. "So she wasn't harmed?"

"No. She looked great actually."

"Oh? How great?"

"Not 'great' as you're thinking of it. 'Great' as in 'great shape'."

"Oh?" she snapped.

"I mean ... forget it. I mean she had no cuts or bruises and spoke coherently."

"That's better."

"You're such a tease," he said. "But you know, Jean, it just doesn't make sense to me. Why wasn't she more shook up about it? Locked in a warehouse for two days for heaven's sake. Wouldn't you be? I mean, still freaked out?"

"Maybe she was but didn't show it."

"Hmm ... I suppose."

"Maybe she's been through it before. Spying; that business of *Vérité's* seeking the truth; high stakes institutional stuff; international competition. Who knows? That's a different world from ours."

"I doubt she's been kidnapped before or it would have come out." Paul scratched his finger. "But throwing her little shindig might have helped. Anyway she's back and the group wants her to tag along with Vincent and me. We leave for Elba at 8:30 or 9 tomorrow morning."

"Tomorrow? Already?"

"Already. Then it's on to Helena. Which reminds me—I may not be calling you every day for a while. But don't worry. I'll be careful, and you be too."

Jean indicated she understood and they ended the conversation with their usual expressions of love.

It wasn't long before Paul wondered why she hadn't objected to Sylvie's participation in the trips. Then again, wonder, confusion and surprise were nothing new to him ever since Leon's e-mail message had arrived five days before. It seemed like five years.

Chapter 11

Monday, May 22
1:35 p.m.

During the entire five-hour flight to Elba, Sylvie had uttered no more than a sentence or two; she slept most of the way. So much for her managing on a cot in the warehouse. Paul took his own share of naps too but in between, brushed up on the history of the island, referring to some folders he'd brought in his briefcase. This was the start of his *Elba Phase*. Such a start would be unnecessary in the *Helena Phase* later on, since he had covered it enough in his book, *St. Helena: Napoleon's Final Defeat*.

At one point he flipped through the pamphlet Frère Dominic had given him, then read the introductory section:

> Elba is an island in Tuscany, Italy, twelve miles from the coastal town of Grosseto. A popular tourist attraction, it is the largest island of the Tuscan Archipelago and the third largest in Italy after Sicily and Sardinia. Many of its picturesque landscapes are circled by woodlands and small coves beneath towering

rocky cliffs. It is a favorite for divers, hikers and mountain cyclists.

Elba is divided into eight communes including Portoferraio, its capitol, and Monte Cristo, the island which became famous through Alexandre Dumas's novel, *The Count of Monte Cristo*. Victor Hugo, the author of *The Hunchback of Notre Dame* and *Les Miserables*, spent part of his childhood on Elba.

During ancient times, the strategic location and rich mineral resources of the island attracted many warring factions such as the Etruscans and the Romans. But its documented history began with the spread of Christianity and the Middle Ages. In the early eleventh century, Elba became a Pisa dominion and soon, Pisa had to defend the island against the Saracens—Muslims from what later became Saudi Arabia, Iran and Iraq. As part of that defense, two fortresses were built: the Mount Volterraio castle and the sea-tower at Marciana Marina, both of which still exist today. The commune of Marciana Marina currently has 2,000 inhabitants including many immigrants who streamed in from the Italian mainland and a few most knowledgeable descendants of the original settlers.

Despite erosion and crumbling walls, the castle is visited by thousands every year. Rumor has it that Napoleon, during his abdication, would spend hours in the castle, meditating and speaking out loud in Italian. What besides echoes of his voice may still be hidden there, in among the ruins?

Pisa domination continued until the sixteenth century except for sporadic periods of Genoese influence. The island was becoming battle-weary. It fell into Spanish hands; sustained repeated attacks and plunder by pirates (Redbeard was one of them); and was overtaken by a Franco-Turkish fleet in 1553. Only Cosmopoli preserved its freedom due in large part to its fortresses, Falcone and Stella.

French and Spanish fighting continued. In 1738 Cosmopoli was renamed Portoferraio, meaning "Iron Port" in Italian. Eventually England entered the mix. During the French Revolution, several thousand French royalists fled to Elba under English protection and in 1796, the island was incorporated into the domain of the king of England. But French forces returned the following year and there followed a sustained period of bloody fighting among the French, the English, the Tuscans and the Bourbons.

In April 1814, following the disaster of the Russian campaign and the Treaty of Fontainebleau, Napoleon was forced to abdicate and a month later, was exiled to Elba. He was accompanied by a personal guard of six hundred men and was made emperor of the island. He remained there for nearly ten months and during that time established a deep relationship with the people and the land. He helped the islanders produce their own food supply, build streets, institute a waste collection system and of particular importance, improve their economy by supporting the development of a mining industry. While on Elba, he resided in a town house in Portoferraio, *Pallazzina dei Mulini*, and an impressive country/summer home, *Villa of San Martino*. Over the years, the people of Elba came to embrace him as a kind of prodigal son.

Paul read the last three paragraphs superficially, his mind still dwelling on two references in the previous one: "most knowledgeable descendants of the original settlers" and "What … may still be hidden there, in among the ruins?" He underlined them and scribbled a reminder in his note pad that he should follow up on them.

Ansel, the pilot, departed within minutes of touch-down. He had assured Paul that he'd be at-the-ready to return to Elba when notified by Leon.

On the taxi ride from the airport to the Fabricia Hotel, along the Porto Azzurro Road, past the archeological site, *Villa Romana delle Grotte*, Paul peered out the windows like a child absorbed in a picture book. He was immediately struck by the sharp outline of gray cliffs silhouetted against a pale sky; the scent of wildflowers; variegated blues and greens reflected in the surrounding waters; sea breezes swaying motorboats and sailboats; lemon-yellow buildings; easygoing noon-hour traffic; the large number of older pedestrians. He studied their wrinkled faces. They appeared happy. Hushed and preoccupied, but happy.

"Interesting looking people," Sylvie said. "Everybody's smiling."

"Taxes must be low around here," Vincent quipped.

Paul wasn't in the mood to smile; Sylvie acted as if she hadn't heard; and the taxi driver, laughing, turned slightly and remarked, "No, they are not."

"You speak English well," Paul said.

"Grazie," the driver responded. "Many here speak like me."

He eased his car into a half-filled parking area adjoining the hotel. Paul paid him and led the other two toward the front entrance. Vincent offered to carry Sylvie's suitcase but she refused. They passed a man in a kiosk who nodded and gave them each a newsletter.

Paul walked back and said, "Tell me, can we rent a car?"

"You tell me when, I order," the man replied. "Or you order inside."

"Also," Paul said, "have you heard of Clive Weaver?"

"Si, everyone knows. He is curator at Napoleon Museum buildings. Long time."

"They're easy to get to?"

"Si. One here. Portoferraio. Then one in San Martino. Easy."

They decided to skirt the awninged entrance and look around. Paul was reminded of a large villa he'd once admired, one of many tucked into the Tuscan countryside. The hotel property was surrounded by vast fields, gardens, olive groves and grape vines and extended to the Mediterranean—the gulf of Portoferraio—where, in the eighteenth century, a wall had been constructed as protection against sea winds. Paul, nonetheless, could still feel the wind against his face. Warm, calm, soothing. Beyond the wall was a private beach and nearer the hotel, an imposing swimming pool, certainly of Olympic size. The area was hardly crowded. Several patrons were having lunch at the pool's gazebo. A few soaked and stretched in the sea waters of two large Jacuzzis. The height of the tourist season had not yet arrived.

In the lobby, Paul was not surprised to see winding staircases made of wrought iron. *Made of what else in Portoferraio?* But he paid little heed to the traditional décor; he was preoccupied with the start of the island investigations. The *Elba Phase* was set in his mind. He wanted to visit Napoleon's main residence, maybe his summer home; the Archaeological Civic Museum; the Museum of the Misericordia; the individual fortresses of Elba's defense system-Forte Stella, Forte Falcone and the octagonal tower of the Linguella; the sea tower at Marciana Marina; and above all, the Castle of Volterraio. He had shared such intentions with the others earlier on the plane.

His luggage bag and briefcase felt light in his hands as he marched straight toward the registration desk. Sylvie and Vincent lagged behind. A receptionist indicated that three rooms were ready for them on the second floor. As she processed their registrations, Paul turned to Sylvie and Vincent and requested that they all meet back in the lobby in fifteen minutes.

"Then we can have lunch at the gazebo and be off to the museum and Weaver."

"A woman needs more than fifteen minutes, Paul,"

Sylvie said, unsmiling.

"You look beautiful as you are," Paul answered.

A bellhop accompanied them to their rooms—three in a row, Sylvie's in the middle.

Once inside, Paul paid as little attention to the room itself as he had to the lobby. But the panoramic view of the gulf was a different story. He recognized the sixteenth century Medici fortresses that he had seen in pictures, and the thirteenth century Castle of Volterraio, the one he was so eager to examine, probably the first thing in the morning. He withdrew a digital camera from his briefcase and snapped his own pictures of the historic structures.

Lunch was quick. They obtained directions to both arms of the museum and, with Paul at the wheel of a rental car, set off for Napoleon's old residence high on a cliff in Portoferraio, a stone's throw from Forte Falcone. They had been informed that weather-wise the day was the same as yesterday, the day before that and most other Elba days: sunny, breezy and warm. All three wore summer outfits: the men, coincidentally, green sport shirts and tan slacks; Sylvie, light blue blouse and lemon print skirt. They had also been informed that the curator's office was in a small one-story annex attached to the two-story main wing.

"Hardly impressive," Paul said as the museum came into view. The others agreed. The annex seemed as old as the main building. The overall wooden "palace" was constructed in typical Tuscan style and probably would never have won an architectural award, yet inside Paul felt a heavy aura of solemnity and sadness as they followed the receptionist, a Miss Sarcodina, down a winding hallway. He tried to picture Napoleon taking the same steps, at once brooding and, perhaps, plotting.

Miss Sarcodina pointed to a closed door with a CLIVE WEAVER, CURATOR name plate, bowed and left. Before entering, Paul motioned Sylvie aside. Vincent stayed behind.

"What's the matter?" Paul asked her.

"How do you mean?"

"You're so quiet. It's as if you're not here."

"Just tired, that's all."

"You even seem melancholic. Is it none of my business?"

"No, that's all right."

"The kidnapping just sinking in?"

"The kidnapping? Yes, that's it. Just sinking in."

When Paul showed no intention of dropping the matter, Sylvie said, "But you know, the promise of tomorrow can make bad days seem long."

Paul gave her a long speculative look. "That's a keeper. I guess if you can put it that way," he said, "there's nothing to worry about. I shouldn't have brought it up."

Sylvie shook her head from side to side. "As long as we're on the subject, Vincent and I have already discussed it, or at least part of it. We think that here on Elba and later on Helena, you should consider us as what you said before—not here. Just tagging along. We'll give input only when you ask for it, and not in the company of others. Unless we feel you're missing an opportunity or not picking up on something, both of which seem highly unlikely. And we'd be discreet about it. But we'll take notes whenever appropriate. In fact we flipped a coin to see who would do it, and Vincent won."

"So he'll take notes?"

"No, I will."

Paul brushed aside the humor, saying, "Well thanks for the confidence. And the freedom."

"That way you can proceed better you know, uninhibited except by your own standards or values or guidelines — whatever you want to call them. After all, you know what you want. Okay? I ... we ... hope you understand."

"Fully. And thank you. But stay alert."

They walked in.

"I'm delighted to meet you," Clive Weaver said, his voice weak and hollow. He had a decidedly British accent. Leveraging himself up from behind an oak desk, his face looked sun-deprived and it sagged as he rose, tripling the skin folds at his neck. It was obvious that he was once a tall man. He made it around to the front — carrying a black letter-size box with both hands — and said, "Yes indeed, very delighted. Here, please sit. Let me guess: you're Paul and you're Vincent. Therefore ...," he tried winking, "... you must be Sylvie!"

Paul laughed nervously and said, "You got it right, Mr. Weaver, and speaking for the three of us, we share that delight."

"How well you put that but no, please — it's Clive. Good old Clive. I trust you had a pleasant flight from Paris?"

All three nodded yes.

After handshakes, both Sylvie and Vincent saying, "Our pleasure," they sat in wrought iron chairs arranged in a semicircle before the desk. Paul was in a direct line with a stained glass double window, the curator to his left, Vincent and Sylvie to his right. Paul and Vincent had removed a stack of magazines from their chairs, placing them on the floor.

"Should I draw the drapes?" Clive asked. "Is the sun in your eyes, Paul?"

"No, it's fine, thanks."

"Do excuse the mess," Clive said. "There simply is never, but never, sufficient room in this blankety-blank office. Why, it's made for a midget. Would you believe I've had it for over fifty-two years? Look at this place. Who else would put up with such nonsense? If they won't raise my allowance, the least they could do is build me a bigger space." The curator patted the three or four strands of white hair that ran across his scalp, as if to ensure they were still there. "By the way, I've always designated it an allowance because its size reminds me of what children receive." He exhaled sharply. "Anyway, enough of that. I was informed you'd be here within a few days and here you are. I believe I have some information that will—how do they say it in America? Fit the bill? And I'm happy, perfectly happy, to be of service. Frère Dominic and I have worked closely for many years, and when he says he believes in something, so do I."

Turning to both sides in his chair, Paul tried to balance a polite concentration on Clive's words with a cursory inspection of a room that hardly fit the curator's description. It was overstocked, giving the illusion of being undersized. It contained oriental carpeting, intricately designed furniture pieces, books, papers, magazines, tapes, fresh flowers and unlit candelabra. Paintings hung on every oak-paneled wall and leaned against some. A floor-to-high-ceiling bookcase spanned one wall; three alcoves had draped archways; and Paul counted at least six closet doors. Crammed here and there were many of today's office essentials: computer, printer, copier, fax machine. And surprisingly, a Global Positioning System unit that didn't escape Paul's attention.

"Ahhh ... you're wondering about my GPS contraption," Clive said. "I'm still a consultant to the Missing Persons Division of our local police department. They gave it to me for my eighty-fifth birthday, but between you, me and an Elba palm tree, I think they just wanted a place to store it. And truth be known, it's never been used since it arrived. That was three years ago."

Paul was astonished at the discrepancy between Clive's physical appearance and his nimble mind. The curator's head was a near-perfect circle, his complexion pale. Incongruously beady eyes and a narrow pointed nose gave him the pinched features of a barn owl. Only his mouth was normal in size and shape but his lips quivered as he spoke. He gesticulated with thick wire-framed glasses, a large ring on his middle finger.

"So," he said, "let's get started, shall we?" He loosened his tie and raised the gartered sleeves of his shirt. "The most important thing I have to offer you, aside from answering any queries you might have, concerns Napoleon's will." Clive opened the leather box and removed several sheets of paper. He looked at Paul and asked gravely, "Have you seen it?"

"If you mean the will, yes. I referred to it in one of my books but since it wasn't part of the theme of the book, I never really studied it."

"Well, there are only four original copies of his will and I have one of them in my hands—English version. I've made a copy of it for you. They're dated April 15,

1821, when he was in exile on St. Helena. These originals differ from all other copies in circulation. The other copies, maybe thousands of them, don't mention a codicil to the will at all. As you will notice, the codicil on the last page in the original is dated April 21, 1821, two weeks before his death. It names a Lady Beckett as the largest monetary inheritor. Yes, the same Beckett that the prior spoke to you about. You see, we do communicate. But the codicil was amended four days before his death and the amended codicil is nowhere to be found. Now Paul, I can't help you with this but you must locate that amendment because I believe it has great bearing on what you're attempting to resolve. I doubt that it's here on Elba but perhaps on St. Helena. Then again, perhaps not. But you must find it. As I've said, it may hold the key you're looking for." The curator's voice had become stronger and louder, with a sense of crisis, of dire necessity. He handed one of the four copies to Paul stating he could keep it.

Sylvie began taking notes.

Paul thought it rude to read through the will then and there, although he was tempted to peek at the codicil on the last page. Instead, he slid the copy gently into his briefcase. But he didn't think it rude to say, "Before we go on, may I ask a question or two?"

"Yes, please."

"Does anyone else know about this?"

"No one, not even Frère Dominic."

"So, to get it straight, you haven't told anybody about the existence of the codicil we have and its amendment which we do not have?"

"Nobody."

"Forgive me, but why not?"

"No one ever asked me about them."

Paul was baffled by what he determined to be flimsy reasoning and was about to pursue the issue when the curator said, "Speaking of Helena ..."

"Yes—Helena." Paul's way of disposing of a subject quickly.

"You know of my colleague there, Thatcher Drinkwell. Fine fellow, fellow Brit. Don't be thrown off by his manner, a bit fidgety. But he's more serious than he lets on. Helena's constable. You'd never think he'd be a bird lover. Younger than I am. Who isn't? But quite a clever chap. And accommodating. That's what you want: intelligence and accommodation."

"And someone on the side of the law." Paul wasn't sure why he made the comment.

"Not much crime there though," Clive remarked. "Let me also say this now because it's the right time to say it. You may notice I like to talk. I've always considered the one listening to me as my victim-of-the-day. Well, Thatcher puts me to shame, so be prepared for it. Talks non-stop; you'll be lucky to get a word in edgewise."

Although Paul had further questions about the will, he wanted to move on but again, the curator directed the conversation. "So that is the sum and substance I've been saving for you on that particular subject. Now, I have another. Lady Beckett? She had an illegitimate child, presumably with Napoleon. A girl. We know that from descendants of what I call her 'covers'."

"Covers?"

"Yes. Through the years knowledgeable descendants have confided in me."

The *"knowledgeable descendants" in the*

pamphlet!

"Some of their ancestors served as covers for Beckett as she slipped onto this island and onto Helena to see Napoleon," he continued, "and as far as a pregnancy was concerned, who better to know about it?"

"And when you say descendants, whose descendants?"

"Talleyrand's."

"*The* Talleyrand?"

"Yes, indeed. Charles Maurice de Talleyrand-Perigord."

"You mean that members of Talleyrand's family helped Lady Beckett have liaisons with Napoleon?"

"It's unequivocal. I must explain and if the prior has already done so, please stop me. Sometimes we secure information that is unequivocal and other times it's what we term 'reasonably reliable'. This—that is, Lady Beckett, the liaisons, the illegitimate child and the Talleyrand connection—is unequivocal."

For the first time during their dialogue, Paul made an entry in his note pad and as he wrote, he could feel the blotches forming on his cheeks and forehead. He hated it when they appeared, especially in front of a relative stranger. His eyes drifted first to Vincent's, then to Sylvie's, and he could tell that each pair was reflecting a gentle reassurance.

Clive, giving no indication that he noticed the change in Paul's face, went on. "I have only one more item to cover. I'm sure the prior referred to both a monumental decision and the hatching of a plan on the part of Napoleon when he lived here. The prior no doubt used those exact words—'monumental decision and hatching of a plan'—the same ones he drummed into me in his preparation calls."

"Preparation calls?"

"Yes. We have them all the time. He has them with all our colleagues around the globe. Dom is a wonderful man but a bit compulsive. That isn't entirely a negative, mind you. It's born of a desire to be faultless."

"I get the picture."

"So we've covered the monumental decision; that is, Lady Beckett's inheritance. The hatched plan is a different story. I have no idea what it's about, but Dom seems to think it pertains to some of Napoleon's battles. Nor do we know where the plan's been all these years. Perhaps it's detailed in the amended codicil. Who knows?"

"Hold it, please," Paul said, his hand raised in a stop gesture. "Okay for two more questions?"

"Certainly."

"First, I know you can't speak for the prior and maybe I should have asked him this directly, but why do you think he believes the so-called hatched plan relates to the battles?"

"Excellent question. Because of what he's been able to ascertain from Talleyrand's descendants."

"Talleyrand again?"

"Yes. But remember I referred to 'unequivocal information'? Well, Dom doesn't much trust the Talleyrand clan. Sorry for speaking this way, but he'd be the first to admit it. So he regards the information as only 'reasonably reliable' and he doesn't hand that kind out freely. And the second question?"

Paul got the feeling that Clive wanted to get off the subject or maybe he was uncomfortable speaking for the prior.

"It's a simple one with two parts: How do you know there was an amendment to the codicil, and how did you come upon an original copy?"

"The answer to the first part is simple too. When you look at the last page of the copy I gave you, you'll notice the phrase, 'See amendment to the codicil.' But there isn't one there. Apparently it's on a separate page. And the answer to the second part is confidential. I assure you, however, that it doesn't bear on what you're trying to achieve, only on our group's process of securing information. It's contrary to the usual methods as our name implies. Contrarians? *Histarians*?"

"Of course. I didn't mean to be nosy. But as to half the question, your answer couldn't be clearer." Paul said. "I should have looked at it before I put it away."

There was a knock on the door and it opened just enough for Miss Sarcodina to stick her head through. "Senanque on the line," she said.

"Excuse me," Clive said, rising in stages. Paul thought he heard more than one joint creak. The curator stood and was already bent to pick up the phone at the corner of the desk. "Dominic!" he exclaimed. "How are you today? Good, good. What? Yes, they're with me right now. That's all? Well let me say things are going well. Yes, I'll do that. Bye for now."

The other three exchanged glances, Paul's lingering the longest.

"He wants you to call him when you get a chance," Clive said.

"Will do," Paul said. "Is he in the habit of checking up like that?"

"Compulsion, remember? Born of faultlessness?"

The curator returned to his chair, breathing hard. "Now, where was I? Oh yes, I was about to ask if you had any additional questions."

"Only two, three more come to mind," Paul said, "and I hope we're not taking up too much of your time?"

"Not at all. You can have the rest of the afternoon. This is a pleasant change of pace for me. Actually, boredom is the usual menu around these parts."

"The Mafia," Paul said sternly.

"La Cosa Nostra," Clive responded. "Yes?"

"Do they bother you?"

"Bother?"

"Do you have to pay for protection?"

"So far, no. Here at the museum we deal with tourists and they like tourists. The more money taken in by restaurants and hotels, the more money they can demand. Same for transportation, dry cleaning, liquor and other retail stores. But it's spotty. I'd say half are victims. Some of the businesses are *run* by the Mafia and that may explain some of it."

"And museums don't have to pay?"

"Not museums. We're not in on their take. Well, except through government taxes that we employees have to fork out."

"That too? They get a cut?"

"Depends on the commune. Portoferraio's one of their favorites, but not, for instance, Monte Cristo. No one seems to know why they leave those people alone. However it's not as bad as in Sicily. There, eighty percent of businesses pay for protection."

Paul consulted a card from the breast pocket of his sport shirt. "I've been thinking," he said, "but before I get to that. What if a business refuses to pay?"

The curator ran a finger across his neck, then jabbed the same finger into his temple.

"Garroted or shot, right?"

"Right, or you might accidentally fall from one of the cliffs. Our topography helps. We read about it in the papers quite a bit, and most of the fatalities involve business owners."

"I see," Paul said. "Now I've been thinking, could they provide us with helpful information? Their type has been around a long time. I read somewhere that La Cosa Nostra had its roots in Palermo in the late twelve hundreds. Maybe they could help out."

The curator was massaging his elbow and stopped short. "But would you dare deal with them?" he asked.

"Only if you thought it advisable."

"It could hurt in the long run."

"How?"

"I don't know, but I wouldn't want to find out."

Paul returned the card to his pocket. "So the bottom line is that you've never had to deal with them?"

"Never."

Paul nodded toward the window. "Then who are those two guys in the black sedan that just pulled up near our car?"

Clive leaned toward Paul and looked out. "Oh them?" he said. "They're Hugo One and Hugo Two. They work for us, our security guards."

"Are they Mafia?"

The curator hesitated, grimaced and replied, "Now you know better than to ask that, Paul."

"Foolish. I'm sorry."

"I understand. You have another question or two?"

"Yes. Do you think Napoleon died of natural causes or was deliberately poisoned?"

The curator responded as if he'd expected the question. "It's very controversial, isn't it? I'm afraid I can't decide."

For want of a better reaction, Paul withdrew the card and faked a notation.

"One more?" Clive asked.

"Yes. The prior urged me to ask about your cartoon collection. Do you …?"

"I know he did and I'd like you to see it. I've donated it to the museum but I keep it here."

The curator struggled up, walked to the nearest alcove and returned pushing a large square cabinet on casters. Paul recognized it as belonging to the French Regency style of the early seventeen hundreds. It held a stack of flat containers filled with cardboard sheets the size of a flip chart. Three-by-five cartoons, caricatures and satirical images were fastened to the top sheet.

Vincent shot up saying, "Here, may I help you with that?"

"No, thank you, but could you bring out the other one?" Clive puffed.

Vincent obliged and they all squeezed into the center of the room around the two cabinets.

"The captions are self explanatory," Clive said. "Some are rather cleverly done. There are larger archival collections for the Napoleonic era to be sure but, I'm told, none as interesting. I'm really quite proud of mine."

For twenty minutes, he guided them through sheet after sheet. "As you can see, Honoré Daumier is my favorite cartoonist or should I say caricaturist? French, don't you know. He often ridiculed political figures. He once drew the obese King Louis Philippe as a giant pear and ended up imprisoned for a spell. After that, he turned to satirizing the rising French middle class, particularly their fashions and manners. And of course Napoleon was a logical target. Daumier liked to exaggerate his hat."

Throughout the session, if there were any special meanings to be extracted from the drawings, they went over Paul's head. Certainly there was no hint of previously unknown enemies of Napoleon or a would-be assassin, as Frère Dominic had suggested. The only vaguely suspicious detail Paul noticed was in the ones mocking the emperor where Talleyrand could be seen looming in the distance or through a thick fog. But this he attributed to the animosity between Napoleon and his on-again, off-again advisor.

The conclusion of the visit was bland. Around 4:15, Paul thanked the curator and expressed the hope that they would meet again. Clive responded with, "Look around the museum. I'm sure you'll find it fascinating. And I trust you'll spend some time on the island."

"That's our plan," Paul said.

"Good. Do visit Volterraio Castle. Well, not exactly the castle itself. It's hard to get to. But you can reach the narrow dirt road circling the base of the cliff. We call it the "rutted road." Then you can have a good look at the castle on top, at least what remains of it. A most extraordinary sight."

Clive nodded to all three and, without a smile, turned and walked into the next room.

That's all? Not even good luck? Paul hadn't expected

such an uninspiring ending but chalked it up to the curator's obvious fatigue. A disconcerting factor however was that the fatigue had become more pronounced once the subject of La Cosa Nostra had been brought up.

Halfway down the hall, Paul said, "Let's skip it. Let's skip San Martino too. I'm not sure why yet, but this whole island gives me the creeps. We need a relaxing dinner tonight and in the morning we can see what's what at the Volterraio Castle. They say Napoleon spent quite a lot of time there. Then we'll decide if we should see more or if we should leave."

As they reached their car, the black sedan sped off. They looked at one another without comment though Paul puzzled over the timing. And a red decal on the car's rear bumper.

"Vincent, you drive," he said, "I'm anxious to look over the will."

Driving away, Vincent asked Paul, "So what's your verdict on Mr. Curator?"

"The jury's still out."

"Does that imply we might run into him again?"

"No. I'm just tired of saying I don't know. Bums me out big time!"

Paul withdrew the copy of the will from his briefcase and hurriedly read through its several pages. He then returned to the sections he judged most significant:

> NAPOLEON
> This 15th April, 1815, at Longwood, Island
> of St. Helena.
> This is my Testament, or act of my last will.
> I

1. I DIE in the Apostolical Roman religion, in the bosom of which I was born more than fifty years since.

2. It is my wish that my ashes may repose on the banks of the Seine, in the midst of the French people, whom I have loved so well.

3. I have always had reason to be pleased with my dearest wife, Maria Louisa. I retain for her, to my last moment, the most tender sentiments—I beseech her to watch, in order to preserve, my son from the snares which yet environ his infancy.

4. I recommend to my son never to forget that he was born a French prince, and never to allow himself to become an instrument in the hands of the triumvirs who oppress the nations of Europe: he ought never to fight against France, or to injure her in any manner; he ought to adopt my motto: "Everything for the French people."

5. I die prematurely, assassinated by the English oligarchy and its tool. The English people will not be slow in avenging me.

6. The two unfortunate results of the invasions of France, when she had still so many resources, are to be attributed to the treason of Marmont, Augereau, Talleyrand, and La Fayette. I forgive them—May the posterity of France forgive them as I do.

7. I thank my good and most excellent mother, the Cardinal, my brothers, Joseph, Lucien, Jerome, Pauline, Caroline, Julie, Hortense, Catarine, Eugene, for the interest they have continued to feel for me. I pardon Louis for the libel he published in 1820: it is replete with false assertions and falsified documents.

8. I disavow the "Manuscript of St. Helena," and other works, under the title of Maxims, Sayings, etc., which persons have been pleased to publish for the last six years. Such are not the rules which have guided my life. I caused the Duc d'Enghien to be arrested and tried, an honour of the French people, when the Count d'Artois was maintaining, by his own confession, sixty assassins at Paris. Under similar circumstances, I should act in the same way.

II

1. I bequeath to my son the boxes, orders, and other articles: such as my plate, field-bed, saddles, chapel-plate, books, linen which I have been accustomed to wear and use, according to the list annexed (A). It is my wish that this slight bequest may be dear to him, as coming from a father of whom the whole world will remind him.

2. I bequeath to Lady Holland the antique cameo which Pope Pius VI gave me in Tolentino.

3. I bequeath to Count Montholon, two millions of francs, as proof of my satisfaction for the filial attentions he has paid to me during six years, and as an indemnity for the losses his residence at St. Helena has occasioned him.

4. I bequeath to Count Bertrand, five hundred thousand francs.

5. I bequeath to Count Marchand, my first valet-de-chambre, four hundred thousand francs. The services he has rendered me are those of a friend; it is my wish that he should marry the widow sister, or daughter, of an officer of my old Guard.

Paul skipped to the last page, paying only slight attention to endless lists of personal properties and possessions.

CODICIL
Longwood, Island of St. Helena, this, 21st April, 1821.

I bequeath to my dear Lady Beckett, three millions of francs.

NAPOLEON

AMENDMENT
Longwood, Island of St. Helena, this, 1st May, 1821.

See amendment to the codicil.

NAPOLEON

Paul's reading was fast but he thought sufficient for the moment. He believed Napoleon's statements, especially those dealing with bequests to relatives, military generals and children of fallen soldiers, made the emperor seem more real, more human. But it was the absence of the amendment to the codicil that most intrigued him. *Where could it be?*

Chapter 12

S oon after their arrival back at the Fabricia, Paul found himself pacing within his room, something he couldn't recall ever doing away from his Connecticut study. He was to meet Vincent and Sylvie in the main dining room in an hour. His mind was teeming with questions: Whom to believe, whom to trust and, the most perplexing of all, was the investigation worth the effort? And the risk? Perhaps soaking in a hot bath would be more soothing than a shower and might even quiet his mind.

It did neither. He put on a bulky hotel robe and was about to leave the bathroom when he heard a noise coming from the other side of the door. He burst out and was both relieved and stunned to see Sylvie sitting on the side of his bed, flipping through the pages of a magazine. She straightened up. She wore a scarlet robe and was barefoot.

"I thought you'd like these," she said, waving the notes she had taken at the museum. "And did you know your door was ajar?"

"It was?"

"Paul, tell me I'm not your mother, but you have to be more careful."

"Thanks, I'll try. But should I worry?"

"Maybe."

"Shouldn't you though? You were the one who was kidnapped."

"We're talking about locking doors, not getting yanked into a car."

Paul eyed the full length of Sylvie's robe and said, "You win." He grabbed the notes and expected her to continue their repartee but she whirled around. Before slamming the door behind her she turned back and said, "See? Like this."

Alone again, he put his hands on his hips and fantasized. He wouldn't have been shocked if she had allowed her robe to drift open.

Dinner was not the respite Paul had hoped for, nor did it turn out to be a review of the day. The thoughts of his companions seemed elsewhere. Sylvie spoke little, Vincent focused on surveillance and Paul absently picked at his food.

It was only 7:20 when Paul reentered his room, too early to call it a night although they had agreed on an early morning start to Volterraio Castle. Vincent had found out where it was. "You can see it on top of a steep hill from nearly everywhere on the island. We had a view of it from our rooms, remember? About fifteen miles from here, no road leading up to it, just to the base of the hill, then the climb by foot, not too long but rugged. Only the most adventurous try it, they say."

Both men had regarded Sylvie simultaneously. "You game?" Paul asked.

"Not really. Lend me the camera and I'll take pictures. Then I'll wait in the car. That is, if you two strong men want to play mountain goat."

Paul, yawning, felt less distracted than two hours before. He glanced at his bed, the phone and finally his briefcase. It was a toss-up but he reasoned that the phone and briefcase had no chance if he chose sleep. Besides, he might awaken in the middle of the night regretting that he had neither phoned the prior, as requested, nor reviewed some old notes on Talleyrand. He had brought them along to refresh his memory, anticipating talk about him with both Clive Weaver and Thatcher Drinkwell. Although no actual discussion had materialized at the museum, the curator had referred to the French statesman twice, adding to the several times his name had surfaced in the last two days. So Paul wanted to review the man's career not only because it would be timely but also because he would insist on some discussion when he got to meet Drinkwater on St. Helena. He had, after all, named Talleyrand in his new manuscript as a suspect in Napoleon's possible murder. Therefore, the phone call could wait another ten minutes.

Paul located the material and picked out the essentials of the diplomat's life, finally coming upon a white paper put together by one of Paul's undergraduate students when *St. Helena: Napoleon's Final Defeat* was in draft form. It dealt with Talleyrand during the Napoleonic years:

> Talleyrand (1754-1838) was a French statesman who was born into an aristocratic family in Paris. Witty, crafty and complex, he became one of the most controversial, influencial and fascinating figures in French history. But his standing with the emperor was erratic at best.

Talleyrand's full name was Charles Maurice de Talleyrand-Perigord, Prince de Benevent. His clubfoot rendered him unable to enter a military career and marked him by his parents as unfit to carry on the family lineage. Early on they thus stripped him of his birthright and any anticipated inheritance. Because he could not follow in the traditional military footsteps of the Talleyrand dukes, he embarked on a religious career, a move acceptable to his family and one which, they felt, would bring him some degree of social standing at least. At age sixteen he began studies for holy orders at the seminary of St. Sulpice and nine years later received his degree from the Sorbonne and was ordained a priest.

He rose rapidly within ecclesiastical circles, combining both theological and political aspirations. But even during his student days, he exhibited a thinly veiled revolutionary philosophy. This eventually became more overt and after participating in activities considered radical by the Church (celebrating mass on the Champs de Mars to commemorate the anniversary of the storming of the Bastille; spearheading the confiscation of Church property for the national government), he was excommunicated in 1791.

Two years later he fled to the United States after learning of a warrant for his arrest for unspecified charges. He spent three years in the Massachusetts area working in commodity trading and real estate speculation. The warrant was revoked in 1796 and he returned to France where, with the assistance of friends in high positions, he was appointed Foreign Affairs Minister of the ruling assembly. At about this time he caught the eye of Napoleon Bonaparte and, each man sensing the political merits of a friendship, they became allies. There followed a series of key political appointments granted by Napoleon between 1804 and 1814 including Grand Chamberlain and Vice-elector of the Empire; Sovereign Prince of Benevento (a small principality taken from the Pope); and representative of France at the Congress of Erfurt. But Talleyrand was also involved in some shady and sinister developments during this same period and his relationship with the emperor began to deteriorate. They were at odds on several military and foreign policy matters. He publicly condemned what he called the crude treatment of Prussia, he opposed the Franco-Russian Alliance and, later, the attack on Russia. From 1812 on, he became a Russian secret agent. In effect he became a spy for Russia, Austria and England, accepting bribes from them to reveal Napoleon's secrets. He even demanded bribes from the United States (XYZ Affair). His firm stand against the Spanish campaign so infuriated Joseph Fouche, the head of Napoleon's secret police, that it helped convince the emperor that he was plotting against him. This provided the spark for

Napoleon's famous depiction of Talleyrand as "a piece of dung in a silk stocking."

Because of his perpetually shifting loyalties, especially during the French Revolution (1789-1799) — sometimes supporting the revolution, the empire or the monarchy — historians continue to debate whether the man was a consummate diplomat who valued France's survival at any cost or a mercenary who selfishly sought out opportunities to "feather his own nest." One thing was certain: he was a voluptuary who had a passion for sexual liaisons. It is said that he had four illegitimate children including the painter, Eugene Delacroix, and possibly one who was conceived while he lived in the United States. He was furthermore a gourmet and in early 1800 owned the elegant Château Haut-Brion in Bordeaux. In this connection, he hired outstanding culinary personnel and was reputed to acquire only the finest tea and spices directly from the British East India Tea Company.

Paul harked back to Frère Dominic's mention of one of Napoleon's lovers, Lady Beckett, distinctly remembering that he cited her as a top executive with the British East India Tea Company!

Chapter 13

Tuesday, May 23
8:45 a.m.

The next morning, Paul, Vincent and Sylvie hardly spoke during the fifteen minute drive to the "rutted road." Vincent stopped the car and all three piled out. Sylvie began taking pictures. From their vantage point, Volterraio Castle was more imposing than Paul had anticipated, certainly earning by virtue of both its appearance and location the title *Elba Island's Guardian*. It was perched on the summit of a rocky cliff that angled perfectly skyward and contained nothing but a colossal mass of boulders. There were no paths to climb, no living or dead tree stumps to help during any ascent. Paul thought it remarkable that the only vegetation was either around his feet or, as viewed against the morning's darkening clouds, clinging to the castle itself. Blades of yellow grass brushed against his legs clear up to his knees, while the castle appeared smothered in green, brown and yellow like a camouflaged fortress. Paul knew its construction dated back to the eleventh century's Pisan period and that it had likely dwindled to half its original height. Still it looked indestructible to him and there were other words that swept through his mind: powerful, formidable, graceful, dignified. Even timeless.

He hadn't yet discussed it with the others but Paul had every intention of inspecting the castle up close, to glance over an entire sea as the Tuscans had done to spot invading Saracen pirates; to see its underground tunnels firsthand; to walk among its walls much like Napoleon two centuries ago, before the erosion and crumbling began. Then he wanted to observe the blackbirds he'd read about. They had been delivered there as a trick and he understood they were still nesting among the ruins. In the dim light, he could barely make out a few circling about. Theirs were the only sounds he heard. Much smaller than normal, they gave the illusion that the structure was bigger that it was, as viewed from long distances by the French, the Turks, the Saracens or any other enemies.

And who knows, he mused, perhaps they might stumble upon something left behind, something hidden centuries before and now exposed. *The box that Napoleon allegedly carried on his frequent visits there?*

He removed his sunglasses for it was growing darker by the minute. He then asked Sylvie to wait in the car and lock the doors.

"You ready?" he whispered to Vincent.

"If you are. What looks like the best route to the top?"

Paul tweaked his chin. "Let's check around," he said. "You go that way and I'll go the opposite." He pointed to his left and right. "If you find a halfway decent approach, give a holler. I'll do the same."

"Got it," Vincent said. "Incidentally, why are we whispering?"

"So we might hear echoes of Napoleon's voice. The

rumor is that he routinely spoke out loud in Italian up there."

They both chuckled nervously. As Vincent went off, Paul headed right. He passed giant rock after giant rock on his left. Interspersed among them were formations that brought to mind the stalagmites of caves he had explored. He stopped occasionally to survey possible routes to the castle high up. Minutes later he looked back and saw that their car was no longer visible. Up ahead, several rocks formed a mound nearer the road, narrowing it some. Paul rounded the mound and stopped short. *What the!* He thought his heart would race out of control!

Twenty yards ahead three men leaned against the back of a black car. They rose to attention, hands on hips, legs apart. Red hoods covered their heads. The eye and mouth slots were overly large, revealing dark skin and mustaches. All three moved slowly toward him.

Paul had the presence of mind to notice that the car's back bumper contained no decal as was the case back at the museum. But of more immediate concern was what to do. Turn and run? Strike up a conversation? Say, "Excuse me?" He might have done so had they not been wearing hoods.

Suddenly Paul heard Vincent's voice from behind and slightly hillside. He held a pistol in each hand. "Back off!" he screamed at the men. He leaped onto the road and swiftly positioned himself in front of Paul.

The men kept coming.

"Stop or else!" Paul's voice was louder and firmer as he straightened both arms toward the hooded men, now ten yards away.

They stopped.

"Put your hands behind your head, all of you." Without taking his eyes off them, Vincent twisted his mouth to the side and said, "Show 'em, Paul, in case they don't understand."

Paul complied as did the men.

"Now one by one, throw your guns on the ground." Vincent continued. "And don't try anything funny. I've shot these pistols many times before. Shake your heads if you understand me."

They shook their heads. They followed Vincent's command and within seconds five handguns lay on the road.

"You in the middle," Vincent said, "only one gun?"

The man didn't respond.

Vincent tipped his pistol in his direction and the man reached into his back pocket.

"Easy now," Vincent said.

The man flipped a small silver handgun onto the road.

"Thank you gentlemen. Now all of you—on the ground, face down, hands behind your head."

They spoke for the first time, each saying, "Si."

Vincent handed one of his pistols to Paul and said, "Keep them covered. Every second." He picked up the men's guns and hurled them far up the cliff, one at a time. He then walked over to their car and shot out its tires.

"Let's go," Vincent said. "There's enough room to turn our car around. And you guys? We're walking backwards so don't dare get up until we're out of sight. Get it?"

As they inched away, Paul remained stunned over

Vincent's skill in taking control of the situation. Leon was right. *What a bodyguard!*

"Why didn't you whisper to me that you'd be doubling back?" Paul asked.

"Because I figured if we were somehow being watched, they'd see that and I didn't want them to. Besides, it wasn't necessary for you to know."

At the car, Sylvie bolted out. "I was so worried! I didn't know what to do. There were four shots. What happened?"

"Nothing," Vincent said. "Just testing my gun."

They got into the car, Sylvie in back. Vincent maneuvered it around and they sped off through a heavy rain that lasted but a few seconds. It reminded Paul of his boyhood vacations in southern Florida.

"You carry a gun, Vincent?" Sylvie asked in disbelief.

"Around here? For sure."

"Back in Paris, you don't seem like the gun type."

"But away from Paris, I can even swallow swords."

"If you don't mind, Vincent, let's level with her," Paul said.

Vincent's expression didn't register disapproval and Paul explained what had transpired, ending with, "Let's get out of here fast and I don't mean this place. I mean the whole damn island. Screw it!"

"Don't fret Paul," Sylvie said. "Maybe they're just trying to throw a scare at us."

Paul had heard her utter that line before. Still, he couldn't tell if she meant it or was merely trying to console him in his moment of uneasiness.

In the hotel lobby, the conversation was totally one-sided. Paul's words gushed out as if he couldn't wait to get rid of them: "When I took on the assignment, I never bargained for this kind of stuff. I've hunted for stolen treasures all over the world, six continents, never faced this. I'm calling Leon. Let's see when the plane can get here. I'm sure you're wondering about St. Helena. That's still open but I've got some deep thinking to do. After Leon, I'm calling Jean. I'll let the two of you know what's going on as soon as I know myself."

Before they broke up Vincent led Paul into a side room. He unstrapped his ankle rig with its Heritage Stealth 9 mm. pistol and offered it to Paul together with an extra six-round cartridge taken from his pocket. "Here. I hope you'll accept these," he said.

Paul stared first at the rig and ammunition, then long and hard at Vincent. After a deep breath, he accepted.

It was 11:30 when Paul got through to Leon. With uncharacteristic emotion he summarized what had happened including Vincent's heroics. The more he spoke, the more fired up he became. This eventually eased up, however, when he came to the curator's revelations. Leon underplayed the castle incident and instead stressed the importance of what they had learned so far; of Paul's being the principal investigator in an historical investigation; and of keeping Vincent close at hand.

"But as you can imagine," Paul said, "I don't have good vibes around here anymore and I want to leave. I met with Clive Weaver and that's enough. He was helpful—a little strange—but helpful. When can the plane arrive?"

"I understand, Paul. It can leave here anytime you

want."

"Is *now* too soon?"

"Not at all. Ansel can be there in, say, six hours. Is that okay?"

"Okay."

"And, Paul? I say this like a father. Anything worthwhile has its distractions, and some are more serious than others."

"Serious?" Paul countered. "You mean deadly. Yeah, that's it: deadly serious."

Chapter 14

A half hour later, Paul put in a call to Jean. It was around 6 a.m. in the States. As he waited for the connection he considered distancing himself from the mission for awhile, yet hoped that something would come along to change his mind. And it did—in the form of Jean's persuasive words, a complete reversal of what she had said four days earlier.

"Hello, Jean?"

"Paul! I thought I wouldn't hear from you for days. Where are you?"

"Elba. We're leaving for Paris late this afternoon. I decided to cut short our stay here."

Once again he summarized what had happened on the "gutted road." He even told her about the pistol and ankle rig Vincent had given him. Jean said nothing. Paul felt some facial blotches and wondered why none had appeared during the confrontation there. *Were his emotions and their effect on his nervous system playing tricks on him?* Ever since early boyhood, he had come to predict with great accuracy when he would turn blotchy.

He made a point of mentioning Napoleon, Lady Beckett and the illegitimate child and then said, "I don't know, Jean. I think I'm all f... , all screwed up. This is getting to me: the stalking car, the kidnapping, the note, the mysterious call Vincent got and now this. For a moment there, I was thinking of bowing out."

"Wait a second. What note, what call?"

"Oh, someone left a warning under my door the other day. Then a couple of days later, some guy called Vincent and told him I should mind my own business. I didn't say anything because I didn't want to alarm you, but since the armed men in their cutesy hoods came into the picture, all bets are off."

"What did the note say?"

"Leave Paris *tout de suite*."

"Listen to me," Jean said. "What did you do when Vincent gave you his pistol and the holster?"

"I brought it back here to the room and strapped it to my ankle."

"And the extra bullets?"

"In my pocket."

"So there you are: dilemma solved."

"What's *that* supposed to mean?"

"Paul, darling, you can't turn away now. Intellectually and emotionally you can handle it. All the negative stuff may just be attempts to scare you off but the fact that you armed yourself tells me you're ready for anything. You just have to be extremely careful from now on. And you have Vincent, God bless him." Her voice quivered. "I know you, Paul. You're not a quitter, so go on to St. Helena as planned. Please!"

He couldn't believe it. He clearly remembered his first call home, when Jean had expressed so many misgivings about the mission. And now, the reversal. A reversal that made her advice more cogent.

"You may be right," he said. "I mean whoever

thought I'd be packing a gun? Thanks, Jean. What is it they say? I needed that. And I love you." He ended their conversation with a reminder that she wouldn't hear from him for several days. "Maybe not until we get back from Helena."

In spite of the encouraging call, Paul was still glad they were leaving Elba. True, there were sites he'd wanted to visit but the chances were slim that anything significant would have been uncovered: the old adage about a needle in the haystack.

He made copious but disorganized notes about the information he'd garnered from Clive Weaver. That occupied the first hour of the flight back to Paris, a point when he thought he was too restless to sleep. Four hours later, minutes before touchdown, he found he was wrong.

Leon was waiting at the airstrip, standing on an open platform adjoining a shabby, window-laden building. He wore the biggest trench coat Paul had ever seen. He would have wagered it was custom-made.

"Welcome back, my boy," Leon said, "or should I say boys and girl—our island travelers?"

Paul began sheepishly: "Leon, please forgive ..."

"No need to explain. I'm certain another day on Elba wouldn't have yielded much more anyway. St. Helena is the real place for the nuggets."

After Leon had shaken their hands, Sylvie and Vincent led the way toward the entrance. Leon signaled Paul to hang back. "I realize it's not exactly warm out here," he said, "but I want to add to what I said on the phone a while ago. In your travels around the world in your—shall we say—your secondary job ..."

"Primary now."

"Primary. You must have come across people of all kinds including double-dealers, undercover operatives, sharks, shakedown artists."

"Yeah, all kinds, but none with deadly weapons."

"None that you could see."

Paul wiggled his toes, feeling the ankle rig. "I suppose that's accurate."

"So? Now you see them."

"Believe me, Leon, I respect what you're driving at but it wasn't that I was shook ... and surprised ... per se; it was that I didn't expect it where it occurred—on a godforsaken imitation of a road near a bunch of ruins. And that's not the whole story. Couple it with Sylvie's kidnapping, with the warning note, with the cars tailing me, all of this in a few short days. But I'm okay now. In fact I'm more determined than ever. As long as I know the ground rules, or lack thereof, and I now know them. I say, 'Bring on the bastards'."

Paul had spoken as though he had a message for the whole world to hear. "While we're on the subject," he said, "one other thing: I'd swear those guys were Mafia."

"They no doubt were. Hired guns."

"Well I've never dealt with them directly before, but that's okay too. I'll be on my toes."

Leon peered through one of the windows. "Sylvie and Vincent look impatient," he said. "but one other thing before we join them. You must have your own network, don't you? I ask because if you do, it may soon be time to rely on them. For tips, don't you know."

Paul felt the cold through his thin jacket but wanted to hear more, away from the others. "Tips?" he asked.

"How do you mean? For leads?"

"That and warnings of people lurking. Your antennas. Here in France, in England, in Italy, wherever you go. I guess I'm asking if you have some contacts of your own."

"Some."

"I suppose you could call it a network?"

"I suppose."

"Global?"

"Possibly."

"Sizeable?"

"Possibly."

"I'll take that as a yes on all counts. So you've verified what we at *Vérité* have discovered."

Paul scratched his finger. "Sounds like I've been vetted," he said.

"You've been thoroughly vetted. That's not a bad thing, is it? As I've assured you in the past, you have exactly what it takes to accomplish what we've engaged you to do."

Paul didn't answer. He smiled wryly, opened the door and allowed Leon to walk through first.

The truth was that Paul had very little of what he would term a network: a few contacts here and there, a few gratified clients, a few fellow hunters of missing treasures.

Inside Leon stopped to ask, "Can you trust them?"

"Some of them. You mean regarding what the mission's about?"

"Precisely."

"No need to. I could just say I'm working on something important and potentially dangerous and let it go at that ... if I have to explain at all."

"As you wish. I'm simply trying to make it easier for you."

"I know that and I appreciate it. Believe me, I'm ready for anything." Paul held back a qualifying phrase, however, "At least I hope so."

"Fine. And you're ready for St. Helena?"

"Ready. Okay to leave tomorrow or do we wait till Wednesday?"

"I've already checked and it's no problem arriving a day earlier than we'd planned. I've made arrangements with both the R.A.F. and the folks at the Farm Lodge Hotel. It's fifteen minutes from the center of Jamestown ... very nice ... very private, I'm told. As for Thatcher Drinkwell, he'll probably be at the Police Service building."

Paul took out his pad and scribbled in the name of both buildings.

He didn't take Leon's advice lightly. Upon arrival in his hotel room, however, he decided to take it one step further. He recalled having traveled to The Netherlands three or four years ago to help locate two misplaced paintings, a Rembrandt and a Pieter de Hooch. They were found but Paul had played a minor role. He had worked closely, however, with one Victor Frelinghuyens, an art dealer in Amsterdam who had once casually mentioned that organized crime was prevalent in his city because members of the Yugoslav Mafia had moved in. He had even met with some of them. Since then Paul had often speculated about possible ties between the dealer and those members. There was a favor to be returned because he had waved his fee in exchange for a promise to assist in any of Paul's future work in Europe.

"Hello, Victor?"

"Yes, this is Victor."

"Paul D'Arneau here."

"Paul! My goodness, how *are* you?"

They exchanged stories about their past joint venture, laughing along the way. Paul made a point of mentioning his dismissal from Yale and the welcome beginning of a full-time career in treasure hunting.

"I don't know exactly how to put this, Victor, but I'll take a stab at it. And forgive me if I sound too presumptuous."

"Come now, Paul—anything at all, you know that."

"Okay. I'm about to travel to St. Helena on a job I accepted that might carry with it some, ah, dangers."

"St. Helena, the island? Napoleon and all that?"

"Yes." Paul paused to search for the right words. "Now, would you be in a position to arrange for some underworld figures to look out for my welfare and that of my two traveling companions? That is, if any exist there? I don't want to hire private bodyguards. This is very hush-hush and the privates don't have the same code as, say, the Mob. Plus different factions of the Mob recognize each other and that would help in tipping me off about some—I hate to say it—some strike aimed at one of us. Or of keeping the bad guys at bay."

Silence at the other end prompted Paul to shift the one-way conversation somewhat. "I can't believe I'm talking like this, Victor, and I do hope I'm being clear."

Finally a response: "You're being very clear, Paul. This is not the first time I've been asked to help in the exact same way. And yes—what a coincidence—I *do* have a contact on Helena—I've vacationed there several times. He has some friends who are just the type you have in mind. Give me the particulars of when you'll arrive, where you'll be staying, when you expect to leave—and of course the names of your companions. Then leave the rest to me. The man's name is Smit—Jules Smit. One way or another he will contact you. There will be a red convertible waiting dockside. I'll see to it that the driver wears a white cap. He'll take you and your friends wherever you want to go during your stay there."

Paul gave him the information, thanked him profusely and indicated he would be notified about how things went, "if I make it out alive."

"Don't worry," Victor said, "my man Smit is most dependable. If he works it the same as before, he'll have three of his pals helping him. Most of the Saints, as the islanders refer to themselves, are dark-skinned—some darker than others. These three tend to stand out. They're all fair and blond—two men and a woman. They'll be, as we say, 'In and out, around and about'. If there are individuals after your skin, ah, forgive me, I mean who are interested in you, having these people there will fend them off. The underworld on St. Helena isn't large so they all know one another. They realize that if they dare hurt you, there will be retribution. Plus you've heard it before and it does exist: there's a certain honor among thieves."

Paul disregarded the honor reference. "What you mean is that if I get killed, someone will get even? Quite a comfort." He managed a laugh.

"That's not the point—it's a deterrent thing."

Paul was mildly reassured but also had some more than mild doubts about the whole deal. *This is one for the books: a fired college professor with a gun strapped to his ankle, in the middle of nowhere, about to be protected from the underworld by the underworld, while he investigates the strange death of one of history's greatest generals. Surreal!*

He wasn't certain why he believed the deal would work effectively only if no one else knew about it—not Sylvie, not Leon, not even Vincent. A question perhaps of too many people "in" on a secret and therefore too many chances for a slip-up? But aside from effectiveness and slip-ups, he didn't want others to think he was in bed with criminal elements. After all, he had to consider assignments that might come his way in the future: life without Napoleon.

Paul was preparing for bed when something suddenly dawned on him. He phoned Leon.

"I forgot to ask how we get back from Helena," he said.

"Oh that?" Leon replied. "Yes, certainly—totally slipped my mind. Sorry. It's been taken care of. I've chartered a special ship to leave from Capetown and arrive at St. Helena four days later, five at the most. Then the whole trip in reverse: Ascension, R.A.F. and so on. The only hitch is—and you'll see when you do the math—if you want to leave the island sooner than two or three days after arrival, you won't be able to. Does this sound reasonable to you?"

"No, not at all," Paul said, disturbed. "If possible I'd rather an emergency plan be in place. We know what happened on Elba. What if we want to—let me rephrase it—what if we *need to* leave earlier than anticipated?"

Paul tapped on the receiving end of the phone. A

moment later, Leon said, "Well I hope that's not the case but, okay, to be ready for that decision, let's do it this way. I'll contact Thatcher Drinkwell and he'll have a separate ship on alert to depart at any time you want. It's asking a lot of him but I'm confident he's up to it. Is that better?"

"Much better. I have this funny feeling but I'm sure Elba sensitized me."

Chapter 15

The three island travelers began the long and arduous journey to St. Helena the next morning, Wednesday, May 24. Ansel flew them to London where Leon had arranged for a car to drive them to Brize Norton airbase, an hour away. There they boarded an R.A.F. plane which landed on Ascension Island three hours later. After a seven-hour wait, the Royal Mail ship, *St. Helena*, set sail for the seven-hundred-mile, day-and-a-half trip to Jamestown. They were provided with separate cabins that were unexpectedly roomy and contained a lower and fold-away upper berth, large window, two wardrobe units, an armchair, a dressing table with over-lighted mirror and a bathroom with shower.

It was remarkable how little they communicated with one another throughout the entire ordeal. Paul felt as though he were part of a multinational secret operation during which friends were suspect, light fixtures bugged and all strangers including military pilots and sea captains possible espionage agents.

The lone exception to their relative silence was an encounter between Paul and Sylvie aboard ship. Once again she made a move that left little doubt about her intentions. It began when Paul answered a knock on his cabin door several hours after dinner. Sylvie stood there, smiling roguishly. And once again she wore a robe, this time black. And she carried a leather bag. *But why the high heels?* She entered and checked that the door was shut behind her.

"Thought you might like some company," she said. Her breath smelled of alcohol.

"You've had a drink?" he asked with a tinge of jealousy. "Where'd you get the stuff and what is it?"

"I brought it along. I was sure we'd never have anything as nice on a damn mail boat."

"So what is it that's so nice?"

"Armagnac Napoleon."

"What's that?"

"A cognac but not as dry. Want some?"

Paul didn't hesitate. "Yes, by all means. I like the Napoleon part."

Sylvie reached into the bag and withdrew a small colorful bottle and a wine glass. She filled the glass with the cognac and handed it to Paul but not before taking a small sip from it and running her tongue around her lower lip.

"C'mon over," he said. "Have a seat. Aren't you having a drink of your own?"

"I had enough in my room." She stepped closer to him while he took in the drink's bouquet and swished the cognac around. As he did so, he never took his eyes off her.

"Careful, don't bump into me," he said. He downed the drink in one swallow.

She moved even closer and breathed, "But I want to get near enough to see if you take tiny gulps ... or big gulps." She corrected herself, raising her voice. "That's dumb. If they're tiny they're not gulps. My mistake."

"Your mistakes are charming," Paul said. He sidestepped her and signaled for a refill. "What the hell," he added, "I'm tired of being cautious all the time."

She complied.

The last Paul remembered was the glass being refilled several more times and his leading her to his bed and pulling her onto him.

The following morning after separate breakfasts, Paul confronted her. "Ah … well, I … ah, tell me," he whispered, "what happened last night?"

"Nothing," she said, peering down her nose.

"Literally?"

"You fell asleep. Life is whizzing by, you know."

Paul thought of Jean back home but had to admit he was in a quandary over Sylvie's obvious desire. "It may come to pass, Syl, but please, not on this trip."

"No one's ever called me Syl."

"Now someone has."

Paul used the day's remaining hours to organize his summation notes and to review the history of St. Helena and Napoleon's exile there. The notes had become less detailed now that he was more "into" the mission. Later he let his mind drift, reliving for the first time in weeks the circumstances surrounding his dismissal from Yale. Despite a flimsy reservation or two he was more convinced than ever it was for the best. He had been forced into a new and unpredictable life style.

He picked up a flyer he had obtained outside the ship's galley. Titled *St. Helena and Napoleon,* it was one in a pile available to all passengers. Other piles dealt with services on the island such as banking, transport, communications, immigration, shopping and medical care. He browsed through the flyer and realized he knew nearly everything in it, having written so extensively about the emperor. Nonetheless he returned to the beginning and reviewed its facts word for word:

St. Helena, a British island in the south Atlantic, is situated 1,200 miles off the southwest coast of Africa and 700 miles southeast of Ascension Island. The Portuguese discovered St. Helena in 1502 but it became part of Great Britain in 1673. The island is approximately ten miles by seven miles in size or about half the size of Napoleon's former home-in-exile, Elba. Rough and mountainous, it is composed mainly of volcanic wasteland. The highest peaks—Diana's Peak and Mount Actaeon—rise more than 1,000 feet above sea level. An area of past volcanic activity is Sandy Bay which contains fertile soil, ideal for the island's fruit and vegetable production. Three columns of Basalt in this area are called Lot, Lot's Wife and Asses Ears.

The island's only port and village is Jamestown, the capitol. Its population is about 5,600, principally Europeans, Africans and East Indians. Its main bay is called James Bay.

The chief crops are flax and potatoes. For a century or more, the flax was used to make mail bags for British Post Offices but this process has declined because of the availability of cheaper synthetic materials. Other industries there include fish curing and the manufacture of lace and fiber mats.

For many years, it was an important port of call for Portuguese sailors to replenish their supplies and to receive medical attention. At one time both the British and Dutch claimed the island as their own as they visited it on their voyages to India. In 1659 the East India Company colonized the island. Fourteen years later, the Dutch attacked and took over the island but the British retook it within six months.

Napoleon Bonaparte of course was its most famous resident. After his defeat at Waterloo, he signed a second abdication at the Élysée Palace. Three weeks later he surrendered himself to the captain of H.M.S. *Bellerophon* which took him to Plymouth. From there, he embarked on the H.M.S. *Northumberland* bound for St. Helena, arriving October 15, 1815. He was allowed a retinue of thirty people. Napoleon stayed at a small house, the Briars, while his eventual home, Longwood House, was being readied. Shortly thereafter he moved into Longwood and lived there until his death.

Three frigates and eight other vessels continually patrolled James Bay or were kept on standby. Gun emplacements and guard posts were established throughout the island.

A year later, Sir Hudson Lowe was appointed governor of St. Helena and it quickly

became apparent that he and Napoleon had
little respect for one another.

Napoleon died there on May 5, 1821. The
cause and manner of death remain in dispute.
Some claim he was poisoned by arsenic, either
intentionally or by accident. Others state he
died of stomach cancer as did his father. He
was buried in the island's Sane Valley where
his body remained until 1840. It was then
transported to Paris and currently lies in the
Hotel des Invalides.

It was a sketchy article but Paul filled in the gaps
with information he'd accumulated in preparation for his
St. Helena: Napoleon's Final Defeat and even for his yet
untitled manuscript. The 1815 to 1821 St. Helena period
was his least favorite in the saga of Napoleon Bonaparte
but now, soon to set foot on the island for the first time,
he reflected on what he might discover. More specifically,
if Elba were any kind of reference point, what on earth
would Helena bring?

Paul was on deck as the ship headed into its
southerly approach to James Bay. He had seen numerous
photographs of the island but when it came into view in
the slightly hazy light, he was amazed at how photography
had failed to capture its sheer darkness. From a distance it
resembled a massive black iceberg. As they sailed closer,
he could make out its irregular upper border and what he
considered a "slit" down the middle where a collection of
whitish buildings stood. There were more off to the right,
on higher ground.

Upon docking at 8:20 a.m., Friday, Vincent called

Paul aside and said, "I've never asked you directly but what's your agenda here?"

Paul scratched at his temple. "What else? Surprise: another interview! That and a visit to Longwood; maybe to Napoleon's grave site; and to wherever else Drinkwell recommends. But because of what happened at the castle, let's refuse any sightseeing he might suggest, only don't tell him why. Besides, we're not tourists. This is our *Helena Phase* and that means business not pleasure."

"Uh-huh. Couldn't we have simply phoned the guy, though—saved all this time and effort?"

"Believe me, Vincent, that would have been my choice, but you heard the prior—they release information only if the conversation is eyeball to eyeball. So we had no choice."

They caught up to Sylvie who was one of the first to disembark.

"Okay, you two," Paul said. "Let's stick close together while we're here."

"Which is how long?" Sylvie asked.

"As long as it takes," Paul replied. He chose not to mention the "emergency" ship.

"That's what I was afraid of," she said.

"Come now, I thought you were looking forward to this trip."

"I was until last night."

"What happened last night?" Vincent asked.

"I had a bad dream."

"I guess I didn't mention it," Paul said, glad that Vincent was nearby, "but Leon arranged transportation for us. Either of you see a red car?"

"There's one," Vincent said, pointing toward a

parking space a few shops up. A street sign indicated, "Napoleon Street", difficult to read in the eye-blinding light of the morning. It appeared to be the main—the only—street in town, quiet, narrow and congested with all makes of cars, their colors in sharp contrast to the light buildings hugging the street. Most of the buildings were one-storied with cement facades. Sidewalks were similarly congested with dawdling people, none of whom looked suspicious. Paul had made it a point to check.

A tall man emerged from the red convertible and walked up to them. He wore sunglasses and a white cap. "Is one of you Dr. Paul D'Arneau?" he asked with a slight accent. Paul couldn't pinpoint the country, probably European.

"I am," Paul said.

"May I speak with you privately?"

"Certainly." Paul followed the man for a short distance, just outside of earshot.

The man extended his hand and Paul shook it. "Good morning," the man said, taking off his cap. His hair was strikingly blond, his face mottled and his bare, muscular arms tanned. "I am not a professional driver. I am Jules Smit."

"You?" Paul exclaimed. He glanced at Sylvie and Vincent who seemed to be having their own conversation. Lowering his voice he said, "But I thought this would be secret."

"It will be just that. Do not worry. I will drive you around—as you Americans say, at your disposal— and my people have been alerted. They will not be conspicuous."

"Will I be able to identify them in the

background?"

"Maybe … maybe not. But their skin is light. Especially the men. Two: Gregor and Gunnar. There is also a young lady: Katrien. Sweetheart of Gunnar. Very attractive, but do not let that fool you. I would not want to fight with her. You lose your eyes."

Another handshake followed, this time Paul initiating it.

When he rejoined the others, Vincent said, "What was that all about?"

"He wanted to know where we'll be staying and for how long. Said he'd be at our disposal at all times."

"How long did you say we'll be staying," Sylvie asked.

"As long as it takes, remember?"

They piled into the car, Paul in the front passenger seat. He indicated they should first check into the Farm Lodge Hotel and from there proceed directly to the Police Service building.

"For Thatcher Drinkwell?" Jules asked.

"Yes. You know him?"

"A little. Everybody does. Good constable. Even better bird expert. He will tell you about that if you let him."

They swung onto a metal railing-lined road, past "Jacob's Ladder"—a seven-hundred-step climb to a fort above—past a bird sanctuary, an elongated tree-fern thicket, stretches of grassland, rows of sunflowers and an occasional foreshortened redwood. The warm damp air—a little cooled as the convertible sped up—became clearer once Jules veered up a steep slope and leveled off on higher ground. Stark contrasts came into view: lush pastures, bare slopes, flax plantations, sea cliffs. Paul stared straight ahead. It had been a long time since he had felt so impatient. Still, if he hadn't warned the others about sightseeing, perhaps he would have asked Jules to slow down and point out some highlights: Ladder Hill, the turtles at the Governor's residence, the Half Tree Hollow neighborhood. Certainly though there would be later stops at Longwood House where Napoleon lived out his last six years, and his tomb in Geranium Valley.

"The lodge is ten minutes from here," Jules said.

Sylvie and Vincent said nothing. Paul hated to reason why, but he wished the car were not an open convertible. He also wished to talk.

"Do you know the ... the other side here?" he asked Jules.

"How do you mean the other side?"

"Your rivals."

"Yes. Very well."

"Oh?"

"Not so well that we work together. We talk sometimes but we have different purposes."

"Are they Dutch?"

"Dutch? Yes, Dutch."

"And you?"

"Dutch."

"Nice country, especially Amsterdam."

"Thank you, but we live here now."

"I see," Paul said. "You mentioned purposes. How are they different?"

Jules cast a brief look at him as if to say he would be uncomfortable providing an explanation. "They bring in some girls—specialize—you know?"

"I suppose. Prostitution?"

"Yes. We like gambling, the numbers, loans. Clean. Also offer protection. Sometimes that is not as clean — but we never murder. The 'Fish Truck'? They do."

"Wait," Paul said, "let's back up. What's the 'Fish Truck'?"

"That's the name the Saints gave them — the other side. They operate out of a big black truck. The back has a high canvas cover. Sometimes they haul fish. Other times they haul men, their own men."

Paul paused to digest this news. "I guess I understand," he said. "Is your side then called the *Red Car*?"

Jules tightened his grip on the wheel as he roared with laughter. "This? No, this is payment for a loan. Two years ago."

"Okay. And you used the word 'murder'. They murder? I mean, ah, the *Fish Truck?*"

"If they have to. We can tell when they might because their victim is also in trouble with us."

"But you never hire them to do your dirty work, do you?" Paul had decided to take a chance. His collar felt sticky despite the breeze which stiffened as Jules nearly floored the accelerator.

He looked at the other two in the rearview mirror before responding. "Now we go too far, Dr. D'Arneau," he said, "but the answer is no."

Paul wasn't entirely convinced. Why hadn't Sylvie and Vincent chimed in with a question or two? Then he figured out that they had probably heard little of the conversation over the noise of the motor. *Just as well!*

The Farm Lodge Country House Hotel appeared to Paul to be a misnomer. A squat two-story wooden structure, it had only five rooms but was surrounded by manicured lawns and tropical gardens. A plaque near the entrance indicated it was built in the late 17th century as a British East India Company planter's house. He read the plaque twice. *There's that company name again!*

A stout phlegmatic woman behind the registration desk said that two rooms were being held for a certain Paul Darmieur. There was hardly any debate in settling the mix-up in names and within minutes Paul and Vincent were booked into a twin room and Sylvie, a double room. The accommodations were simple, clean and ample enough for what Paul anticipated would be minimal time spent there. "See you both in ten minutes," he said.

Conversation during the return trip to Jamestown was sparse. Sylvie complained, "There was no time to change," her voice louder than usual as a chilly stiff wind kicked up. She wore the same green cardigan as when they had disembarked. She crossed her arms tightly against her chest.

"Why do women always cross their arms like that when it gets cold?" Vincent asked in a loud voice.

"I didn't think you noticed things like that, Vincent, but to answer your question delicately, we have more to cover."

"Oh," Vincent replied.

"Oh?" Paul said from the front seat.

At 10 a.m. Jules dropped them off at the entrance to the island's Police Service building. It was situated on a quiet side road, straddled by a small neat park and an empty lot.

"I'll be waiting out back," he said, "but take your

time. I have a book to read."

The outside of the building looked like a one-room schoolhouse in rural New England. Before walking in, Vincent said to Paul: "Just like on Elba, Sylvie and I will hang back. You do the talking. We'll listen and try to catch the nuances."

"Agreed," Paul said, "but speak up if you think it's necessary."

The inside was plain, containing little more than a wooden desk, four wooden straight-back chairs, a filing cabinet that faced the door and a cramped holding cell. The main room smelled old but scrubbed, antiseptic. An overhead camera seemed out of place as did a red leather chair behind the desk. A simple glance was sufficient to take it all in. From the ticking and clicking in a small back room, Paul assumed it held the usual electronic equipment associated with police departments.

A man of average height and weight stood at the filing cabinet, rifling through some folders. He had short brown hair, a fair complexion, sharply defined features and a faded tattoo of a bird on each forearm. Glasses dangled from an eyeglass cord. He wore a print short-sleeved shirt and khaki pants. He didn't notice Paul and the others entering and he stood plumb straight, even though his suspenders gave the impression of pulling him down.

Paul faked a cough. "Excuse me," he said meekly. "Constable Drinkwell?"

The man looked up and smiled. "I like that," he said. "Good to hear once in a while. Usually it's just 'Thatch'. But maybe I shouldn't complain about it—I'd hate to hear 'Constable' all the time." Though he spoke rapid-fire, his keen gray eyes seldom blinked. "May I help you?"

"Well my name's D'Arneau—Paul D'Arneau—and this is ..."

"Paul!" he shouted, giving Paul a firm handshake. "I should have known. I was told you'd be arriving today but I'm so blasted preoccupied. We have these two gangs on our hands, on *my* hands. Each side claims the other is too greedy. Nothing big yet ... just smoldering beneath the surface. Through the years we've had very little crime but we're expecting that to change. Heaven help us. And we're a small operation—only a handful of officers to scatter around town, and me. That's it. The gangs are at each other's throats and creating all kinds of problems, but that's not your concern. What is, and I congratulate you for it, is that you're here to inquire about Napoleon. You know, I've been constable on Helena for twenty-six years, sometimes busy, sometimes not, sometimes training officers for Ascension Island, sometimes not. And—get this—not once, not *once* has anyone asked me about Napoleon. Oh, they might ask for directions to the museum—his residence here, Longwood House—but that's about it. I should feel honored that you're here, and I am. Now, let's see, these are your associates, are they not?"

"Yes," Paul said finally. He introduced them and they shook hands.

"Happy to meet you," Sylvie said.

"Good to happily meet you," Vincent said. The other three gave him a bewildered look. "I mean to say, whatever Sylvie said," Vincent added, flustered. "I apologize. I wasn't trying to be funny. It's just that Sylvie and I haven't had a chance to say much recently. We rushed in and out of the Farm Lodge and our voices didn't carry well in the convertible so we stopped talking. Couldn't hear much for that matter."

"Wait a minute," Drinkwell said slowly. "A convertible? A red convertible?"

"Yes," Paul interjected. "Why, does that mean anything?"

The constable stroked his thin mustache. "No," he said, "not at all. I thought for a split second, but no, couldn't be. We have several red convertibles on the island."

Paul expected him to walk to the window and see Jules waiting in his car, but he didn't. *Not yet.*

"Anyway," Drinkwell said, "Let's sit and talk, shall we? You've probably heard that I like to talk. But what do people expect? My wife does most of it at home and some days no one drops in here. I should go out to lunch once in a while but I keep bringing in a damned sandwich. In twenty-six years, I still keep track. That means I've saved the cost of over six-thousand lunches. Maybe, what, fifteen-thousand dollars? I always say saving money's good for the soul—as long as you use the savings wisely. *All* money should be used wisely."

The three sat and Drinkwell, rounding his desk, patted his leather chair. "Take this chair for instance. One of our school groups gave it to me for my twenty-fifth year on the job. Can you believe it? Now why'd they go and do that? Coulda put the money to better use. There isn't a lot of it around these parts. You certainly know we're what's called a British Dependent Territory and as such, two-thirds of our budget comes from the U.K. You'll never guess where we get a good chunk of the other third. The sale of postage stamps!"

It hadn't taken Paul long to realize he liked the constable and found himself unwinding. He looked over at a more relaxed Sylvie and Vincent.

Drinkwell reached down to the bottom desk drawer and withdrew a loose-leaf binder. "Let's see," he said, putting on his glasses. "I have what I wanted to cover." He flipped through a few pages. "Yes, here it is. I must confess, I've been waiting for this opportunity and I've made an outline so I wouldn't miss anything. I also have some quoted passages to read you. They really get to the heart of how Napoleon felt when he arrived here ... so here we go. By the way, how was your voyage?"

"In a word," Paul said, "exhausting."

"Yes, I know. Unfortunately that's one of our rules. Nothing by phone or mail, only in person. The 'rotten rule of the *histarians*' I call it. Really gets the prior's goat. Speaking of him—and understand, I totally admire him—but did he tell you that when we work with a client, we coordinate our efforts?" He referred to the binder again. "Yes, coordination. What that means is I'm aware of what he covered and what my good friend, Clive Weaver, covered, so for your benefit we eliminate duplication, and for our benefit we have a division of labor." He stared at Paul. "Make sense?" he asked.

"Yeah, real good sense," Paul replied. He removed a note pad from his briefcase and said, "You have your notes. May I ..." He checked with the other two and saw that they already had pads and pencils poised, "may we take notes?"

"Yes, indeed. And speaking of others, how's my friend, Guy Martin? And Leon Cassell? I met Guy some years ago in Paris—tops in his field. We've helped a lot of researchers, thanks to him. And what can I say about Leon? A wonderful person, very committed. I remember the first time he came to Helena …."

"Hold on! Please!" Paul exclaimed. "He's *been* here?"

"Why yes, twice that I know of. Once for business, once for pleasure. At least that's what he said at the time. Is it a surprise?"

"No, not at all. I must have him confused with another of my Parisian friends."

Paul had to fumble with his note pad to keep his composure. That and asking Sylvie if she had a sharper pencil. He noticed Vincent studying his shoes.

What's going on? I asked Leon if he'd been to Elba and St. Helena and he said neither, didn't he?

Despite the disconcerting revelation, the last thing Paul wanted to do was spoil the rest of their time with the constable. It was hard flashing Drinkwell a what's-next expression, especially while wishing he had a cracker to munch on.

The constable let it pass. He returned to the binder. "The serious matters, the reason you're here, we'll get to it soon. But I should mention what they invariably say about me: 'Talk, talk, talk. Birds, birds, birds.' I already spent time on the talking. Now for the birds and I'll cut it short. Anyone else—not as busy as you three—would not be so lucky. Yesiree, the *Birds of St. Helena*—that's the title of my book. I don't keep the little darlings, I just know about them, made a study of them, their history, their habits and so forth. So I must dispense with that first."

It was as if he had a compulsion that had to be satisfied, an overture to a symphony. Without consulting his notes, he spoke with authority—and in a deeper voice. "Not many seabirds here. They shun us and I don't know why. There are plenty off Ascension but we only have Tropic Birds and Black and Brown Noddies. Some call the Fairy Tern a seabird—I don't because it nests not only on cliffs but also in trees and on some of our buildings. You may spot some … they're interesting birds with translucent wings and eyes that seem too big for their heads. As for land birds, most seem to fly around Jamestown primarily. I maintain they're social creatures—they like to be around people. We have ten species here, only ten in all, like Waxbills, the Common Myna, the Malagasy Fody and Swainson's Canary. But my favorite is the Wirebird, can't miss it; it prefers to live on a ridge above Longwood House, but some come down and race around the grounds. They have long spindly legs and no way will you catch one—they're too quick and fast. They'd rather run than fly. I would have named them Ground Wirebirds."

Drinkwell stopped. "You know," he said, "I should have offered you some coffee or tea. Would you like a cup?"

All three shook their heads no. "I thought of coffee," he said, "because I was afraid I might'a been putting you to sleep."

"No, no—not at all," Paul said. "It's very interesting. Migration and all that."

"Well, I didn't get into migration or more important, when and how certain birds were released here and decided to stay, and don't worry, I won't. In fact, that's enough on that. It's putting *me* to sleep!"

He turned the page and unclipped a smaller piece of paper. "Next, the quoted material. The only reason I want to read it is that I never had it printed out or I'd give you a copy. It's in my longhand hieroglyphic scrawl. And the reason I'd like you to hear it is because it creates a mood and, what shall I call it? A poignant picture of one of the great personalities in history? Forgive me if I sound biased, and certainly you, Paul, know the character of the man you've scrutinized, but to assist in this mission of yours, perhaps this might help explain why the emperor behaved as he did. Not in wars, mind you, but off the battlefield."

Paul's attentive demeanor matched that of Sylvie and Vincent. Spellbound? The constable took a deep breath, stood at attention and began:

"I took this account from the diary of the Comte de Las Cases. He was in the small entourage that accompanied Napoleon into exile. The Comte wrote:

'We were all assembled around the emperor, and he was recapitulating these facts with warmth:'

> For what infamous treatment are we reserved! This is the anguish of death. To injustice and violence they now add insult and protracted torment. If I were so hateful to them, why did they not get rid of me? A few musket balls in my heart or my head would have done the business, and there would at least have been some energy in the crime. Were it not for you, and above all for your wives, I would receive nothing from them but the pay of a private soldier. How can the monarchs of Europe permit the sacred character of sovereignty to be violated in my person? Do they not see that

they are, with their own hands, working their own destruction at St. Helena?

I entered their capitols victorious and, had I cherished such sentiments, what would have become of them? They styled me their brother, and I had become so by the choice of the people, the sanction of victory, the character of religion, and the alliances of their policy and their blood. Do they imagine that the good sense of nations is blind to their conduct? And what do they expect from it? At all events, make your complaints, gentlemen; let indignant Europe hear them. Complaints from me would be beneath my dignity and character; I must either command or be silent.

Drinkwell slowly removed his glasses and let them drop to his chest. "Powerful," he said. "At least I think so. He was certainly controversial but I admired the man. I felt sorry for him—the way he ended up—though many other people didn't. Not at all. Oh well, let's proceed. I've editorialized and given you my pet stuff long enough. Thank you for your patience."

Paul, anxious to comment, responded: "But I thank you, and I'm sure Sylvie and Vincent do also." They smiled their approval.

"You're very kind. Kinder than some of the demanding researchers who occasionally pop in: the mariners, the astronomers, the weathermen."

The constable put on his glasses again and searched through his notes. "With your permission, Paul, I propose to give you some background and related facts as we've been able to assemble them, then offer you my interpretation. You can take it from there and hopefully piece it all together. So just to be sure we're on the same page, we're trying to establish whether Napoleon died a natural death or whether he was murdered. Right?"

"Right," Paul replied, "and if he was murdered, who did it?"

"Okay. I have much to say about it—it's all outlined here in my binder—I've actually rehearsed the things I want to say to you—but interrupt me if things don't seem clear."

Paul had the feeling there wouldn't be any need for interruptions.

"And expect to hear the same language others have used in describing things because we've conferred on them so often lately. You've spoken to most of them."

"Who?"

"The prior, Clive Weaver, Leon Cassell, Guy Martin, other *histarians* you haven't met—middle management so to speak. They do much of the legwork, the endless confirmation work."

"Perhaps I'll meet some other *histarians* before it's all over."

"Perhaps. It depends how far along you get. Now, first off, the poisoning thing. I know Guy Martin feels Napoleon was fed arsenic from 1812 on, that some wanted it to be a slow death so he would fail in his battles. And when he didn't die that way, they finished the job here on Helena. I'll return to that in a minute. My thoughts on hair samples with high concentrations of arsenic … and the silly idea that it came from dye in the wallpaper at Longwood? Nonsense. In my opinion, there's no final proof the samples were his, and if the wallpaper did him in, why didn't it happen to anyone else who lived there?

"But regarding the slow death theory, we have to bring in Napoleon's marshals. His most trusted one was Michel Ney. As you no doubt know, Paul—but maybe not Sylvie and ... Vincent, is it? —he had switched allegiance away from Napoleon and to the Bourbons, that is the Royalists or backers of King Louis XVIII, but then switched back in time for the Waterloo campaign. I believe the prior mentioned this to you. Anyway, after that disaster, Ney was put on trial for treason and executed. Four of the marshals voted against Ney and for the execution." The constable read from his notes, "Perignon, Marmont, Victor and Jourdan. Jourdan was president of the court that handed down the sentence.

"Now here's the point. Before the trial—much before—these four men were conspiring to kill Napoleon. It's not clear whether they had voted for Ney's death for political reasons or because they heard he'd somehow learned of their plan to do away with the emperor. References to the plan are here in excerpts from the minutes of their secret meetings. I translated some sections into English for you." He produced a manila envelope from the back of the binder and stabbing the air with it for emphasis, went on, "I got this from the memoirs and personal letters of each marshal. When you have time, you can read some of the statements—quite incriminating. But do notice that even though their meetings were secret, they were probably worried about reprisals, so their suggestions were indirect. Seems to me they would have been better off not taking minutes in the first place."

He handed the envelope to Paul who inserted it into

his briefcase and said, "The bottom line then is that you *do* believe he was being poisoned?"

"No doubt about it."

"Enough to kill him?"

"That's different. I can't say definitely. No doubt you know who Montholon and Lowe were."

"Yeah, Montholon was his aide-de-camp and Hudson Lowe was governor of the island. He and Napoleon despised each other."

"Maybe those two guys gave him a big swig of arsenic near the end. Or maybe they just saw to it that he received no more of it."

"Come again?"

"I knew you'd ask, so I brought along a statement one of our *histarians* sent me from Romania. I hope I'm not overwhelming you with all this." Drinkwell removed a card from the top drawer of his desk and read from it:

> In Europe arsenic was used by some as a mind-altering drug. In small doses it produced a feeling of well-being and strength. When a man has once begun to indulge in it he must continue to indulge or ... the last dose kills him. Indeed the arsenic eater must not only continue his indulgence, he must also increase the quantity of the drug, so it is extraordinarily difficult to stop the habit; for, as the sudden cessation causes death, the gradual cessation produces such a terrible heart, knowing that it may probably be said that no genuine arsenic eater ever ceased to eat arsenic while life lasted.

The phone rang. "Excuse me," Drinkwell said picking up the receiver. "Yes? No, tomorrow. Well, have it your own way then. Later today. Bye."

His face showed no emotion although he shook his head from side to side. "Sorry for the interruption but I'm a one-person operation in here." He scanned his notes. "Alright, you ready for more?"

"Yeah, you're on a roll, Thatcher." Paul had eased up on formality but he couldn't bring himself to call the man "Thatch."

"Now we have the critical issue of Lady Ashley Beckett. Not too many people know about her and her carryings-on, and I'm aware of others briefing you on her: Guy, Clive, the prior. So there'll be some overlap here, some repetition. But that's okay because it's a rather complicated tale. She was an English lady who, as you Americans would say, had the 'hots' for Napoleon, so much so that for many years—we haven't been able to determine precisely how many—she followed him, stalked him, stayed with him, whatever. Not that he resisted. Especially when he occupied Longwood, he would welcome her there. It's reported that she would stoop to anything just to be near him; even bothered him when he was in battle; would buy her way with cash or sex to get to him. Now the ever-present Talleyrand fits into the picture. Some of his family helped her see Napoleon here on Helena. They and no doubt Talleyrand himself received the same things in exchange."

Sylvie uncrossed her leg and craned forward. "When did you say Lady Beckett took up with him?"

"Probably around 1814, near the end of the campaign in France. For the record, that followed the humiliating

Russian campaign a year or so before. Napoleon lost badly in France. Paris had been besieged; he abdicated for the first time; said goodbye to the Old Guard at the Château of Fontainebleau; and was banished to Elba. That about right, Paul?"

"On the money."

"I love your American expressions!"

The constable poured himself a glass of water from a silver decanter. "Want some?" he asked the others. They said no in unison and appeared happy for the break, for the chance to bring their notes up to date. After draining the glass, he said, "I hope I'm not going too fast," but didn't wait for a response.

"Carrying on then, two important points must be included in the Lady Beckett story. One is that she had an illegitimate child, a girl, most definitely by Napoleon. We've traced her lineage to a woman who lives in Brussels. We can have our *histarian* there arrange for you to meet with her if you wish."

"We'll see," Paul said.

"And, two, that she was one of the top executives with the East India Company. I'm sure all three of you are familiar with that company: tea and spices; long sea journeys from England to India and back; stopovers at islands including St. Helena. Now bear with me." He examined his notes carefully. "During our extensive research, the names of five men surfaced over and over again. They all worked for the East India Company. I have their names and a comment about each of them if that would help you: William Balcombe. He also owned "The Briars" which is where Napoleon stayed while they got Longwood in shape; Thomas Brooke. He was the company's secretary. Next is …"

Paul looked up abruptly.

"A problem?" Drinkwell asked.

"No, it's just that I vaguely remember those names as being in my own notes when I was at the university. Only there were seven names. I grouped them together under one of my 'Unknown' headings."

"Well, I'll soon add two more to the five and they may very well be the same seven you came up with. There's no indication that the extra two worked for the company but we have reliable evidence they were tied in with the group and specifically with Napoleon after his death."

"Curious," Paul said, "but please continue. Number three is?"

"Let's see, we have Sir William Doveton, the company's treasurer; Robert Leech, its accountant and Thomas Greentree, its main storekeeper. Now add to them one Captain Bennet who allegedly donated a dining table to help make Napoleon's coffin and a Mr. Rutledge. And what did he do? He guarded Napoleon's body!"

"So we have five officers of the same company who presumably answered to Lady Beckett, and two men who may have played key roles in stealing Napoleon's body. But we'll get to that in a second. For now, let's say we have definite proof that Bennet and Rutledge were paid handsomely to assist the other five in whatever schemes they came up with. Helping Lady Beckett penetrate this heavily guarded island in order to see Napoleon? Stealing his body and replacing it with someone else? If so, we're not yet sure why. Maybe you can beat us to the punch in finding out, but we'll keep trying. Those middle management *histarians*, remember?"

"That's a key question, isn't it," Paul asked. "Why steal the body?"

"Yes it is, and as I said, I don't have an answer."

Paul wanted to stay on the subject. "On a related matter, what's your take on the theory that Napoleon isn't in the tomb at Invalides at all, but that a double is there? Those who propose it claim all sorts of circumstantial evidence, such as, he frequently used impersonators throughout his reign. Some conspiracy buffs even believe he escaped from Helena early in his exile and was replaced by some man in the end stages of stomach cancer. Hardly seems possible but if it's true, where did Napoleon escape to, when did he die and where did his body end up?"

Drinkwell sat quietly for a few seconds, rubbing his forehead.

"I find it hard to believe he's not in the tomb at Invalides, but there's only one way to find out."

Paul, jolted, looked at Sylvie who looked at Vincent who looked at Paul who stared at Drinkwell before following up with: "I'm sure we have the same thing in mind. Could it ever be done? In a million years?"

Thatcher squirmed in his chair. "Your Leon can arrange *anything*," he said. "The number of important friends he has goes, I'd say, beyond the pale. Politicians, heads of state, public officials, military men, curators, educators, media moguls, opinion makers—you name it. Current and former. Inside France, outside France. Even in the States. A huge undertaking, but Leon's the man who could pull it off. And I'll let it go at that."

The constable's body language indicated he was uncomfortable with the subject so Paul didn't pursue it.

"But let me ask a question of my own," Drinkwell

said. "Why did Lady Beckett inherit the most money in Napoleon's will?"

"Because she made him happy?" Paul responded.

"C'mon Paul, and I say this with all due respect—not to Napoleon but to you—but many, many women made him happy. Two he married, others were mistresses, and they were all over the map: Josephine, Marie Louise, Désirée, Pauline, Marie Walewska, Mademoiselle Georges, Giuseppina Grassini, Madame de Stael. He liked to flaunt his mistresses." Drinkwell quickly found a quote in the binder. "In fact he once said, 'I am not a man like others and moral laws or the laws that govern conventional behavior do not apply to me. My mistresses do not in the least engage my feelings. Power is my mistress'.

"But he wrote love letters to all of them and each one sounded more convincing than the others." Again the constable went to his binder. "Here are samples to four of them: Josephine, Marie Louise, Marie Walewska and one I'm not certain of. You may find them interesting, and they'll also give you a flavor of other things on his mind."

Paul had read many of Napoleon's love letters before; nonetheless he accepted the samples and inserted them in the envelope in his briefcase.

"So I say," the constable continued, "we'll probably never know why Lady Beckett ended up with the largest inheritance. But speaking of the will brings me to my last point and I know you'll want an answer and it's very simple: I don't know. The question is where's the amendment to the codicil? None of us has any idea. The prior talks about a 'decision' and a 'plan hatched on Elba.' We now know the decision was Lady Beckett's inheritance but the plan? He seems to think it's what the amendment's all about. I can't begin to guess. And just in case you're wondering, Clive Weaver told me he gave you a copy of Napoleon's will and its codicil, which I was told refers to—but doesn't include—an amendment. To date, then, we have three questions with no answers: Why would anyone want to steal the body, if that actually happened in the first place? Where's the amendment? And the big one, did he die of natural causes like stomach cancer or was he killed by arsenic or otherwise? Correct?"

"Correct, but with all due respect—the shoe's on the other foot now—really, with all due respect, Thatcher, you keep forgetting. If he didn't die a natural death, or an accidental arsenic death—the wallpaper theory—who was the murderer?"

"Ah, of course, that is, if the four marshals weren't responsible."

"Yeah, that's it."

A uniformed officer rushed in and, after spending a few moments in the back room, rushed out muttering, "Forgot my flask."

"Tea, not whiskey," Drinkwell said.

Paul seemed oblivious to the intrusion. "Another question," he said. "What did Napoleon do with most of his time here besides what we've all read about? You know, like walking, gardening, billiards, cards, chess, dictating memoirs?"

"Well, for the conqueror of most of Europe, nearly six years in captivity must have been pure hell. He was miserable, became melancholic and didn't do much more than what you mentioned. He apparently sat a lot, staring off into space. The prior believes he was turning schizophrenic even before he abdicated. And there are some hints that as time wore on, he began suffering from a kind of paranoia." Drinkwell opened yet another drawer and brought out a second binder. "I have a collection of entries to his diary, word-for-word. I'd like to read three to you. Takes a while but I think worth it, to shed light on his mental state and even, when he talks about his conquests, to get a sense of the enormity of it all. Of course, keep in mind that it's hard to tell when changes in his mental status began—during his last military defeats or once he was settled in here.

"I penciled in asterisks for the three I'd like to read." He rifled through several sheets of paper. "First we have '*A questa casa. O in questo luogo tristo, non voglio niente di lu*'" :

> I hate this Longwood. The sight of it makes me melancholy. Let him put me in some place where there is shade, verdure, and water. Here it either blows a furious wind, loaded with rain and fog, *che mi taglia l'anima*; or, if that is wanting, *il sole mi brucia il cervello*, through the want of shade when I go out.

"His use of Italian rather than French: is it a sign of abnormal regression—back to his childhood? As to the second entry, I'm no psychiatrist but it strikes me as weird. You be the judge":

> Man loves the supernatural. He meets deception halfway. The fact is that everything about us is a miracle. Strictly speaking, there are no

phenomena, for in nature everything is a phenomenon: my existence is a phenomenon; this log that is being put in the chimney is a phenomenon; my intelligence, my faculties, are phenomena; for they all exist, yet we cannot define them. I leave you here, and I am in Paris, entering the Opera; I bow to the spectators, I hear the acclamations, I see the actors, I hear the music. Now if I can span the space from St. Helena, why not that of the centuries? Why should I not see the future like the past? Would the one be more extraordinary, more marvelous than the other? No, but in fact it is not so.

"And the third one is exceptional—in more ways than one. The words convey such scope, such grandeur, but they can also be the words of a paranoid. The emperor was always prone to grandiose proclamations but none like this":

You want to know the treasures of Napoleon? They are enormous, it is true, but in full view. Here they are: the splendid harbour of Antwerp, that of Flushing, capable of holding the largest fleets; the docks and dykes of Dunkirk, of Havre, of Nice; the gigantic harbour of Cherbourg; the harbour works at Venice; the great roads from Antwerp to Amsterdam, from Mainz to Metz, from Bordeaux to Bayonne; the passes of the Simplon, of Mont Cenis, of Mont Genevre, of the Corniche, that gave four openings through the Alps; in that alone

you might reckon 800 millions. The roads
from the Pyrenees to the Alps, from Parma
to Spezzia, from Savona to Piedmont; the
bridges of Jena, of Austerlitz, of the Arts, of
Sèvres, of Tours, of Lyons, of Turin, of the
Isère, of the Durance, of Bordeaux, of Rouen;
the canal from the Rhine to the Rhone, joining
the waters of Holland to the Mediterranean; the
canal that joins the Scheldt and the Somme,
connecting Amsterdam and Paris; that which
joins the Rance and the Vilaine; the canal of
Arles, of Pavia, of the Rhine; the draining
of the marshes of Bourgoing, of the citentin,
of Rochefort; the rebuilding of most of the
churches pulled down during the Revolution,
the building of new ones; the construction of
many industrial establishments for putting
an end to pauperism; the construction of the
Louvre, of the public granaries, of the Bank, of
the canal of the Ourcq; the water system of the
city of Paris, the numerous sewers, the quays,
the embellishments and monuments of that
great city; the public improvements of Rome;
the re-establishment of the manufactories of
Lyons. Fifty millions spent on repairing and
improving the Crown residences; sixty millions'
worth of furniture placed in the palaces of
France and Holland, at Turin, at Rome; sixty
millions' worth of Crown diamonds, all of it
the money of Napoleon; even the Regent, the
only missing one of the old diamonds of the
Crown of France, purchased from Berlin Jews
with whom it was pledged for three millions;

the Napoleon Museum, valued at more than 400 millions.These are monuments to confound calumny. History will relate that all this was accomplished in the midst of continuous wars, without raising a loan, and with the public debt actually decreasing day by day.

"Sylvie and gentlemen, just his referring to himself not as 'I' or 'me' but as 'Napoleon' should raise an eyebrow, don't you think? But there's more than that. The tone of the boasting has meaning. Granted it was no doubt directed against those who would defame him, but I think there's a possibility, even a probability, the man was mad. Nuts. He wrote these in the ninth month of his confinement so I have to ask, 'Was he already deteriorating when he arrived and if so, was it because of the defeats or because of arsenic? If arsenic, was it self-administered or secretly fed to him?'"

The constable was breathing as though he'd just finished a foot race. He took a long drink of water. "So those are the questions, some answered, most not. Sometimes even digging out the important questions is progress. And there are probably more—more than we even know about." He glanced at his watch and then at the clock on the wall. "As of 10:47 on May 26."

Vincent straightened saying, "So we keep coming back to the same questions."

"Yes, and to repeat myself, they'll probably generate others as you think about them."

Vincent twisted his lips in a smile and said, "I have one that's not really related and it's a bold one, Constable, but only if you take it the wrong way. May I ask it?"

"By all means. Nothing's too bold in this business."

"How do you know so much about Napoleon? I mean, you have extensive notes you keep referring to but …"

"Vincent, I've made a study of him. As I said, I admire him—despite his greed, his bravado, even his mental collapse. And I'm not even sure about that. There can often be a fine line between brilliance and insanity. I'm happier believing he was brilliant but I can't discount madness."

And while Paul's mind was in silent overdrive, Sylvie chimed in, "Let's not forget he was also the Father of Sexism."

Paul had to stand and stretch. "Thatcher," he said, massaging his upper arm, "you may or may not know about my new manuscript and that I included Talleyrand as a suspect in Napoleon's possible murder."

"Yes, indeed. Got you suspended from Yale I heard."

Paul shrugged and held out his arms in a gesture of helplessness. "I have no secrets anymore," he said. "You guys really communicate."

The constable's eyes narrowed as he shook his head smugly.

"Well," Paul said, "what's your opinion?"

"Talleyrand as a murderer?"

"Uh-huh."

"Honest answer?"

"Honest answer."

"No."

"That's what I thought you'd say and just to be accurate, I wasn't suspended. I was fired."

Vincent looked as though he had another question for Drinkwell. He raised his hand this time.

"Another bold one?" Vincent asked.

"As many as you want."

"Why did you become an *histarian?* There's no apparent financial reward. No public acclaim. No increased social status."

The constable leaned back and clasped his hands behind his head. "Ah, but there are other rewards, more important ones. And these apply not only to me but to my colleagues as well—all over the world. I know because we've talked about them. It's remarkable how some motivations can be the same in different countries, among different peoples. And what are these rewards, these motivations? To know you're helping in worthy causes. We'd never take a project that was dishonorable. To satisfy historical curiosity. To be like a mountain climber who climbs simply because the mountain's there. Or like the sculptor whose work is mediocre, yet stays with his craft because he considers it art for art's sake." He transferred his hands to the top of the desk and with his eyes drifting over his three visitors, said softly, "And that's why we're *histarians.*"

Paul rose. "On that note we'd better be going. We can't thank you enough, Thatcher, for your time and for all the information you've given us. I hope we can return the favor someday."

"It's been my pleasure. I only wish you didn't have to pay the price of listening to my bird lecture!"

At the door Paul said, "Thanks again and if you ever

come to the States, do look me up. Come to think of it, I totally forgot to suggest the same to the prior and Clive Weaver. Will you tell them for me?"

"I'd be glad to. Maybe we'll make the trip together. Who knows?"

Outside, as they strolled along a graveled driveway toward the parking area, Vincent said, "Bright fellow."

"Self-taught I would assume," Paul said.

"From the looks of it," Sylvie said, "he must have plenty of time to read while on the job."

All three froze. Up ahead the red convertible was parked against a chain link fence that surrounded the parking area. The door was open on the driver's side. Jules Smit's body was half in, half out of the car, his upper body slumped awkwardly across the seat, his legs touching the ground.

Paul felt as though the air had been sucked out of his lungs but he managed to lean down and withdraw the Heritage 9 mm from his ankle rig. Vincent said nothing as he yanked out his Beretta .45. Each held his pistol with both hands as the three inched forward.

"Stay close behind us, Sylvie," Paul whispered.

At the car, he bent over the body and saw an apparent bullet wound on the side of Jules's head. A trickle of blood was caked down to his shoulder. There were no signs of life.

Chapter 16

When they rushed in to tell the constable of their discovery, he pounded the desk with his fist and exclaimed, "Damn it! I knew it, I knew it. I knew it would happen sooner or later. Now what? Retaliation?" He stood, walked over and put his arm on Paul's shoulder. "I'm so sorry you had to find the body," he said.

"Do you think it's a signal for us to stop what we're doing?" Paul asked innocently.

"Good point," Drinkwell said. "I never gave it a thought. But who would go this far?"

Paul didn't want to elaborate.

"Just in case though," Drinkwell added, "I'm giving you police protection while you're on the island."

"But Thatcher, there's no need for …"

"Nonsense. I insist and I'm in charge here, right?" He gave a thin smile and jabbed Paul's side with his elbow. "Now let's go out and check on the body, process the scene. Then I'll have to make some calls and take a brief statement from you, Paul. I apologize but that's the protocol … Christ, I sound like this is an everyday occurrence around here … we have our share of vagrants and swindlers, but not many murderers. By the way, what's the victim's name?"

"Jules Smit."

"*That's* the man, or at least one of them. Active with

the 'Pins'."

"The 'Pins'?"

"It's what we named them. The other gang's the 'Needles'."

Instead of laughing Paul said, "So it's pins and needles. Right now, that's about the way I feel. On them." He was confused over the difference between the "Pins', or the "Needles', and the "Fish Truck" but he let it drop. He had gotten the overall picture.

Drinkwell grabbed a camera, tape measure and a notepad and led the others out back. On the way, Paul eased to the constable's side and whispered, "One last thing, Thatcher. The ship that Leon spoke to you about— he did, didn't he?"

"Yes. It's docked and ready to go whenever you give the sign. I hope you decide not to and can stay a bit longer."

"In that connection, what's the value of visiting the grave site or even Longwood?" Paul asked. "I was thinking of it as a sightseeing opportunity but now, under the circumstances, I just wonder."

"In the case of Longwood, who knows? There are documents under glass there and other artifacts. You might be able to decipher some things that no one else has. Even extract a tiny clue. Regarding the gravesite in Geranium Valley—some call it the Valley of the Tomb—I wouldn't imagine there are many clues there now, but it's a lovely experience. Napoleon selected the site himself, you know. Or at the very least, you can say to your friends back home that, yes, you saw where Napoleon lived and where he was buried on St. Helena. Speaking of that tomb, I also gave you a description from the papers of Sir Hudson Lowe. It tells of the complexity of constructing the grave. So yes, the governor was generally considered a vile person—I for one thought so—yet he apparently orchestrated the burial and went to great lengths to keep the casket airtight."

But the last things on Paul's mind were the details of grave construction and impressing friends. Besides, none of them knew of his secret mission. One thing that was on his mind, however, was what Vincent and Sylvie thought about Drinkwell's reaction, his choice of the word "retaliation" and his reference to gangs. Paul decided that with Smit now gone he would address the issue directly. Drinkwell had moved well ahead.

"You should both know," Paul said to Sylvie and Vincent. "that Jules implied he had some friends who were members of a gang here. Said he was sympathetic to their cause and that they never resorted to murder."

"We couldn't hear what either of you were saying from the back seat but I for one got that impression once Drinkwell spoke up," Vincent explained.

"Same here," Sylvie added.

Not only had the constable supplied the officer in a police cruiser that followed the trio, but he also managed to have their rental car arrive within a matter of minutes.

This time Paul drove, his hands tight on the wheel, claiming he was more rattled than the other two and that it would help calm his nerves. Seldom had he admitted to such weakness as he termed it. He also reflected on the sobriquets "Pins" and "Needles" and "Fish Truck." He hated the sound of them and that too upset him.

"You're entitled to it and I don't blame you," Sylvie said from the passenger seat. "It's really *your* mission and they know it. Whoever 'they' is. Let's pray it's part of the gang violence the constable talked about."

Aside from a comment by Vincent that the killer must have used a suppressor—"No one calls them silencers anymore"—Sylvie was the only one who said anything more during the entire drive back to the Farm Lodge Hotel. She asked question after question, running most of them together in an unemotional monotone as if she were thinking out loud. "Are we up to having lunch? Should we do anything more today? Why bother with Longwood and the gravesite? Isn't Drinkwell too intellectual for the work he does?"

But it was those about Paul's safety that *did* reflect emotion— deep and dolorous. "Must we worry about you, Paul? We had a scare on Elba, and now Helena. What about Paris when we return? Can't we leave here earlier? I'm worried about you, Paul, or did I already say that?" She received no answers and seemed to expect none.

They parked to the side of the hotel and got out of the car. Paul waved thanks to the police officer who had parked near a stone wall below, conspicuously visible from the main road.

As they walked in Paul said to Sylvie, "I appreciate your concern and I have my own about you."

"Isn't anyone around here concerned about me?" Vincent asked, with an obvious stab at humor. It fell on deaf ears.

"About eating lunch, Syl, I think we should try. Let's ask Miss Cheery Face over there if she can recommend a place. And just for your peace of mind, and yours too, Vincent—yes, we can leave earlier. Thatcher said he's got a ship ready to sail if we decide. I didn't mention it to you. Don't ask why except I didn't really think it would be necessary."

"You've made up your mind then?" Vincent asked.

"Yeah, and the way to answer you is to say I haven't broken my record."

"Meaning?" Sylvie said.

"Meaning there were two islands to investigate and two islands to get the hell out of!"

Paul could hear the other two sigh. "We should leave in the morning," he said. "Let's have lunch, go visit the other two places, have a decent dinner—the policeman will be nearby just like he is now—then get an early start tomorrow and carry on with business in Paris, or wherever else we have to go."

"Paul," Sylvie said, "you sound more resolute and that's good but please, please be careful."

"Resolute's my middle name. Haven't you heard?"

Ann's Place was exactly as the receptionist had described: quaint, near the pier in Jamestown, in the middle of an expansive garden. It boasted a variety of popular "Saint" dishes such as curry, pumpkin stew, fishcakes, pilau, black pudding and coconut fingers. It was noisy, jammed to capacity and filled with pleasant food aromas. They were told that a corner table would open up in a few minutes and took temporary seats on a leather sofa near the door.

"To answer another of your questions back there, Syl," Paul said, "my heart and brain tell me not to be in the mood but my stomach's hungry."

Soon they were seated. Paul didn't waste any time. "Any bets on the most burning item we all want to bring up?"

"I'll go first," Vincent said. "Drinkwell's remarks about Napoleon's tomb."

"Ditto," Sylvie said.

"Unanimous," Paul announced. "Think Leon has the wherewithal to set it up—if we decide to go ahead? You're both in a better position to make that judgment than I am."

"No doubt about it," Vincent said. "Whether or not he would do it is another thing though. He may think it's unnecessary. We'd have to make a convincing case for it."

"I agree," Sylvie said. "I think if we can present the reasons for going to all that trouble, he'd cooperate. He wants very much for the mission to succeed and you, Paul, are the … the … pivotal person here. He has great faith in you—you must know that by now."

"I have to admit," Paul said, "in listening to this, you both already favor having a look-see."

"If there's any question about who's there," Vincent said, "we'll have to."

They each ordered fishcakes and black pudding and raced through the meal as though they were late for a job interview.

Back at the hotel when Paul was informed that dinner reservations for St. Helena's finest restaurants had to be made in person, he threw up his hands and almost shouted a word he only used privately, like after the time he accidentally smashed his thumb with a hammer. "We could have made one while we were there!" He stared at Sylvie and Vincent. Finally he said in his most contrived voice, "Ann's Place will do, right? Good food."

They nodded in the affirmative. "And nice atmosphere," Sylvie said.

"I didn't notice," Paul responded. "Look, we'd better make the reservation before we go to Longwood. I'll drive back to town now and get it over with."

"Tell the officer to go with you," Vincent said. "We'll be fine here."

"You sure?"

"We're sure," Sylvie answered.

"Okay, I won't be long."

Giving his name and desired time at the restaurant's reservation counter took all of a minute. As Paul turned to leave, a young woman holding a portable phone approached him and said, "Are you Paul D'Arneau?"

"Yes?"

She handed him the phone. "It's for you."

"Yes?" he repeated into the phone.

A masculine voice at the other end sounded muffled: "Listen hard, my friend. Leave the island immediately or your pretty girlfriend gets hers. Smit didn't listen. We know she's at the hotel and the cop's with *you*. Understand?" Before the click Paul heard a trailing hyena laugh.

He hurled the phone onto the counter and burst out the door. "To the hotel! Quick!" he screamed as he ran past the police cruiser. He could hear his heart pounding and feel his legs weaken as he leaped into his car and sped off. The police officer eventually overtook him and led the way, his siren blaring. Paul had no trouble keeping up though his mind churned wildly and his hands felt moist.

He came to a dusty halt at the hotel and before bolting from the car yanked out his Heritage pistol. He outraced the officer to Sylvie's room and banged on the door.

"It's me, Paul," he shouted. "Are you there?"

Seconds seemed like minutes before the door opened and Sylvie wrapped in a white robe appeared and said, "What's wrong? You're sweating."

He pushed past her into the room and looked around before dropping onto the edge of her bed, barely able to catch his breath.

Vincent appeared in the open doorway. "What's all the commotion about? What's going on?"

Paul was wiping the back of his neck with his handkerchief. He related what had happened.

Sylvie explained that she had just taken a shower and was fine: "No, there were no phone calls or unusual noises. No, I never left the room." She went on to say she still believed they were bluffing—using threats to get him off the mission, for whatever reason.

"Really?" Paul said sarcastically. He knew better, but having just experienced a monstrous scare—on her behalf no less—he felt her last point trivialized what to him was a matter of life and death. "And what would you say about the castle incident?"

"You told me they didn't show their guns; they just kept coming toward you."

"And today's murder?"

"A turf war. Nothing to do with us."

"Your kidnapping?"

"A scare tactic."

"Over what? We've never been connected."

"I know. Too bad."

Paul was in no mood to get into *that*.

"What's your opinion, Vincent?" he asked.

"I think we have to take them seriously."

Paul, still emotionally bruised, thought Vincent was hedging—perhaps for Sylvie's sake. "Whatever," he said. "We leave early in the morning, like at six."

"I thought that decision was a done deal," Sylvie said.

"But I never figured so early; guess I'm just itching to get going. Or maybe a tiny voice is telling me the bad guys are still sleeping at that hour."

The police officer, who had been leaning against the door jamb, came to attention and said, "You're leaving us so soon?"

Paul tried to soften a piercing look as he replied, "Officer, you heard it all just now and you know about the murder. Wouldn't you leave now?"

"I suppose. But what's the murder got to do with you?"

"I wish I knew for sure." He also wished he could fathom the subtle change he saw in Sylvie: her sharp views, her demeanor, the tone of her voice. He attributed part of it to her way of bolstering his spirits, but the rest? He had no clue. Since the murder, however, he sensed that she was observing him differently, holding her gaze, eyes haunted, like someone who had something more to say but dared not say it.

But Sylvie's disposition aside, Paul wanted to remember St. Helena as a timeless culture, a jewel. And it probably was, yet for less than a day it had turned out to be a treacherous and deadly one.

Chapter 17

1:22 p.m.

The two men agreed with Sylvie to reassemble in an hour and they retired to their room. Paul immediately called Thatcher Drinkwell. Without mentioning the phone call and its aftermath he indicated they'd like to sail at 6 a.m. The constable assured him the ship would be ready.

Paul could still feel the perspiration and thought a long hot shower might be both necessary and therapeutic. It ended up being less than long, however, for he was anxious to review some material about Longwood House and Napoleon's gravesite before they left for both locations. He couldn't decide if it were a case of nervous "overkill" or if it would serve as a distraction from thoughts of the murder and the threatening phone call. But even more nagging was the continuing question of whether or not Napoleon's tomb at the Les Invalides was occupied by a double. Furthermore, if Leon agreed to have the casket opened, Paul wondered if the nearly two-hundred-year-old remains would be clearly identifiable. He had read about Napoleon's body being viewed by several individuals in 1840 when the casket was opened on St. Helena preparatory to its being transferred to Paris.

This was nineteen years after the emperor's death and the body reportedly appeared well preserved. This finding was disseminated by many to bolster their contention that Napoleon's wine had been murderously laced with arsenic, both a poison and a preservative.

When it came time for Vincent to shower, Paul turned to a section in the introduction of his latest book about the emperor, St. Helena: *Napoleon's Final Defeat*. He read:

> I have visited neither Longwood House nor the emperor's former grave but I have read about them, studied photographs and film and consulted with other historians who have made the difficult voyage to St. Helena. What follows came from a distillation of all the above. The principal characters in Napoleon's entourage on St. Helena were Louis-Joseph Marchand, his personal valet; Count Charles Tristan de Montholon, his aide-de-camp; Henri Bertrand, his Grand Marshall; de Montholon's and Bertrands' wives; Count Emmanuel Las Cases, his secretary and literary advisor; Gaspard Gourgaud, his orderly officer; and confidant, Franceschi Cipriani. In addition, three or more physicians attended Napoleon during his six years of exile (1815-1821), the most important of whom were Francesco Antommarchi, Barry O'Meara and Alexander Arnott. It was Dr. Antommarchi who performed the autopsy on the emperor in Longwood's Billiard Room and Dr. O'Meara who coaxed him to spend time gardening.

If someone were spiking the emperor's wine with the intention of murder, that person logically came from this group. But we must also toss in the British governor of the island, Sir Hudson Lowe. Their mutual antipathy was a poorly kept secret and, in addition, Lowe was in constant fear that Napoleon would escape captivity.

The property's well-maintained gardens are said to be a near duplicate of those that existed during the exile. They feature the original pools, trees and various flowers reportedly seeded by the emperor himself.

The Billiard Room, the first you come upon at the front entrance, was also the one that served as a reception room, map room and a retreat where Napoleon would spend endless hours playing billiards. It is painted in its original green color with a black Greek design background. In one of the shuttered windows is a small round cutout through which he allegedly spied on the English guards. The room contains two display cases containing among other things: the Legion of Honor and Iron Cross of Italy; one of his snuffboxes; a lock of his hair; billiard balls; a small infantry sword; miniatures of the King of Rome; and a Sevres medallion showing Napoleon and Marie-Louise, his second wife and the one who bore him his only child, a son. The room also contains a white marble bust of the emperor, the wooden world globe he used for some of his writings and, of course, the billiard table.

Some of the other rooms are: a living room where Napoleon died on May 5, 1821 in his small canopied campaign bed. Here we find his death mask, portraits of Marie-Louise and his first wife, Josephine, and several original furniture pieces; a study containing more original furniture and copies of Napoleon's frock coat and hat; his bedroom with its simple furnishings; the bathroom containing the large copper tub in which he would soak for hours, often reading and writing; the valet's bedroom stocked with personal letters, books, medallions and drawings; the library displaying samples of Napoleon's reference books; and the Will Room where he drew up his will in April, 1821.

Within the beautiful Valley of the Tomb, a metallic fence surrounds the burial area and a cement slab is positioned atop it. A variety of trees adorns the valley and I cannot improve on the government of St. Helena's concise commentary regarding their historical significance: "His tomb remains there to this day although his body was later exhumed and taken to France. The twelve cypress trees that surround the tomb were planted in 1840 in memory of Napoleon's twelve great victories. The Norfolk pines were planted when France became the owner of the valley, the olive tree was planted by the Prince of Wales in 1925, and the wild olive was planted by Prince Phillip in

1957. In 1921 an olive tree was planted in the name of Marshall Foch to mark the centenary of the death of Napoleon.

At 2:30 when they met outside for their trip to Longwood House, the air was cool and Paul could feel the breeze ruffling his hair. Only Sylvie was dressed appropriately. She was decked out in a dark brown poncho layered over a lighter brown print skirt and white leggings. Paul and Vincent ran back to their room and returned wearing identical blue blazers.

They found Longwood overrun by tourists and after pausing to view the magnificent gardens, a small gazebo and the sunken footpaths that Napoleon had ordered to hide him from guards, the police officer obliged Paul by accompanying them inside. By now he and Vincent had developed a kind of sign: Paul would gaze down at his ankle and Vincent would pat the left side of his chest.

Vincent and Sylvie took time examining everything on display while Paul moseyed about but discovered nothing unexpected except the profound smell of dampness. What's more he wasn't that interested and certainly saw nothing in the way of a clue as Thatcher Drinkwell had put it. The visit simply rekindled the haunting possibility that Napoleon had either been deliberately poisoned or stolen—or both.

Within twenty minutes, Paul said, "Okay, let's clear out." The other two reluctantly followed him to the door. The policeman nudged Paul aside saying, "I'll go out first."

An overcast sky and breezy air did little to accentuate

the serene beauty of the Valley of the Tomb. Paul took notice of the brook, the geraniums and especially the trees, many of the originals gracefully bent toward the tomb. Again he called on his reading and his own writings to recapture the details of Napoleon's funeral at the site on which they now stood. The services were conducted by the Abbe Vignali and held four days after the emperor's death. Three thousand English soldiers of the twentieth regiment participated. *His enemies! Astounding!* Twenty-four of them had carried the coffin down the path to the gravesite. Yet it was the slab of concrete that intrigued Paul the most as it symbolized in his own mind the bitterness between Napoleon and Governor Lowe. The emperor's associates had requested that the word "Napoleon" be inscribed on the slab but the governor refused, insisting on the word "Bonaparte" instead. As a result, the slab remained unmarked for nineteen years.

They spent less than twenty minutes there. It was not Paul's style but he realized without apology that the twin visits had been nothing short of perfunctory.

It was about 4 p.m. when they arrived at the hotel. "There, that's over," he said. "Two down, one to go."

"What's the third?" Sylvie asked.

"Dinner." Paul was tired of setting the time for when they should be ready for what. He checked his watch. "Remember," he said, "we're boarding at six. So Vincent, you decide — we eat when? It's now four."

"Five-thirty," Vincent said. "Let's leave here at five."

"Okay by me," Paul said. He turned to Sylvie. "Does that allow enough time for a lady to get ready?"

Sylvie didn't respond but her expression said it all.

Once in their room Paul stated he had two phone calls to make: to Leon in Paris and to Victor in Amsterdam.

"You don't think the time difference amounts to much in either city?" Paul asked.

"No, I don't," Vincent replied.

"And in case you're wondering, you don't have to make yourself scarce."

It took about fifteen minutes to reach Leon.

"My goodness! Paul! What's up? How's it going?"

"Hi, Leon," Paul said soberly. "It went fairly well and I use the past tense advisedly. We're still on Helena but we're sailing back at 6 in the morning. A couple of ugly things happened that I'll get to in a minute, but we learned more than we expected, even more than we did on Elba."

"You said 'ugly'? Like what? Are the three of you all right?"

"Yeah, considering. But I *must* get something cleared up with you. That's a polite way of saying I have a bone to pick and, frankly, I'm pissed."

"You heard then." It was a statement, not a question.

"Yes, I heard you visited the island at least twice but you told me that you'd never been here. Remember?"

"That's correct and I'm sorry about withholding it from you, Paul, but the truth is I didn't want you to depend on my information. I wanted a completely fresh approach. Clear the board as it were. Then if you needed anything that might fill in some blanks later, I might be of help. Though I doubt it because I never found out anything I didn't know in the first place. It was some years ago. I went there for the same purpose as you but the *histarians* were just getting off the ground then, so compared to you I was at a great disadvantage."

Pretty lame excuse.

"Well, okay," Paul said, "but from now on we stick with, you know, he truth. Like the name of your organization, *Vérité?*"

"Of course. That was bad judgment on my part and again, I apologize."

Paul said he was satisfied with the explanation, then spent considerable time first on consultation with Victor Frelinghuyens; second, the shooting death of Jules Smit; and third, the threat on Sylvie's life. "The bottom line is we're ready to scram. On the other hand, as I said, we learned plenty. Thatcher Drinkwell was terrific. Very talented. We think he's wasted on this … this lonely island. What do they call it? An emerald set in bronze? More bronze than emerald, I'd say." He next summoned up what the constable had covered: from arsenic to the notion of Napoleon's body being impersonated or stolen; from Michel Ney to Talleyrand; from Lady Beckett to the British East India Company executives; from her illegitimate child to Napoleon's love letters; from her inheritance to the codicil. But Paul did not mention Drinkwell's reference to opening the tomb at Invalides.

Paul couldn't tell whether or not Leon was taking notes but he had a gut feeling that he was.

"I knew the constable would prove valuable," Leon said, "so all in all the trip was worth taking?"

"I'd have to say yes—all in all. If it weren't for those two setbacks, we'd probably be staying longer. But no way now."

"Did you happen to take in Plantation House?"

"Where the governors live? No. Hudson Lowe was a son of a bitch I hear, and that alone eliminates him as a murderer or body snatcher, as I see it. He was very much despised and I think if he were guilty of anything so horrendous, he would have been found out a long time ago. The secret wouldn't have held up."

"Good logic, Paul."

Paul was unmoved by the compliment and had said all he wanted to say. The conversation ended with Leon's guarantee that the R.A.F. would be waiting for them on Ascension Island and with a brief exchange that apparently delighted the head of *Vérité*:

"I can't wait to get home," Paul said.

"To the States?"

"No, to Paris."

"I like to hear that, my friend. Do please consider it your adopted home."

The next call would be less confrontational but more painful.

"Paul, it's you?" Victor had answered the phone at once.

"Yes. We're about to leave St. Helena and, Victor, I have bad news. Your contact here, Jules Smit? He was found murdered earlier today."

"Murdered? Oh, no! How?"

"Shot in the head. Looks like the work of a rival gang."

"Uh ... who found him?" It was obvious Victor didn't know what to say next.

"I did."

"I feel bad about this, Paul. The murder, of course,

but for you to find the body, to promise you that you'd be protected, and it just … it just broke down. I feel terrible."

"Don't. It's not your fault. Apparently there are some things going on that are new to the island. We spent some time with their constable and he's completely frustrated."

"Paul, answer me honestly. Two questions: one's easy to ask. The other? Well I hope you don't misunderstand. Did this ruin the trip for you? I mean in terms of the goals you set out with."

"No. Except for the damper it put on the situation, we did fine. And your second question? I think I can guess."

"Could this in any way have anything to do with …"

"With me and my companions snooping around? Could be. Who knows?"

Dinner was not memorable. None of the three ordered a drink and all of them poked at their food. Even their conversation—what there was of it—was "under wraps", for they had invited the police officer to join them.

Halfway through the meal, Paul said to him, "You know, we never got your name."

"Smith. Oliver Smith," the officer replied.

"That's Smith, not Smit, right?"

"Smith, sir. If it was Smit, I'd be off grieving somewhere over the killing."

"Do many Smits live on the island?" Vincent asked.

"He's the only one that does … did."

"Did you know him?" Sylvie asked.

"Only *of* him. He was with the 'Pins'."

"The other gang's the 'Needles', I understand," Paul said.

"Yes, sir."

"Then what's the difference between, say, the 'Needles' and the 'Fish Truck'?"

"Same thing. But strictly speaking, the 'Fish Truck's' been here forever. Longer then I have and I was born here. And the 'Needles' just joined them. They're not as violent."

Paul took a moment before framing his next question. "So, using your best judgment, do you think it was old guard 'Fish Truck' that was behind the murder?"

"Yes, sir, no doubt."

"One last question, officer," Paul said, "and forgive me if I sound like a prosecutor, but do you think the 'Fish Truck' might have been around in Napoleon's day?"

"Most likely."

Chapter 18

Saturday
11:15 a.m.

The ship was named the Argos, a small Greek freighter that hauled roll-on/roll-off vehicles, packaged lumber and containers. It had cabin space for twelve passengers in square units that were surprisingly well furnished and comfortable. Paul had no idea when the ship had docked in James Bay, probably during the night. Nor had he asked, but Thatcher Drinkwell had made good on his promise. They set sail at 6:10 a.m. There were no other passengers on board.

Now, having grown accustomed to the pitching and yawing, Paul had mixed feelings. He wanted desperately to figure out how to fill the next thirty-six hours at sea. And although time was moving slowly, he didn't really mind: the pace on St. Helena had finally caught up to him. He took frequent naps, sat thinking on deck and exchanged stories with the crew. There were no games, lectures or entertainment aboard the Argos. The dining area was a continuation of the galley in its metallic composition: steel walls, steel floors, steel tables, steel benches. The food was filling and Sylvie and Vincent, obviously in the same throes of boredom as Paul, drew out their meals to the last morsel. But, as on the voyage south a few days before, none of the three spoke much about the mission: just the positives and negatives thus far and, particularly, what needed to be learned, visited or flushed out. Paul wasn't sure about the other two but he could sense the urgency of these initiatives.

At this point his only concrete activities were to update his summations and organize his briefcase. To "sanitize the sickening thing", in his words. He was about to open it when he heard a light tap on his door and Sylvie walked in. She wore blue jeans, a loose pink sweater and no makeup or jewelry.

"It's not what you think, Paul," she said, seeing his expression. "This is different. It'll only take a minute. I couldn't handle any more than that right now."

He pointed toward the chair and she sat down softly. He remained standing, his hands in the pockets of his khakis, wondering what was about to happen, on guard for anything.

Sylvie said, "I've been holding things in and I've decided not to do that anymore. I know this may be unexpected and a bit dramatic but I'm bothered by it and maybe telling you will help." Her fingers trembled as she fumbled with her watch strap.

"Bothered by what?" he asked.

"You."

"What?"

"And me."

Paul held his hands up in a stop gesture saying, "Now hold it, Sylvie. Is this what I think it is? A new approach?"

She didn't answer the question, instead studied her

loafers tapping the floor. She then stammered her way through their mutual experiences since he had called on her at the Institute. And she put a spin on each of their meetings. A romantic spin. Her voice took on a plaintive quality.

"Oh Paul, I'm all confused, but don't you see? I'm afraid I'm, ah, falling in love with you. I know that sounds stupid and I know where I stand. You're taken and I know you'll probably always be taken and there's nothing I can do about it. But that doesn't mean I can't tell you about my feelings. Yesterday the threat on my life upset me more than I let on, it put those feelings in perspective, and I wanted to share that with you before it's too late. Can you understand?"

Paul stood, speechless. He clenched his hands in his pockets.

"And believe me," she continued, "I'm not asking anything of you, and I won't embarrass you. I just wanted you to know. And I'll say it again: maybe this will help me."

Paul crossed over and put his right hand on her right shoulder so he could avoid direct eye contact, afraid he couldn't sustain it.

"Sylvie," he said, much like a father, "first of all, as you've indicated more than once, those threats are just that—threats—meant to scare us away. And second, what you just told me is impossible. I'm flattered, very flattered, but it's impossible. Fond of? Maybe. Attracted to? Maybe. But love? We've known each other a little more than a week."

"That's all it took for Josephine with Napoleon."

She dabbed her eyes with a tissue, pushed herself up, walked to a tiny porthole and stared out. "Yes, you're taken," she said, visibly dispirited, "and I wish you great happiness, but if you ever become ... untaken, I'll still be in Paris."

Paul couldn't resist: "You mean like Bogey and Bergman and 'We'll always have Paris'?"

"I wish we did. That at least."

Sylvie turned and faced Paul squarely. "There's more to it, I'm afraid, but I've said enough already. For the sake of the mission, let's pretend this conversation never happened, okay? Over and done. I got it off my chest." On her way out the door she stopped to kiss him on the cheek.

Paul sat on the edge of the bed, perplexed. *Was this all an act?* If so, why? Even if it were, he was concerned about the comment, "There's more to it, I'm afraid." And beyond that, he was curious about how Sylvie would conduct herself from now on.

A full five minutes passed before he resigned himself to the fact that there were no clear-cut answers. The episode—he preferred the word "confession"— was just one more thing to worry about. Yet he was determined not to be sidetracked by Sylvie's behavior. He couldn't afford the drain on his psyche. It helped to compare her admission, real or not, to that of a schoolgirl's. But a schoolgirl was not what Paul wanted at this stage of the investigation. *Maybe she'll step aside? Should I ask her?*

There were things he wanted to tend to. His summations. Reorganizing his briefcase. Examining what Drinkwell had given him in an envelope. Paul forced himself to concentrate.

He took hold of his briefcase as if it contained garbage and emptied its contents onto the bed. It *did* contain garbage. He surveyed the pile in disgust: the envelope, Napoleon's will—the important things—jumbled in among notes, cards, pencils, pens, paper clips, elastic bands, loose coins, a legal pad and other clutter. Plus a small box of saltine crackers. He decided he wasn't in the mood for "sanitizing" after all so he slid the envelope and love letters aside and threw everything else back into the briefcase.

The overriding issue, however, was not the love letters or the envelope—not even Sylvie's startling disclosure—but his long overdue summations. So much had transpired since his last one that he wanted merely to *list* highlights, not *interpret* them. And no questions. The value of this exercise far outweighed the time it took to formulate; it helped him take stock on any given day, to assess where he was coming from and where he might go. He removed the legal pad, sat at a small table and vowed to be concise as he recorded the following from memory:

KEY REMINDERS since 5/19:

> Sylvie kidnapped; only delegation knows she is spy for *Vérité*. Warning under door. Vincent on board full-time. Guy arranges monastery visit with Frère Dominic. To monastery. Dom calls Napoleon schizo. He elaborates on *histarian* network. Says N's postmortem disappearance a possibility. Mentions Clive Weaver at Elba & Thatcher Drinkwell at Helena; Lady Beckett & E. India Co; decision & plan; cartoons; Marshal Ney & the 4 who planned N's death; Talleyrand. Mysterious call to Vincent. Review N &

career. Sylvie returns unharmed, throws party; says she's game for Elba & Helena. To Elba. Clive provides N's will with codicil & notation of amendment; mentions Beckett, illegit. child, descendants of Talleyrand who acted as covers for N/Beckett liaisons; the inheritance; Mafia connection. Cartoon view. Confirm amendment reference but none there. Obvious Sylvie come-on. Review white paper on Talleyrand. Confrontation with Mafia types at castle. Decision to leave Elba, maybe the mission. Call to Victor in Amsterdam; will arrange Helena protection, Jules Smit. To Helena. Another Sylvie come-on. Review history of island. Driver turns out to be Jules Smit. "Fish Truck". Thatcher Drinkwell says Leon <u>did</u> visit island; at variance with Leon's statement; arsenic theory; slow death theory; Ney & marshals; Beckett & illegitimate child; child's lineage traced to Brussels; E. India Co. & 5 officers; issues of stolen body & double; inheritance; N's mental state; love letters. Smit found shot in head. Thatcher provides us police protection. Pins & Needles. Issue of opening tomb at Invalides. Call threatening Sylvie. Review my own account of Longwood & gravesite. Call to Leon, weak explanation re his Helena visits. Notify Victor re Smit murder. On Argos, Sylvie's strange revelation.

There! At last! Paul felt more proud than relieved. He had never actually consulted the summations during one of his cases. But the mental review required to chronicle the issues and events were sufficient to continue the practice.

He wasn't through with his paperwork however. He opened the envelope and withdrew its contents: three pages labeled "Marshals", a stack of Napoleon's love letters, and a single sheet over the top of which was scrawled, "Lowe description." Paul read the latter first:

> A pit was dug sufficiently capacious to allow a wall of masonry, two feet in thickness, to be built within it around the sides. The dimensions were, depth twelve feet, length eight feet, and breadth five feet. At the bottom of the pit, there was also a layer of masonry, a large white stone was placed and the coffin on eight stones one foot in height. Four other large white stones were placed on each side of the grave, and the whole cemented together. The top was enclosed by an additional large white stone let down by pulleys and firmly cemented with the other portions of the grave, so as to form a stone coffin or sarcophagus; two layers of masonry were then built over, joined, and even clamped to the side walls. The remaining depth of eight feet to the surface of the ground, was filled up with earth, and above the surface, flat stones were laid over the grave, the length of which was … twelve feet, and the breadth, eight feet.

He found Lowe's account interesting but couldn't

decide why the constable had included it with the other materials, unless he wanted to mitigate against the harsh words he'd leveled at the governor earlier.

Next Paul picked up the "Marshals" papers. He didn't attempt to decipher the French sentences, instead reading only what Drinkwell had translated in the margins.

> Would it not be best for France, for Europe, for the world to be rid of him once and for all, to be done with the conniving, the meddling, the transgressions too numerous to count? Besides he has lost his grip.

> They say he partakes in the poison of kings and the king of poisons, albeit in small amounts. The opportunity and its consequences are there to seize.

> It is after all a recreational drug, but one that can go too far and continue to overcome even if it has been stopped.

> Arsenic can do it. What would be the outcome if the dose were to be strengthened or if either amount were taken with more regularity?

> Are we agreed as to how to proceed or must we await further evidence of that which seems apparent? It would be for the glory of France and all its dominions and all its newly vanquished.

And then samples of Napoleon's love letters:

To Josephine: I have not spent a day without loving you; I have not spent a night without embracing you; I have not so much as drunk a single cup of tea without cursing the pride and ambition which force me to remain separated from the moving spirit of my life. In the midst of my duties, whether I am at the head of my army or inspecting the camps, my beloved Josephine stands alone in my heart. Occupies my mind, fills my thoughts. If I am moving away from you with the speed of the Rhone torrent, it is only that I may see you again more quickly. If I rise to work in the middle of the night, it is because this may hasten by a matter of days the arrival of my sweet love. Josephine! Josephine! Remember what I have sometimes said to you: Nature has endowed me with a virile and decisive character. It has built yours out of lace and gossamer.

To Marie-Louise: You have sent me a very beautiful com-fit box with the portrait of the King of Rome at prayer. I want you to have it engraved with the caption: "I pray God to save my father and France." This little picture is so interesting that it will please everybody. I am sending you Mortemarte with 20 flags captured from the Russians, the Prussians and the Austrians. My health is good. The Emperors of Russia and Austria, and the King of Prussia were at Pont, at Madame's; they went from there to Bray, and their headquarters were to have been at Fontainebleau on the 18th. They are now making post-haste for Troyes. My troops have entered Nogent and Sens. Give my son a kiss, keep well, and never doubt my love.

To Marie Walewska: I saw no one but you, I admired no one but you, I want no one but you. Answer me at once, and assuage the impatient passion of N. Ah! Grant a few moments' pleasure and happiness to a poor heart that is only waiting to adore you. Is it so difficult to let me have an answer? You owe me two. There are times—I am passing through one now—when hope is as heavy as despair. What can satisfy the needs of a smitten heart, which longs to throw itself at your feet, but is held back by the weight of serious considerations, paralyzing its keenest desires. Oh, if only you would! No one but you can remove the obstacles that keep us apart. Marie, my sweet Marie, my first thought is of you, my first desire is to see you again. I want you to accept this bouquet: I want it to be a secret link, setting up a private understanding between us in the midst of the surrounding crowd. We shall be able to share our thoughts, though all the world is looking on. When my hand presses my heart, you will know that I am thinking of no one but you: and when you press your bouquet, I shall have your answer back! Love me, my pretty one, and hold your bouquet tight!

The fourth read:

You have made my last years tolerable, even
more so than during the several before while
I expended my full energy upholding the
desires of many in the battlefield. And now I
must fritter away the minutes, my heart, my
soul trapped here until you steal to me once
more. I await that time with more impatience
than you could ever know, my darling. Your
smile and golden locks fill my waking hours.
I feel strange and weakened but he would be
a fool who turned away from the inevitable.
The Valley of Geraniums would be my choice
if I could not but have my final resting place
in your English gardens, beside you for an
eternity.

Paul read the letters carefully. Something seemed
fishy but he couldn't immediately put his finger on it.
And then two things hit him like slabs of concrete. The
fourth letter held no salutation, and referred to an English
garden. It had to be written to Lady Beckett! *A secret love
letter to a secret lover!*

Of course he had heard of Beckett and he knew she
was English. He also knew it wouldn't be long before he
would tap the mental note he made of Beckett's garden.
But why would he—they—want to be buried in a simple
garden? He reread the letter. "Gardens", not "garden."

The three passengers had five meals aboard the *Argos*. They saw little of one another except on those occasions. At the first meal Sylvie and Vincent handed over and editorialized on their notes and during the others, they dominated the conversation with talk of world history and general scientific matters. Paul got the impression they had conspired to divert his attention away from the mission for a change. But it didn't work. He contributed little more than a disingenuous smile and some idle chatter.

Actually Paul was waiting for Sylvie to return to her admission of love for him— alleged or otherwise and certainly not in the presence of Vincent—but after the third meal, dinner, she gave him the usual peck on the cheek and said goodnight.

He allowed an hour to pass before knocking on her cabin door.

"Well, this is a switch," she said, ushering him in. She wore the same casual clothes she had worn at dinner—a baggy brown jersey and beige slacks—while Paul, barefoot, tried to appear blasé in a blue robe. He had rolled up his sleeves and trouser legs to make it appear as though he wore nothing underneath. He sat on the edge of the bed and gingerly crossed his legs so as not to give the charade away. She pulled over a chair, turned it around and straddled it, resting her arms on the back. She stared at him, smiling but not laughing.

"You're making fun of me," she said.

"No I'm not. I'm just trying to lighten a time when you seem cold as ice." He lowered his sleeves and trouser legs, put on a pair of soft slippers he had brought with him and removed the robe. "Guess it didn't work," he said.

"Good try but I just don't think it's a laughing matter."

"I totally agree. I didn't intend to belittle the matter — only to humor you. But are you okay?"

"I'm okay now. I got it off my chest."

"You weren't serious though, were you?"

"Silly fellow," she answered, probing his eyes, "as serious as I could be. What do you think?"

"I can't say. I've been trying to make some sense out of it."

Sylvie pulled back. "Look, you've got too much on your mind as it is. Let's drop it for now. I said what I had to say, and the Paris thing still stands. I meant it." She cupped her hand over her mouth briefly, then took it away. "You talk serious? That's serious."

Paul did the same thing with his hand before saying, "I guess." He resisted the urge to jump up and hold her close, for no other reason than to create the right mood for what he was about to say next.

"I realize you may want to leave well enough alone," he began, "but I think this needs to be said on my part. Yes, as you put it yesterday, I'm taken. But — and God I hope this comes out right — you would have made a great wife. I want you to know that, Syl."

"Would have?"

"I mean mine."

Sylvie got up stiffly and rubbed her arms in front of her chest. She turned, walked to the door and wheeled around. "Paul," she said, her voice taut. "I said I'm okay. Let's not stir things up."

He stood but remained near the bed. "You're right," he said. "Sorry. Guess I didn't stop to think it through. And as long as I'm screwing things up tonight, I might as well ask. You said before that there's more to it. Is this a good time to elaborate, or is it too touchy a subject?"

Sylvie took a step closer and broadened her stance. "Well, I don't know. I don't know if I should. Under the circumstances ... that is, once I realized myself how I felt about you ... I definitely planned on telling you. But I needed to get up enough courage first."

"Aw, come on now, how bad can it be?"

"Real bad. You may not like me anymore."

"Try me." Paul felt like crossing his fingers. He sat back down gently, hoping she would explain what was still an enigma to him.

Sylvie sighed and let her shoulders drop at the same time. "But there has to be a promise in return," she said.

"Like what?"

"Like keeping this a total secret. If anyone in the delegation gets wind of it, I'm ruined with *Vérité*. I'd be crushed because I believe in *Vérité* very, very much, although you may not think so once you hear what I have to say."

"I promise—I swear. If I thought it would help convince you, I'd cut my finger with a knife to draw a little blood."

She walked back to her chair and again straddled it. "Here goes," she said. "You do know I've been a spy for *Vérité* against the Institute, right?"

"Right."

"Well, the reverse is also true. There, I've admitted it. I've been a double agent— that's the simplest way I can put it."

Paul stared at her. "You mean you were spying on

Vérité on behalf of the Institute?"

"Not really spying. Helping them. And this is the hard part, Paul. Forgive me. If you have it in your heart, please forgive me. I was helping them dissuade you, to get you off the case. But I was in a bind. In a way, I had no choice. It was either that or ..." Her words were tumbling out.

"Wait, wait! Let's back up. Two questions here. No choice—why? Dissuade me why?"

"I had no choice because they would have fired me."

"But why did they want me off the case?"

"The Talleyrands."

"Who?"

"You know his history, Paul. Every historian does." Sylvie waited for a response.

But Paul was too astonished to give one. He scratched his finger. "The Talleyands? I can't believe it. How did they come into the picture?"

"It's a long story but I'll condense it. You see, I've rehearsed this, figuring I'd tell you some day, not now, though. But the same thing with how I feel about you. I didn't want to tell you so soon. They go together, Paul. If I love you, and I do, and if I want to tell you, and I do, how can I not level with you now. Does that make sense? It does to me."

"Yes, it does. Don't worry about it. Please get to the Talleyrands."

"In the late 1790's, Talleyrand was deported from France—I won't go into why—and he fled to your country. He was allowed back two years later. The Institute of France was just beginning at the time and it was struggling, real bad. Somehow he came to its rescue. The upshot of it all is that from then on he developed strong ties with the Institute and all its branches, including the one I work for, the Academy of Sciences. This has carried on for years and years so that his present day relatives have terrific pull with the Institute."

"And they're pissed—sorry—upset that I named Talleyrand as a suspect in Napoleon's murder, correct?"

"Yes. That is, the theory of his murder."

"But how did they know that? It's in my unpublished manuscript."

"That's where Yale comes in."

"Yale?"

"Oh yes, this gets more intriguing by the minute. You won't believe how many things we've been dealing with that are all tied together like a ball of, what, string? We've got Elihu Yale, the East India Company, Lady Beckett and spices to cover yet."

"Now I'm confused. What the hell do spices and the guy Yale was named after have to do with it?"

"You'll see, but let me finish with the murder theory. The Talleyrands are afraid you might come to a definite conclusion that Napoleon was murdered. They want the public to think it was a natural death and have been pushing that for years. Unnatural death equals an ancestor as a possible killer. Natural death? They forget about the ancestor as a killer."

"But why didn't you tell me this sooner?"

"Because I was caught in the middle. My job was at stake, but when I saw what they were doing to scare you away, and how much my feeling for you was growing, I thought enough is enough."

"So it was his relatives who were behind the, let's

call them, 'incidents'?"

"Yes, all of them."

"Would they have resorted to murder?"

"I don't think so on their own, but once the Mafia comes in, who knows? Signals could get crossed or the hoodlums could get careless."

"What about your kidnapping?"

"A complete hoax. Again, to put a damper on the mission."

Paul sprung up, paced between the bed and door several times and sat back down. "Boy, that had me fooled, all of us. What I don't understand though is how did the Talleyrands know I was in on the case?"

"I told them."

"But …"

"It was part of what I had to do at the time."

"Okay, understood. Elihu Yale and spices?"

"Talk about irony! Your former employer and alma mater, right? You indicated it was named after this Elihu Yale fellow. I take it he was the college's largest benefactor, but he was also an official with the British East India Company. Well, Talleyrand was not only a great statesman but also a renowned gourmet and wine connoisseur. He once owned the fancy Châteaux Haut-Brion and hired the finest chefs around. And he also bought the best tea and spices from Yale's East India Company. That's how Talleyrand and Lady Beckett happened to strike up their friendship and develop the 'covers' used for her to see Napoleon. And all the rest."

"So Yale and the Talleyrand clan are close?"

"Hand and glove, even to this day. And that's how the clan knew about what's in your manuscript. Ahead of anyone else. Then when they read who you put at the top of your suspect list, I bet the Yale people contacted them on the spot. In fact, I've got to believe that's why you were let go. For that more than for the mythology excuse."

Paul got up again and walked slowly to Sylvie's side. He held out both arms at the same time she began to cry. She took his hands and he gently pulled her up.

Now in his arms she said, sniffling, "I wish I didn't have to tell you all that, Paul, but I care about you terribly and you deserve to know."

He kissed her on the forehead and said, "You're a brave woman and I won't breathe a word about it to a soul. You can bank on it."

She pulled away and raised her chin. "But one thing you *don't* deserve," she said, "is listening to some sniveling French broad who can't control her emotions. You're engaged for heaven's sake!"

For the duration of the trip back to Paris, Paul couldn't dismiss Sylvie's revelations from his mind. Only the encounter with Leon, who was waiting at the de Gaulle Junior airstrip, interrupted his stream of consciousness: from her complicated dual role, to Talleyrand, to the Institute, to Elihu Yale, to the British East India Company, to exotic spices, to Lady Beckett, to trysts with Napoleon and back to Sylvie. He had paused to dissect each issue, over and over. *What to do? For now, file it away along with everything else in this head.*

Sunday, May 28
7:40 p.m.

"Getting to be a habit, folks," Leon said.

"Good to see you, Leon," Paul said, "and good to be back."

As before, Sylvie and Vincent walked ahead into the only building at the airstrip. Leon tugged on Paul's jacket and gestured for him to stay behind.

"So the trip was worth it despite those two unfortunate incidents?" Leon asked, using his last cigarette to light another.

"Definitely. A bit scary and a bit distracting, but not enough to wipe out what we learned. I'm happy we went, but even happier it's over."

"Drinkwell's already called me, filled me in on everything. He thinks you're topnotch, by the way." He didn't give Paul a chance to respond. "So what's next?"

In contrast to the weather in Paris upon their return from Elba, the night was still and balmy. Paul removed his traveling windbreaker and slung it over his shoulder. He had Leon hold his briefcase while he did so.

"This thing weighs a ton," Leon said, handing it back. Again he didn't give Paul a chance to respond, instead answering his own question. "Next I would guess is Belgium?"

Paul gave him a quizzical look.

"I told you Drinkwell filled me in," Leon said apologetically.

"Well, you happen to be right. I want to check out the 'lineage woman', for want of a better name. The constable said she's a direct descendant of Lady Beckett and Napoleon. She may have some important things to say. Plus I may want a DNA sample if she's willing."

"Come again?"

"A DNA sample. I'll explain in due course. Later. Some other things have to crystallize first. Just trust me for now."

It was Paul's first hint that he intended to prove Napoleon had a living relative, and he realized that if Leon considered the logic, the emperor's DNA would also have to be obtained. In addition, if the decision were made to see who occupied the tomb at Invalides—Napoleon or an imposter—and if in either case the body were unrecognizable, its DNA must be extracted. He wondered if Leon would comment. He didn't. Perhaps because he appeared eager to pass on more of what he'd learned from Drinkwell.

"The name of the 'lineage woman'", Leon said. "is Sophie Bauer. She's well liked in the Brussels area. Retired school teacher. Spinster. Nearly everyone around knows of her possible link to Napoleon—even that she may be a descendant of an illegitimate child of his. She's apparently reluctant to talk about it; refers to the child as her unofficial forebear. And there was no mention of a Lady Beckett."

Paul took out his note pad and abbreviated the information. "How did the good constable know all this?"

"He called the *historian* in the region, actually right there in Brussels, and simply inquired."

"I see. So she *does* exist. Well, can you set up an appointment with her for me? We'll take the Bullet there in the morning. I'll ask Sylvie to come. With her background, she's no doubt had plenty of experience taking buccal smears for DNA."

"Glad to and I'll call you later to confirm it. In the meantime you'd better consider having Vincent go along too. He can wait in the taxi if you'd prefer."

Chapter 19

It was just after 8 p.m. Sunday when Paul arrived at his room at the Meridien Montparnasse. He felt as though he had just come home from a war. A war that was still raging. Even before unpacking he called Jean and spent some initial time talking about how she felt and what was happening at her end. He then launched into a detailed report of the *St. Helena Phase* of the investigation and his latest conversation with Leon. When he got to the Jules Smit murder, it didn't appear to bother her. Either that or she didn't want to show it. Paul next explained why it might become necessary to open Napoleon's tomb and acquire a DNA sample from his remains. Similarly he was planning a visit to a descendant of Napoleon's alleged daughter for a sample of her DNA to confirm the emperor's identity.

"Now review with me, Jean. You gave me a rundown once but I can't keep the DNAs straight. You were talking about tracing someone's ancestry. And no fancy terms."

"You mean nuclear DNA and mitochondrial DNA? They're both used to identify people. Mitochondrial doesn't degrade as easily as nuclear—so it's better for those who died hundreds of years ago. The only problem is that it's passed on from generation to generation only in the female line of the family. You told me Napoleon had no female heirs except possibly that child with Lady Beckett. So that's the route to take."

"The route to take?"

"Mitochondrial. And taking the sample from bone or teeth in the tomb."

"And in Brussels, swabbing the inside of the cheek?"

"Yes. See, the technicians will be dealing with Napoleon's DNA—if it is Napoleon and you use mitochondrial analysis. Then using the descendant's DNA as a reference sample and employing a concept called 'the most recent common ancestor through matrilineal descent', the lab can be the hero in all of this."

"Whoa! I said no fancy terms. But I get the idea, and you think we're going about this the right way?"

"Yes I do, but leave it up to Sylvie. She must be very familiar with the whole process. She's going with you?"

"I hope so."

Leon called a half-hour later. "All set for tomorrow," he said. "Two-thirty at 2004 Muller Street, just off the center of the city. The taxi driver will know. The woman's anxious to meet you and will be glad to answer questions, though she said she doesn't know what all the fuss is about—she's certain she's related to Napoleon. Seems like a nice person. Also she knows about your wanting a DNA sample."

"How did she react to that?"

"She'll cooperate but wanted to know why."

"And?"

"I kept it vague. I'm not even sure myself. But I said we have some new information about Napoleon and the sample might help determine how he died. And she dropped the subject. When you get there you can elaborate if you wish, but I don't think you'll have to. So to repeat the address, she's at 2004 Muller Street."

Paul wrote it down, his mind already on something else: There was still no indication that Leon suspected the tomb-opening idea. And Paul wasn't ready yet to broach the subject. He first wanted to discuss it with Guy and Maurice, but that would have to wait until tomorrow.

Paul was exhausted but before retiring he phoned Sylvie's apartment. She agreed to accompany him to Brussels on the condition there would be no talk about their relationship except as it applied to the mission.

Monday, May 29

The Thalys Bullet trip to Brussels took an hour and twenty-five minutes and the taxi ride to Sophie Bauer's apartment took another fifteen. Paul had reasoned that the fewer people conversing with the woman, the more comfortable she would be; hence he had convinced Vincent not to go along. Meanwhile Sylvie, from the moment she put a swab kit into Paul's briefcase, was more talkative and upbeat than usual. Paul had slept till nine and felt well rested for the first time in days.

Of his dozen textbooks over the past twenty years, the first was the initial installment of a series devoted to European history. It dealt with northwestern Europe. Paul considered Brussels one of the most important cities of that region for two reasons: one, its location—along with neighboring Antwerp, Bruges and Ghent—smack in the center of major trading partners France, The Netherlands, Germany and, across the North Sea, the United Kingdom.

He wrote about the peculiarity, as he characterized it, of the country's sharp division into the Dutch-speaking *Flemings* to the north and the French-speaking *Walloons* to the south. Within Brussels itself, both French and Dutch are spoken.

The second reason and the one having greater impact on other major countries including the United States was the key role of Brussels in international politics and economics. It provided—and continues to provide—headquarters for both the North Atlantic Treaty Organization and the European Union.

Thus, while Paul had written extensively about Brussels, he had never been there; and now, if he hadn't been wrapped up in his "mission within a mission"—the DNA sample—he would have preferred to explore the city and its environs for a few days. He regretted having once written the ill-conceived sentence: "The smells and sounds of a bustling Brussels were not unlike those of New York City, only in miniature." He could still feel the sting of those historians from universities other than Yale who roundly criticized him for writing about some countries he hadn't observed first-hand. Eventually, in a guest editorial, he answered those critics by unleashing a salvo of his own: "Some academicians I know have written about hell, but have they ever visited it? Not yet anyway."

In any event, this was not the time to see the many historic sights of Brussels. The taxi left them off at a major intersection near an alley which the driver pointed to as Muller Street. And in their short walk, they came upon no suspicious characters. No one stalked or tailed them; no one regarded them with murderous intent. Paul scrutinized them all as they passed by. He peeked into shop and restaurant windows, glanced at rooftops and even looked hard at a beggar to whom he gave an American five-spot. He still packed the Stealth 9 mm at his ankle, however, but since Sylvie had "come clean" he doubted there would be a need for it.

The weather had turned blue skies nippy since they had crossed into Belgium, and Paul wore the best of three suits he had packed for Paris, a dark pinstripe. Sylvie wore a cropped blue jacket over a white blouse and a print skirt.

It was 2:05 when they arrived at the small complex on Muller. Sophie Bauer ushered them into the living room of her second-floor apartment, an airy, colorful five-room space laid out in an L-shape. Paul and Sylvie bumped into each other as they maneuvered to determine who should lead the way.

"Don't be nervous," Sophie said in a husky voice. "You have a friend in this seventy year old. Anyone who might show me my true ancestors is welcome here." Smooth complexioned and cosmetic-free, she was short, trim and straight, all features that Paul would have attributed to a younger woman. She was dressed casually and colorfully: loose tangerine jersey, loose tangerine slacks, tangerine slippers.

They sat in a grouping of three easy chairs, each a different shade of soft red. Paul and Sylvie declined tea or coffee.

"You speak very fluent English, Ms. Bauer," Paul said.

"Please, I'm Sophie. Your kind formality brings me back to my students, first and second graders. They were all dear to me but I'm retired now."

There was an awkward gap in the conversation before Paul said, "You do know I'm sure, ah, Sophie, the difference between a European and an American?"

"There's a difference?"

"Yes, the European speaks more than one language."

All three chuckled.

Paul decided not to waste any more time. "Well," he said, "here we are, hoping to make history. I should begin, Sophie, by stating we're not about to identify your family tree scientifically. We're assuming that Napoleon is indeed your forebear. And that a certain Lady Beckett bore a child by him, a baby girl. Now when we get your DNA analyzed—Mr. Cassell mentioned that, didn't he?"

"Yes, he did."

"Well after that analysis, we'll work backwards to confirm or disprove your direct line to those two individuals. You've no doubt heard of Lady Ashley Beckett?"

"No doubt," Sophie answered. "The golden-haired beauty." She grew pale around the mouth.

Paul, momentarily taken aback, looked at Sylvie.

"She had golden hair?" she asked.

Something began to gnaw at Paul.

"Yes, definitely," Sophie responded.

"Why are you so certain?" Paul asked.

"Because my grandmother told me. She knew everything about the four or five generations before her."

Paul wasn't sure how to phrase what he had in mind, nor where he would take it once he started. "Did she ever say that each of the succeeding generations produced at least one female offspring?"

"All of them."

"No males?"

"Not a single one. I always thought that was unusual, but maybe not."

"And from your grandmother to the present?"

"Well, she had only a daughter—my mother. And my mother had two children, a girl and a boy. The girl was me, obviously. A year after I was born, my mother disappeared, leaving me to be raised by dear Ada, a distant cousin by marriage. I miss her. She told me my mother had another child sometime later: the boy, my brother. As for good old mom, I have no idea whatever became of her, and Ada—except for the child thing—never talked about her or my brother. I got the feeling she knew about their whereabouts but for reasons of her own, didn't want me to know. Maybe after all was said and done, it was the right thing. She was a bright and caring woman."

Sophie's voice had gotten huskier. Thick. Gravelly. "Would you excuse me for a minute?" she asked. "I'm going out to the kitchen for some water. May I bring you some?"

"No thank you," Paul said and Sylvie shook her head no. Sophie took a tissue from her pocket as she left the room.

Upon her return, she said, "That must have been a verbal rat maze for you. Let's go back to Ashley and her golden hair. When it was described to me, I remember thinking of the English fairy tale, *Goldilocks and The Three Bears*. I used to read it to my students every year.

That's it! Golden locks! Paul reached onto his briefcase and fumbled through the samples of love letters before finding the one supposedly written to Lady Beckett. He ran his finger down to the line, "Your smile and golden locks fill my waking hours," read it aloud, then handed the letter to her.

"Have you ever seen this, Sophie?" he asked calmly.

She scanned it. "No," she replied.

"Could you please read it? And do take your time."

Sophie read the letter quickly and went back to reread specific sentences. "That's her all right. I mean it was meant for Ashley, without question."

"How about the English gardens?" Paul asked.

"Sure. That's Beckett Gardens in London. They're still there I hear."

"Have you ever seen them?"

"No, never."

"Why not, may I ask? Or is it too personal?"

"Heh… this is *all* too personal, but that's okay." She swatted away some imaginary lint from her thigh. "I suppose I should be proud that I'm a descendant of Napoleon Bonaparte. Most days I am, but I'm also ashamed that my own blood may be unofficial. And, you know, it's one thing to learn that my grandmother's birth was unofficial—I can accept that. But to see where her golden-haired ancestor might be buried, I'd just as soon not go near there. One thing is what— hearsay? But the other is real. You can see it, touch it. It's oh so hard to explain my feelings." She looked at the ceiling pensively. "Let's just say I've stayed away from the gardens in case her grave is there."

They chatted briefly about things irrelevant from Paul's perspective. He looked toward Sylvie who then reassured Sophie that the procedure would be quick and painless. She deftly swabbed Sophie's inner cheek and smeared the swab onto a microscope slide. Next she allowed both the swab and slide to air-dry before packaging them and placing the package in Paul's briefcase. They stayed to chat for only a few more minutes. He asked for and received Sophie's phone number and stated that she would be kept apprised of any significant results. Sophie hailed modern science and wished them luck. Both Sylvie and Paul thanked and hugged her warmly before leaving.

As Paul inserted the key into his hotel door, Vincent ran toward him from a near corner of the hallway. He looked like one who had just spotted a long-lost brother.

"Am I glad you're back!" he exclaimed.

"Why? What's up?"

"The prior's been looking for you. Says it's important."

"Oh? How many times did he call?"

"Only the one time but I could read urgent in his voice. I almost tried to contact you and would have if he'd called a second time. Here's his number." He handed Paul a slip of paper.

Inside, Paul flung his briefcase onto a chair, but suddenly recalled that it contained the DNA sample. He hurried over to straighten and pat the briefcase as if it held a chunk of kryptonite. He then marched to the nightstand and sitting on the edge of his bed, put in the call to Frère Dominic.

"Paul? Good. Earlier today I received disturbing news that a group left London to seek you out there in

Paris."

"Seek me out?"

"That's the expression he used."

"Who's 'he'?"

"Graham Radford. Our *histarian* there."

"Where did he get the information?"

"He has a whole bevy of informants."

Paul scrunched his lips. "What kind of group? Did he say?"

"He used the word 'unsavory.' When I asked him to explain, he said 'known mobsters.'"

"Here we go again," Paul said, cradling the phone in his shoulder and scratching his finger. "Sounds like a posse in reverse. How big a group?" He really didn't want to hear the answer.

"Four men. They left this morning. One of them had supposedly spent half his life in prison for shooting his girlfriend and for two attempted murders on the same day. Goes by the name 'Alec the Assassin.' Look, how far along are you in solving your … your conundrum?"

"Not far. A few more pieces have to fit into place."

"Well, may I suggest you have a bodyguard?"

"I have one. Vincent. He was with me when we came to the monastery, remember?"

"On second thought, could you arrange full police protection? I mean twenty-four-hour coverage. Leon could help with that, couldn't he?"

"Yeah, I'll ask him. I guess that's the thing to do. You know, Dom, I should be unhinged, but I'm beginning to get used to it and that's what worries me more than anything."

"I can understand and I'll do some praying, but what

you just said is why you need help—protective help. I don't think we should hope for dangers to blow away, and because you've got so many things bubbling up in your mind, you can get careless. Plus you're too close to everything. Let others worry about your safety."

Paul couldn't argue with the logic of this advice and responded, "Thanks, Dom. I'll follow through with Leon provided you follow through with something you just said."

"What's that?"

"Pray."

After hanging up, Paul told Vincent about what the prior had said.

"We have no choice, Paul. We're both armed but if they're hellbent on completing a job, only a heavy police presence will stop them. And I mean heavy. We'll need it anyway if we go ahead at the tomb."

Paul allowed himself to fall back hard on the bed. He ran both hands down his face and said, "Jeez, I'm so tired of making phone calls here, making phone calls there. Interviewing here, interviewing there." He rocked back up and added, "But I admit we have no choice."

He placed a call to Leon whose number he now knew by heart. He gave the nature of the call and Leon didn't hesitate. Shortly he would, as he put it, deploy a counter patrol: two uniformed police officers keeping vigil in the lobby and two more stationed at Paul's door. All four would accompany or follow him wherever he went. Leon also agreed to a meeting in the hotel's coffee shop at two the following afternoon.

Paul next looked up Maurice's and Guy's phone numbers and before calling them, muttered, "See what

I mean? It never ends." By now he thought phone calls were just as sterile as e-mails. He would prefer to see their facial expressions, their body language, even though there was essentially only one issue to discuss. Unless they had others.

Neither man queried the reason for meeting but Maurice said he would be at the coffee shop at 9:30 in the morning and Guy said he would be there at eleven-thirty. Paul figured separate meetings might be more productive.

He stood abruptly and stretched his arms to the ceiling. "What say, Vincent? Time for dinner? I don't know about you but I'm famished." He stripped to the waist. "I also need a shower. You call Sylvie, fill her in and tell her to be here within the hour. Ten-to-one our police squad will also be here by then."

Chapter 20

Paul was right. Forty-five minutes later, just before 7, he answered a knock on the door but only after being satisfied through a series of questions and answers that a police contingent had done the knocking. He invited the four men in. Sylvie had already arrived dressed in black slacks and jean jacket over an azure blue top. Vincent hadn't gone home to change from clothes more wrinkled than matching: blue trousers, light green shirt and a faded maroon jacket. Paul stood awkwardly, wearing only brown pants and a sock on one foot.

Each officer eyed them from top to bottom and then one spoke up: "We've been asked by our good friend Leon Cassell to provide, shall we say, support for three important people, and I assume that means you. Which one would be Paul?"

Paul felt foolish raising his hand. "I am, officer, and I thank you for responding so fast. In case you're wondering, I just came out of the shower."

"Yes, it looks that way," the officer said. "Now rest assured that all of us are trained in this kind of duty. And on top of that, Leon and I had a good orientation talk about some possible danger you might encounter. Leave it to us, sir—we'll be quick to neutralize any threats that might come your way while you're in Paris. So go about your business and we'll handle any and all contingencies. We may not be in your line of vision every second, but you will be in ours."

"Well thanks again, officer. That's very reassuring," Paul said.

With that, the officers reeled around, soldier-like, and walked out.

Sylvie and Vincent gave broad smiles of satisfaction.

The trio had decided on *The Brasserie* for dinner, just down the street. Inside it was the simplest of restaurants — a single room with booths along three walls and a small bar and swinging door to the kitchen along the fourth. Spicy aromas and cigarette smoke hung in the air. At first, Paul disliked the loud echoing conversation they walked through to get to their seats because he thought they'd have to shout to be understood. It had always been a "thing" with him: a crowded room without carpeting and with paperless walls to absorb the "chitter-chatter." But on reconsideration, he concluded the noise would drown out their own talk as well.

Two of the police officers materialized out of nowhere and were seated nearby. They appeared to be kidding a waitress.

At their table Paul said, "Can we eat in peace and not talk about the mission for a change? For the next hour, let's screw the mission!" Vincent agreed. Sylvie thanked a different waitress who dropped off a basket of bread and butter, even though she had gone beyond earshot. Their silence lasted about two minutes.

"He's got to see it's the only sensible thing to do," Paul said.

Sylvie corrugated her forehead. "Who's got to see—and what sensible thing?" she asked.

"Leon. Opening the tomb. There's so much indication for it. Indisputable. I forgot who said what, but things like opportunity to steal the body, substitute a double, imposters are nothing new to Napoleon. Yeah, sure, imposters when he was in his power days—security reasons—but when he's near the end? Why? Then we have all the loose ends. The amended codicil. Where the hell is it? Beckett Gardens. Should we check it out? Lady Beckett's golden hair. It's in the love letter. Sophie referred to it too. These point to something significant but I'm not sure why. Is it because ancient DNA—with a few mutations thrown in—can't prove beyond a reasonable doubt all by itself, and the golden locks can't do it by itself either? But taken together, they can prove the body is Napoleon's? If that's who's lying at Invalides in the first place. So Beckett had golden locks. Big deal. But then again, it shows that she was Sophie's great-great-great-whatever. And we have Sophie's DNA. I don't know. I really don't know. One minute I think I understand it and the next, I don't. One thing I'd swear to though: we've gone as far as we can go, short of opening that tomb."

Sylvie and Vincent had let him ramble while taking it upon themselves to order a bottle of red wine for the three of them. Paul hadn't noticed the waitress with pad and pencil.

"You know what?" he said. "I'm talking in circles. Let's just eat."

The following morning at precisely 9:30, Maurice hobbled into the coffee shop to join Paul who, a minute before, had winked at the police officers as he passed by them and then claimed one of two unoccupied tables. Maurice greeted Paul by doffing his black beret. Settling into a chair opposite him seemed to be a major undertaking for the Frenchman, who rested his cane on the chair between them. Paul detected no alcoholic smell this time.

"Glad you called, Paul. Maybe you'll bring me up to date. I mean from your point of view. Leon does a pretty good job, but I like to hear important things right from the horse's mouth."

Paul gave a synopsis of the events at Elba and St. Helena but concentrated on the visit to Brussels. He detailed the value of DNA in identifying ancestors and the necessity of opening the tomb to obtain a sample. Before he had a chance to mention Sophie's comment about Lady Beckett's golden hair and how it squared with Napoleon's love letter, Maurice spoke up.

"I'm in favor of that, Paul. Going right to the tomb itself. Yes, I am. The man was poisoned, no doubt about it, but why would that mean there's an imposter in his tomb? Did they ever think back in 1840 that someone would have the audacity to check his burial site sometime in the future? And if they did, did that mean they had to cover up and substitute someone else? Would arsenic stay in his bones all this time? Did they think it would last forever? It can, come to think of it. But that's not the point. The point is who's in there and how did he die? I mean Napoleon. I don't give a hoot about any impersonator. But is going in there to get a reliable sample of his hair worthwhile? All those hair samples that have suddenly surfaced—who's to say they're really his? Go right to the source, I say. See if it's Napoleon, then do whatever the scientists say to do to see how he died. Take a fresh look. And if it's not him, then we have to ask why not, and that I can't answer as we speak."

Paul wondered how it all would have sounded if he *had* smelled alcohol on Maurice's breath. "You make some good points," Paul said. "So welcome to those of us who vote to open the tomb. It's unanimous thus far. Guy and Leon are left."

"What does the young whippersnapper have to say?"

"Vincent? All for it." Paul believed Maurice had asked the question only to get another dig in. "The one I'm concerned about though, Maurice, is the president of *Vérité* himself."

"Leon? He'd be a fool to object, and he's no fool."

They both ordered rye toast and coffee.

"Once he's on board and he will be, he'll arrange everything because he's got more connections than a power plant. And rest assured, I'll pitch in. I think there should be a military presence, not only for added security but also as a fitting symbol of what Napoleon represented for so long. Also some crack soldiers should be stationed nearby just in case, and I can see to that."

"In case of what?"

"In case of anything."

Paul hoped the session with Guy at 11:30 would be a duplication of the one before but with neither a sermon nor a dig. The journalist listened intently to Paul's synopsis and plan of action.

"I've been thinking about it," Guy finally said, "and

I'm not surprised at what you recommend." He turned his attention to the waiter who had just come over and said to him, "It's almost lunch time. Why not bring me a ham and cheese sandwich and a glass of milk? You want anything Paul?"

"No thanks." He hadn't finished his rye toast two hours earlier.

"My value in this project," Guy said, "is in a way you might not have anticipated. I don't care how secretive you are, and by 'you' I mean everyone involved—the planners, the workers, the politicians. Especially the politicians. There are bound to be leaks. Even unwitting leaks by the insiders. Mistakes. Talking too much. Bragging. You don't want these leaks to lead to what I would call speculative stories right now. Getting the media, the tabloids all whipped-up. I've seen it before: the leaks, then the frenzy. If you find things that are very historic, let's say, you want the story released later and you want it to be a nice neat one, not one that appears as a result of a leak. That's one under a cloud, no matter how you try to tidy it up later. So getting back to my value? I can block most any leak from becoming a story. It wouldn't be the first time. I'd say I have a ninety-five percent success rate. Remember what I once told you regarding my relationship with the prefecture and my getting tipped off? They'd be the first to pick up any leaks and I, in turn, would be the first to be notified. And I could squelch any story. As I said, I've done it before and I wouldn't hesitate to do so in this case."

Paul was even less hungry, yet craved a cracker. "That would be valuable, Guy, and you're right, I wouldn't have anticipated something like that."

"So go ahead," Guy said, "you have my blessing if

you need it. And you can count on my vigilance over the old leak-to-story routine." He bit into his sandwich. "And I hope it's Napoleon in there," he added, "although the world would have a more shocking story if it's someone else."

Chapter 21

Paul sat at a table in the same shop. It was after two. He untied and retied his shoelace. The only difference from the morning was that the cigarette smoke odor had turned visible.

In the morning he had wanted to obtain not only Maurice's and Guy's input but also their backing before he spoke to Leon. A matter of more ammunition, of shoring up support. And though he was prepared, his mind grew foggy as Leon lumbered in ten minutes late. Suddenly Paul felt the giant was a stranger who needed convincing about jumping over the Grand Canyon.

"Sorry, Paul. Traffic snarl," Leon said, squeezing into a chair, cigarette dangling from his lips. Paul had never seen him wear a sweater before, jet black and vertically ribbed in design, unsuccessful in conveying an impression of slimness.

"Thanks for coming," Paul said, "and I'll get right to the point. You asked me about two weeks ago to undertake a monumental task. I did and I've spent more hours on this case than I have in locating stolen diamonds in Zaire, artifacts in Morocco and paintings in Germany—all combined." It was a line he'd planned on using.

"And you've accumulated vast amounts of

information."

"Yes, I have."

"And that information has led you to a *sine qua non* in your investigation."

"You might put it that way."

"So you want to open Napoleon's tomb."

Paul shot upright in his chair, his face feeling glazed with shock. "But ..."

"So do I," Leon said. "There never was a question, to my way of thinking, that it would come to that. And I knew all along that you were thinking the same thing. Don't ever get serious about the game of poker, by the way."

Paul summoned whatever adrenaline hadn't been siphoned off into the emotion of the moment. "I, ah, that's about the sum and substance of what I wanted to talk about. And you knew all along. May I call you a rascal?"

"Yes, I knew all along. And yes, you can call me a rascal if you'll permit me to use an old expression that I believe originated in your country: 'What d'ya think I am? An empty suit?'"

Their laughs were lusty, genuine. And, in Paul's case, filled with relief.

Leon went on. "But, yes, it's got to be done, and with Maurice's help, we can arrange it. The sooner the better. We'll get the proper permissions from our government and from any other group they counsel us about. We'll use personnel from the *Prefecture de Police* including the proper equipment and workers experienced with blowtorches. We'll bring in military personnel if Maurice thinks it's necessary. We could consult with cemetery people and the like but I'd rather stick with the police and the military. They can keep a confidence. They're used to it. We'll shut down the area, you know, for repairs. Rope it off, canvass it off from floor to ceiling, keep visitors away."

"Can it be done in one day?"

"I believe that's plenty of time."

"A lot of unsoldering and unsealing. Six coffins in all, one inside the other."

"Yes, I know, but it shouldn't be a problem."

Paul liked the pace of their conversation. It screamed speed. He tested it.

"When can we go ahead?"

"How about tomorrow? Early. Say seven? That'll give us three hours before the tourists stream in. Meanwhile, I'll get workers to shroud the area tonight after seven, closing time."

"You can set it up that quickly?"

"Why not. A call here, a call there."

"What if you meet some resistance?"

"Believe me, it doesn't matter. If I do, I proceed a different way." Paul sensed the big man wanted to elaborate and he was right. "Someday," Leon said, "I'll explain, but for now let's just say I have all kinds of chits out there and if I can't call one in for whatever reason, I call in another."

"So the bottom line is that you'll have everyone ready to go at 7 in the morning and all I do is show up?"

"You got it—with one exception. Don't minimize your role. We'll see to it that Officer DuBois will direct the operation. I'll be there too, but in the background. He'll be instructed to answer to you, not me."

They shook hands. Leon walked out and Paul sat there, pondering. The police officers at the opposite end of the coffee shop saluted him and he saluted in return. He noticed they were munching on biscuits.

Paul started for his room but decided to step outside for a dose of healthy air. He felt energized, for never in his wildest dreams could he have imagined the meeting with Leon would be a cakewalk. *So much worry for nothing.*

Outside he waved to the other two officers who were sitting in a police cruiser diagonally across the street. As he took a long deep breath his head lifted and he casually looked up. The top floor of the five-story office building straight ahead was lined with windows, all closed shut save for one at the far left end. He tried to avoid the glare from reflections off the glass—he had forgotten his sunglasses—all the while guessing that the single window was cracked open about a foot, at most two. At first it didn't register as anything important and he even thought little of a linear flash of light coming at him from that single crack but upon shielding his eyes, he confronted the light head-on and observed it changing shape—to a smaller, sharper ball of fire. *A rifle! The shiny steel barrel! Then the muzzle!*

Paul darted behind a car parked at the curb in front of him, turned around and pressed backward against it and waited to allow his breathing to slow down. The specter of his body rolling into the gutter tore through his mind. Then he pushed himself off and raced into the hotel, shifting his weight from side to side like a football halfback zigzagging through tacklers.

Once in the lobby, the outside officers approached him from behind. "What happened?" one of them asked. "You looked like you were staggering."

"Just a little dizzy spell. I get them now and then.

Tension."

"And you're sweating."

"It's a hot day." For a moment, Paul thought about describing what he had seen but dismissed the idea out of hand. He was too focused on the morning ahead, as menacing as the incident was. And he even decided he would withhold mention of it to anyone else, fearing it might somehow jeopardize the plans for Invalides.

Paul had visited the Church of the Dome and Napoleon's tomb twice before but had never imagined he'd one day be involved in taking the tomb apart. He, Sylvie and Vincent arrived at the marble gallery overlooking the sarcophagus at 6:55 a.m. Leon had led them through a slit in the massive canvas curtain outside the gallery. Sylvie carried a Styrofoam container, presumably to secure a bone fragment taken for DNA profiling.

They were introduced to Leon's wife, a small woman by comparison. And to Officer DuBois, some government officials and several historians attached to the Hotel des Invalides. Maurice and Guy were there. Two members of the clergy were there. A woman with a videorecorder was there. Off to one side, twelve uniformed policemen stood at attention as did six medal-laden military officers on the other side. In the crypt below, ten workers in white jumpsuits and black caps circled the tomb, their eyes trained on DuBois like a starter in a road race waiting for the signal. He in turn stared at Leon. Two of the workers wore headlight sets similar to those used by coal miners, although the lighting was more then sufficient. Two ladders leaned against the elevated tomb. Metal scaffolding was in place on two sides. Various tools lay on a wooden platform an arm's length from them: hammers, circular saws, wedges, crowbars, chisels, screwdrivers, blowtorches. Conversation was sparse and hushed.

Paul remembered his last visit when he had stood almost in the same spot gathering material for his latest Napoleon book. Clipboard in hand back then, he was making notes and sketches of what he was observing and of what he had previously read. And now, he took out a card containing notes he'd used for the final draft of that book. He read:

> At crypt level, the sarcophagus, consisting of a casket within and a scrolled cover, and made of red porphyry, a variety of granite, rising high toward the double cupola and pendentives of the dome. The elaborate bronze door leading to the tomb is flanked by two colossal bronze figures that bear symbols of imperial power on a cushion: the crown, the sword, the globe and the hand of justice.

> At gallery level, the six chapels around the gallery but currently outside the canvas recently installed.

> At the base of the sarcophagus, a multicolored, star-shaped mosaic recalling Napoleon's eight most famous triumphs: Rivoli, the Pyramids, Marengo, Austerlitz, Iena, Friedland, Wagram, and Moskowa. And circling around, twelve winged statues in Carrara marble, symbolizing victory.

Paul, at the time, and again now, imagined the emperor enclosed in six coffins placed one inside the other. He knew their composition by heart: the first of tin-sheeted iron, the second of mahogany, the third and fourth of lead, the fifth of ebony and the sixth of oak.

What followed was a series of nods. Leon nodded imperceptibly in Paul's direction. Paul's nod was more obvious. "Proceed," Leon said to DuBois who nodded to the workers below. The dismantling began.

The men worked swiftly and in harmony. They freed the tomb off its support structure and lifted it onto the scaffolding. Their grunting pierced the dead silence. They managed to move the tomb to ground level. Later, when they reached the final coffin, Paul felt unsteady as he slid sideways for a better viewing angle. Sylvie took hold of his hand. He believed the answer to the question was moments away. *Please let it be Napoleon and not an imposter.*

Four of the workers lifted off the lid and gasped in unison.

Paul turned marble white. "There's no one there!"

Chapter 22

After recovering from the shock, Paul and the delegation huddled at the rear of one of the empty chapels. Leon deferred to Paul who, despite the somberness of the occasion and their meeting place, barked out requests and instructions.

"If my hunch is correct," he said, "a little visit to London will go a long way in wrapping this up."

"Where in London?" Sylvie asked. "Beckett Gardens?"

"You got it." Paul answered. "You'll come?"

"Absolutely."

"And bring that DNA container?"

"Yes, of course."

"And you, Leon, you can contact the *histarian* there? Radford is it? We need to notify whoever's in charge of the gardens to expect us. Give us permission to look around. Snoop, if necessary. I'll take care of any request to dig after we get there."

"Yes, Radford. Very efficient. He'll set the scene."

Paul excused himself, said he'd be right back and broke away. He walked out the door, through the slit in the canvass and, hardly noticing the workers collecting their tools, fixated one last time on the empty coffin, as if to verify what he had seen only minutes before. Or what he had *not* seen. He ran a finger slowly over his lower lip, wheeled and walked back into the chapel. For the first time, he felt as challenged—obsessed—with locating Napoleon's body as he was in determining the manner of death. The corollary, he reasoned, was that the body itself might offer major clues as to whether he had died naturally or was murdered.

The Beckett estate, once an expansive tract of floral land with mansion, riding stable and assorted outbuildings had been deeded to Edenshire Township in the early 1900's as part of a nasty and well-publicized foreclosure. The mansion and other structures were gone now, the entire tract having been converted into a cemetery abutting London's northern edge. The designation "Beckett" was retained, however, and the area variously identified as "Beckett Cemetery and Gardens" or "The Cemetery at Beckett Gardens" or simply "Beckett Gardens."

Lady Ashley Beckett had been the mansion's most famous occupant. "Famous" as in "infamous", for to some she was an outcast; to her family members a disgrace. Her prodigious appetite for amorous alliances was never a secret and even a possible affair with Napoleon Bonaparte had been mentioned as a seduction on *her* part.

Nonetheless upon her death, her heirs buried her there on the land she treasured and erected a massive headstone rivaling that of Henry Fielding's in Lisbon. Its inscription read:

Lady Ashley Beckett
Entrepreneur and Friend to Many
1795-1845
May She Rest In Peace

At 4:00 p.m., Ansel, Leon's personal pilot, landed the light plane on an Edenshire airstrip not unlike the one in Paris. Paul, Sylvie and Vincent were aboard. Through *historian* Graham Radford, Leon had arranged for a supervisor and three-man digging crew to accompany the trio to the gardens for an "inspection." The supervisor had raised questions about such a designation but was silenced and rewarded in no uncertain monetary terms.

The cobblestone entry drive to the gardens was bordered on both sides by stone pots on rock pedestals, pachysandra, rose geraniums, towering sycamores and plain trees. Far off in the distance were row upon row of gravestones in a sea of the yellows and reds and blues of early flowers that Paul couldn't identify. Fifty yards in, the supervisor pointed to Lady Beckett's headstone, off to the right. And it was there that Paul stated he wanted to begin their inspection. He urged the inspector to leave after assuring him that no defiling would take place, no damage done. The diggers, he said, would be used only to move away some earth in one or two areas suspected of housing old unmarked graves overgrown with vines, sod or mixed vegetation.

Paul stood studying the area, then moved to a spot directly behind the headstone. In its shadow, the growth appeared thin, a fact other observers might have attributed to shielding of the sun by the ten-foot high marble slab. *But they're not looking for shallow headstones!*

Paul dug an inch into the ground with his foot. Two inches. More as the dirt seemed less compact. Then he met solid resistance.

"Here," he said to the diggers. "Could you please dig around here?"

They complied and within the length of a shovel blade, there was a clang. Paul had never conceived of trying to differentiate between the clang of metal on rock and the clang of metal on cement. But if he were now to place a wager, he would pick cement.

He felt the blotches come, asked the men to broaden the hole, grabbed a shovel excitedly from one of them and outlined a three-by-six-foot rectangular area around it. Before they had completely dug out the space, Paul looked at Sylvie and Vincent and shouted, "Pay dirt! Excuse the pun."

He kneeled down and cleaned off a one-foot square cement block with his hand. It bore an inscription in tiny letters:

WAIT FOR ME, MY BELOVED
IT WILL NOT BE LONG
1840

Paul's words came quickly now as did his movements, almost twitchy.

"The coffin there," he said, "can you—would you—open it? Your boss would give the go-ahead, I swear to it. I'll explain to him later."

The bulkiest of the diggers started in and the other two followed suit. They used tarnished tools taken from a tarnished toolbox. It didn't take long: iron screws dangled from the coffin's rim.

Paul's, Sylvie's and Vincent's eyes stopped blinking as they beheld a mummified corpse before them. There were dirty cloth fragments over most of the wasted body, yellowed ornaments, medals and two swords. And at its feet, a small tin box, blackened as if it had lain in soot.

The corpse's skull had disarticulated from the rest of the body and lay at an awkward angle to the chest, the bones of which were riddled with pockmarks.

Silently the three of them put on surgical gloves. Paul picked up the skull and was about to hand it to Sylvie when he stopped short.

"What's this?" he screamed.

He inserted his thumb into a circular hole in its left temporal side and the little finger of his other hand into a smaller hole on the opposite side of the skull.

"He was shot!" Sylvie shrieked. "That's an entry wound on the right."

Paul's hands shook as he handed the skull to Vincent who had signaled he wanted to examine it. Paul then opened the tin box and withdrew two sheets of rag paper, stiff and brittle with irregular edges. Each contained a message written in the scrawl that, from having studied official French documents, Paul recognized as the emperor's.

The first:

Amendment to Codicil

1st May, 1821

I ask forgiveness for using a terrible chemical
that will over time end my life.

The second:

4th May, 1821

I write this alone without benefit of counsel
and without foreknowledge that it shall ever
be read, nor do I intend it to be, for it is only
an instrument to purge myself of the decision

I have made. If it were not for my dear Ashley
this would not have come to pass this way, nor
did the coercion delay fulfillment of my last
wish. I requested her to supply the weapon that
may or may not be herein included. She would
not, or more properly, could not discharge it,
leaving it for me to complete the task with my
own hand. It was not a hasty decision on my
part, arrived at only after an unsuccessful trial
with the terrible chemical whose name I cannot
bear to write. My guilt has no boundary and I
leave it to others to decide if the ache is greater
over my military defeats, my temptation in the
face of the chemical, or my final act the result
of which has now been witnessed. I await your
coming, dearest Ashley. Long live my beloved
France and its people!

Paul decided not to wait. He took out his cell phone
and called Leon to pass on the news.

The reaction of *Vérité*'s president was more evident
in his voice than in his words: breathless, loud, raspier
then usual. "I can't believe it," he said.

And Paul's voice was just as breathless as he tried
to cover as much as possible before they met again. "But
there it is, Leon. Napoleon's manner of death was neither
criminal nor natural. *It was suicide*. An awful sight. An
awful-looking casket, falling apart, the body deteriorated.
Can we meet in the hotel lobby at about 7:30? I'll give
you my theory of the background. For now I'll just say
the body was stolen in 1840 when it was supposed to be

transferred to Paris. No doubt Lady Beckett was behind it. I see Talleyrand's hand in it too. She wanted Napoleon buried in her gardens and expected to join him there later. Now we have to prove it's definitely his body. The writing looks like his, I must say. The DNA business will take a few weeks in a case like this. Eventually I'll work up a written report for you."

"Forget the written report. You've kept the delegation well informed. I know I speak for them when I say you've convinced us beyond a reasonable doubt. It's what they want in a court of law and we can't ask any more than that. Excellent work! You grew on the job, you know. We all saw it."

"Thank you, ah, sir. Speaking of the delegation, you'll inform Maurice and Guy of what we found?"

"I certainly will. And Paul?"

"Yeah?"

"Thank you so much for changing history."

Chapter 23

Paul entered his Meridian Montparnasse room at 7:10 and immediately called Jean. He parroted what he had told Leon. Her initial response, too, was one of disbelief and then, her voice cracking, she said, "See? I knew you could do it. Wait till the Yale people hear."

"*If* they hear."

"*If* they hear? The whole world will hear."

"I don't know about that. Depends on what Leon and *Vérité* do with it."

"You're meeting with him?"

"Yeah, downstairs in ten minutes."

"Can you call me back after you do? I'm interested in what he says."

Paul looked forward to the meeting, not only to present background details but also to clear up things that dealt directly with Leon. Sylvie and Vincent had both suggested that the two men confer alone, believing more would be accomplished that way. Paul had agreed, thanked them and said he'd soon be in touch.

The men sat opposite one another in relative privacy in the hotel's lobby, Paul's fingers steepled, Leon taking long drags on a cigarette.

"So, Paul," Leon began, "you must be bushed."

"A bit, but euphoric really." Paul seized the initiative, planning to alternate between question and explanation.

"Who do you think was trying to kill me?" Paul asked.

"Not kill, just frighten you away. I can only surmise it was the Talleyrand family for reasons we're both familiar with."

Paul withheld his seeing the rifle in the window even if it didn't fit Leon's description of "frighten."

"As I've indicated, Leon, the DNA analysis, taking into account what they're able to extract from the skull and matching it with Sophie's profile, will take a few weeks, two if we're lucky. I expect it to be positive but even if it is, the result can't be considered one-hundred percent absolute because of possible mutations in the lineage. But Sophie's golden locks story kind of balances that out. Gives the lab result a little more validity. Maybe cancels out the mutation effect. It would in *my* mind anyway."

"And in mine. I'd be satisfied."

"Now next," Paul said. "Are you in a position to say what you expect to do with what we've found out? I mean, I would hope it becomes public knowledge, or at least that it somehow gets to the Talleyrand people. You, yourself, said they were the ones after me and if they finally know what happened—that their oh-so-famous ancestor didn't commit the dirty deed after all—then they'll lay off and I can relax and continue with my treasure hunting interests."

"Don't worry, Paul. One way or another, they'll know. So yes, do relax."

"Good. Thank you. Now next. You've explained the discrepancy between your visiting and not visiting St.

Helena. The truth is that you *did* go there. Am I prying too much by asking why?"

"No, your question is entirely appropriate and if you hadn't brought it up, I would have. I went there looking for my roots."

"Come again? Your roots?"

"Yes. At the time I wasn't at all sure what I expected to find. And brace yourself, Paul, but I must admit to another lie. I call it a temporary one however because I planned on telling you about it at the right time. And now's the right time. It has to do with Sophie. Sophie Bauer in Brussels. You see, I told you that Thatcher Drinkwell gave me her history and that's not true. I didn't need to be told. I know the story well. She's my half-sister."

"Your w … what?" Paul stammered.

"Yes, we're related. After she was born, mother left the family and later had a son by a different man. My father."

"So you're related to Napoleon?"

"Yes. We are — were — are. I can say it with impunity now. And I fairly well know about DNA and how it works, like the mitochondrial kind being better than nuclear for years-old specimens and coming down through families but only on the maternal side. But I also know that the last descendant to show a link to a certain person — the 'last reference sample' or something like that — can be a male. And I'd be happy to submit to a DNA test myself." As he spoke, Leon had embraced the subject with broad sweeping gestures.

Paul, in turn, stood as if shot, waiting to fall.

"So to use your expression, Paul, there it is. As president of *Vérité*, I've wanted the truth. But for more than one reason. To answer two questions: How did Napoleon die? And am I definitely his relative?"

Five minutes later Paul was on the phone with Jean and blurted his way through what he had just learned. He could almost visualize the surprise in her expression. Paul didn't give her a chance to verbalize a thing.

"By any chance," he said, "could you teach me how to speak with a Japanese accent?"

"I've had it all today," she replied, "but okay, I'll bite. Why?"

"Because if someone calls requesting that I sort out the true story about Alexander the Great or Marie Antoinette, I can switch to the accent and say I never heard of a guy named Paul D'Arneau."

EPILOGUE

It took three weeks but, remarkably, an abundant amount of mitochondrial DNA was obtained from the skull. And the reference sample from Sophie showed a definite match. Scientists from the French Academy of Sciences, colleagues of Sylvie, were unanimous in their declaration that the skull therefore was that of Napoleon Bonaparte. Furthermore their forensic anthropologist confirmed that the openings in the temporal portion of the skull were indeed the result of bullet penetration—an entry wound on the right, an exit wound on the left. Each examiner pledged to uphold the Academy's code of ethics and secrecy as to the nature and identity of specimens and any matter concerning a specific case that is not in the public domain.

Paul assured Leon, Sylvie, Vincent, Maurice and Guy that he looked forward to the day he visits Paris again, this time on less than official business, when together they might take in the French Open Tennis Tournament or the Tour de France or even a show at the Moulin Rouge.

As for Frère Dominic, Clive Weaver and Thatcher Drinkwater—*historians* all—Paul promised to keep in touch with them, hoping they would one day visit him in New Haven.

And Paul himself? He and Jean spent three days motoring throughout New York State—laughing, sightseeing, reviewing their two-week-long Napoleonic saga. But mostly laughing. The next day he resumed his search for Fra Angelico's *Golden Saints*.